MIDNIGHT RIDER

A Time Travel Mystery

Book II – Time Passengers

D. K. TILL

To my critique group: Connie, Donna,
Gwennie, and Shirley
I couldn't have done it without you!

To all time travelers everywhere:
Happy Sojourning!

NEL

Some people believe children can't be sociopaths. Kids are innocent, they say. If a kid commits a shocking crime, they say, it's because of society. Or some glitch in their upbringing. Because warped brain chemistry in a kid isn't possible.

Well, those people are wrong. My former friend Nel defied those misconceptions and then dared you to object.

I remember the first time I saw her. We'd moved that summer to a new city. On the first day of school, the confidence she wielded over our fifth-grade classroom captivated me. Maybe because she was the smartest student in the class and she knew it. While my parents rewarded me with five-dollar bills for every A and three dollars for every B, Nel's parents took her to science fairs and Lego competitions. In most of them, she either won or finished in the top three. So when she chose me, the new kid, as her friend, I felt honored she saw something in me worth befriending—me, the shadow to her glow. As long as I remained her shadow, things went just fine. If I ever stole the spotlight, however unintentionally, she'd be right there with a prank or a mocking joke to put me in my place.

I remember that year as a roller coaster of highs and lows, all predicated on Nel's treatment of me, either friend or foe. If she couldn't be the best at whatever she set her mind on, she'd make sure I wasn't, either. I kept the lows to a minimum by never outshining her.

Were the highs worth suppressing myself and my natural talents?

As a fifth grader seeking popularity, approval, to be SOMEBODY—absolutely.

Today, as an enlightened, mature adult—absolutely not.

But in sixth grade, I caught my first glimpse of her cruel streak.

She showed me a bruise on her upper arm. "My dad did it," she said when I asked. Dark red and hard to miss, the bruise remained on proud display as if it were a new tattoo. Word got around, and Child Protective Services showed up at her door, questioned her dad, and placed Nel into foster care.

With Nel attending another school, I missed her companionship, her brilliance. A light had gone out in the classroom. Her intellectual energy was the contagious kind, the kind that made the rest of us smarter too. I couldn't call her. Those weren't the days when kids had cell phones. So I went to her house and knocked.

When her mom answered, I jolted back a step. She looked ten years older than she had the week before. Red streaks marred her face, and her eyes stared at me as if she didn't know who I was. "Nel doesn't live here anymore," she snapped and started to shut the door.

"Wait!" I pleaded. "I want to talk to her and wondered if you know how to reach her."

She gave a bitter laugh. "I can't believe you'd want anything to do with that little b—that girl—after what she did to her father and me."

"I-I thought her dad—"

"She lied. She inflicted that bruise herself. She was mad because we took some of her privileges away after she lied to us about being at school when she was at the mall with her cousin."

"Is that why she didn't go to the Robotics convention?" Nel had been so upset her parents wouldn't let her go.

"Yep. She made up this elaborate story so CPS would take her away. Those people questioned her father, and of course, he denied everything while that daughter of ours stuck to her story. Now he's facing charges, and she's bullying some other poor parents."

Would Nel have been so bent on revenge she'd harm herself to frame her parents?

If Nel's mom was telling the truth or even if she was exaggerating, then Nel's dark side proved far more ruthless than the hints I'd glimpsed.

"Forget her." Nel's mom must've read my mind. "Nel is a little narcissist, and this isn't the first time she's done this. You're better off without her in your life. Because if you ever get on her bad side, she will ruin you."

PART I

IN THE YEAR 2023

June 3, 2023
Portland, Oregon

"Get your tickets out, mates!" my fiancé, Giles, urges us as his BMW approaches the Oaks Amusement Park entrance.

"Done," say Zach and Arias in unison from the back seat.

"Time to go to the future." I show him the ticket already visible on my phone screen, and he flashes an excited thumbs-up.

Dear Giles. He was so pumped for this inaugural trip with the notorious Coltrane McMurray and his Midnight Rider Time Hopper. "Thea!" he said when I told him my newspaper editor agreed to assign me the story and showed him the tickets to prove it. "They're paying my way too? Splendid! This is cause for celebration."

"Bring your Minolta camera. You're our new designated photographer."

Then my bestie and her husband splurged for tickets to join us, guaranteeing a fab time. Everywhere she goes, Ari puts the fun in the dullest of *fun*ctions.

But this won't be dull. I keep wiping my sweaty palms on my black leggings, then squirting sanitizer on my hands. An actual time machine ready to transport us a hundred years into the future? Surreal! I pinch myself to make sure I'm not dreaming.

Nobody's ever done this before. How does one defy the laws of physics and get away with it? What if something goes haywire? My diamond solitaire engagement ring twists back and forth between my thumb and forefinger as if fretting in solidarity with me.

In the sweep of the streetlight, Giles's smug grin flashes. He's not worried. This is his first weekend getaway since his CPA firm wrapped up tax season in April.

His headlights illuminate the narrow lane past the old skating rink—a favorite spot in the seventies to sneak a smoke—to the grassy waterfront field where Mr. McMurray stores his vehicle. At the distant carnival, kids played arcades and squealed on kiddie rides and ate cotton candy mere hours ago. Maybe I'll take Mia next week. Anything to coax her rare smile. Now, the darkened roller coaster keeps watch over the night like a silent dinosaur ready to pounce. Behind me, Ari giggles as she does when she's nervous but won't own it. At least, I'm not the only one. Stars dot the evening sky over the infamous meadow where McMurray made history. "The Orville Wright of Time Travel," the local media dubbed him.

The murky Willamette River peeks through dense brush, and Giles parks beside a dark Hummer with Washington plates. People stand by a round contraption like a modified tramcar, their backs to us. Giles hangs his spendy camera around his neck, and we cross the weedy field to join them under the bright full moon. Zach's ever-present vaping habit mingles sweetness with the odors of damp grass and faint smoke from faraway wildfires.

A tall man steps forward to greet us. "You must be the four we're waiting for. Giles, Thea, Arias, Zach?"

"Yes," Giles replies for us, and our phones diffuse a blue glow over the man's thick glasses while he checks our tickets.

"I'm Coltrane McMurray." He gives each of us a hearty handshake. In the white moonlight, he could be anywhere from thirty-five to fifty-five years old. "Come meet the others."

The other two women introduce themselves as Ellen and Sher from Tacoma.

"Long drive." I sling my pack over one shoulder.

"Yep." Sher, the younger one, wrinkles her nose. "Three hours."

Ellen, short and blonde, nods. "But worth it, we hope." Around forty, she eyes Zach with a slight curl of the lip. Is she one of those Gen Xers who holds contempt for growth-stunted, infantile young men like Zach?

Sher smirks. "I detect a UK accent."

"We're Australian."

"Cool! Ellen, we have a couple of Aussies joining us."

Giles chuckles. "Thea's been in the States for almost six years now. Myself for nearly three."

"What part of Australia?"

"Melbourne," I say.

"Sydney," says Giles.

"Oh, really?" McMurray cuts in. "I spent a couple years in Sydney during my wild youth."

A comparison of memories ensues between our host and my fiancé, but I edge closer to the distracting harmless-looking plastic machine—your friendly neighborhood humongous bouncy ball. Inside, blinking lights turn it into an alien object, and my heart hitches and races yet again. Already the article takes shape in my mind.

Six time-traveling explorers breach the last frontier—the future.

McMurray points to Giles's camera. "No photographs allowed, sorry. You'll need to keep it in your car."

Giles loses all his luster. "Really? But it could get stolen."

A valid fear. The Minolta cost him more than four hundred dollars.

"Fine." McMurray waves his hand. "You can bring it on board, but you can't take it with you once you exit."

"Why not?" I jam hands on hips.

"Where we're going, the people won't recognize it. They could think you're pointing a weapon at them. We don't want any freak-outs on our hands."

Giles tightens his mouth but lets it go, no doubt wondering, like me, what kind of article it will be without photos.

McMurray ushers us all to the machine's small door, accessible by a metal step. Inside the dark window-lined interior, six cobalt blue airplane seats await. It could be a futuristic cockpit, all pulsating lights and complicated instrument panels. They say he built it from scraps and parts of old planes and helicopters.

We settle in, Giles and me in front, as McMurray does a quick roll call. "Zach and Arias Adams, Thea Daniels, Giles Davies, Sheryl Stark, Eleanor Street. Welcome aboard, men and women."

A steady beep accompanies him. Counting down every excruciating second.

"It's fifteen minutes until midnight. Thank you all for getting here on time. In fifteen minutes, your life is going to change." He checks his phone. "In fifteen minutes, you're going to take the trip of a lifetime."

Ari leans forward and mutters into my left ear. "Which is why we had to fork over megabucks for this trip. First time I've ever spent so much for a glorified carnival ride."

Then why did you come? I bite back the response.

McMurray pins Arias and me with a look. "Just a reminder—you all signed a legal release when you bought the tickets. I can't emphasize how important it is you all understand this is an experimental run and inherent risks could be involved. I'll do everything within my power to ensure your safety. However, if anything unforeseen happens, you'll hold me and my company legally harmless."

Enter the time machine at your own risk.

Why such a dire warning? I seek Giles's assurance, but his attention is rapt on McMurray. *Dear Lord, please protect us.*

I slip my sweaty palm into Giles's big, dry hand. Isn't this raising any red flags for him? What's Ari thinking? How about the two ladies from Tacoma? Do they also have the urge to flee this thing right now? What I won't do for an article—oh, why did I push for this assignment?

Because Giles convinced me landing this would launch my career.

Silent, we gawk at our host.

"As my website explains, tonight at midnight the moon's gravitational pull is at its peak, which is the impetus that launches this baby into the future. As far as you're concerned, however, you won't be able to tell you've moved at all. The only movement will be the timewaves all around you." He reaches into his shirt pocket and pulls out a pouch. "Which is why you are required to wear a blackout mask until we reach our destination. The year 2123."

"How do you know 2123 even exists?" Ellen crosses her arms.

Sher adjusts her Mariners cap. "How do you know the world won't end before then?"

"Because I've made trial runs as far as 2130. Yes, the world survives another century and then some."

Zach chuckles. "Whoa, dope. So when will the world end?"

"I don't know. I haven't been there yet." Our host hands each of us black masks that cover our faces except for the hole our noses poke through.

Once mine is on, the darkness is absolute. Shivers crawl up my spine. On the verge of hyperventilating, I lean against Giles's comforting shoulder.

"Hang on," McMurray says.

A strap passes across my body and wrests my hand out of Giles's, binding my arms to my side and my back to my seat, preventing me from touching the mask even if I wanted to. "Here we go. In five seconds, you'll be in the future."

The hum intensifies, and my heart won't stop racing.

IN THE YEAR 2123

From zero to ten decades in five seconds flat.

"Welcome to June 8, 2123," McMurray announces in his best radio-DJ voice. "Please keep your masks on for one more minute." He must have seen me trying to escape the restraining device. But it holds fast. "I need to prepare you for what you're going to see, so it won't be such a shock to your system."

Nobody replies. Even Ari has nothing to say. If only I could cling tight to Giles's hand.

"You might as well leave your American cash here. Nobody here uses paper money or coins. It's all digital. And leave your smartphones," he says. "Or at least turn them off. They aren't going to work. You'll see people who look like they're talking to themselves or to the air around them. What they're doing is talking to holographic images, which you won't be able to see. There's no internet either. Instead, everything is done on what is referred to as the CLOUD. That stands for Communications: Local Or Universal and Discreet. You'll each get an earpiece and access to our group hologram so we can stay in touch. The hologram looks a lot like a computer screen, so it shouldn't be difficult to get used to it. I'll now remove your masks."

Mine whisks off before he removes Giles's. I crane my head at the world outside, but a solid steel, black fence surrounds us on all sides. Before I can even gasp, McMurray runs through a tutorial on holographic technology, and something like a floating smartphone, but an ethereal one, hovers in front of each one of us. He demonstrates how to contact the group, how to open the time capsule door, and most important of all, the 2123 version of the former Google Maps—Mapamatics—which indicates where to find food and all the things our Google does.

Behind me, Ari clears her throat. "Um, how long will we be here?"

"Twelve hours." He arches his thick dark brows. "It's just past noon right now. When you leave, please leave your masks on your seats. You'll need them for the return trip."

Twelve hours? That reality stretches ahead like a week.

The restraining strap loosens, and I shoot to my feet like I've been released from prison. A portion of the steel fence slides open. Free to gape to my heart's content, I freeze at the scene out the window.

Oaks Amusement Park is gone. In lieu of the dance pavilion and old skating rink, tall, sleek buildings assert their right to be there. No roller coaster visible.

UFOs crisscross a sky that gleams an unearthly shade of periwinkle blue.

"You won't see any cars here, either." McMurray drones through the surreal scene. "Folks here drive autopods that fly on remote-control technology."

Which explains the UFOs.

"If any of you ever saw reruns of the *Jetsons*, you know what I'm talking about."

I haven't seen the old cartoon, but I've heard of it.

"If you want a great view of the city, hire a taxipod. Okay, everybody out. Explore all you want but be back before midnight."

Giles sets his camera on his seat. We all grab our backpacks and step out, one by one, into a wall of heat like walking into a sauna. I break into an instant sweat and fumble for my big red sunglasses in my pack's front pocket, the relief from the glare instantaneous. I sniff an unfamiliar odor. A strange mix of metallic and chemical aromas threatens to launch a headache, and the lack of overhead powerlines only emphasizes this new world's alien nature. What do the people do for electricity? Or have they moved on to solar power only?

"It must be a hundred ten degrees out here." Giles slides on the black sunglasses that make him look like Ryan Gosling. He takes my hand, and his thumb caresses the diamond on my finger. My comfort level shoots up twenty notches. Good thing he's here with me.

"It's a hundred fourteen degrees," says McMurray behind us. We all gather round him, reluctant to venture too far from our anchor. "That's why I told you to bring a spare set of warm-weather clothes." He points to a building about fifty feet across the plaza. "You can go change in the public toilets over there."

"Can we get back inside the vehicle to stash our stuff?" Ari twirls a strand of pink hair around her finger. With her pack so stuffed, she won't want to carry it around.

"Yeah, I'll be nearby."

"And what do we do about food?" One of the Tacoma ladies pulls a Clif Bar from her jeans pocket. The package crackles as she opens it.

"You each have a three-hundred-dollar meal allowance as I explained in the email. Use it wisely."

"Three hundred dollars?" Ari glares at Zach as though he's to blame for the high prices. "How much does food here cost, anyway?"

I cluck my tongue. "You guys mustn't have read the attachments McMurray sent us. He warned us a normal-sized sandwich could cost roughly seventy-five dollars." Thus, three meals could add up to three hundred dollars. In light of that, the steep admission price makes sense.

By 2123, inflation will skyrocket by a 1000 percent.

"Why couldn't we bring our own food and get a discounted ticket price?" Zach steps forward and taps his fingers together, as aggressive as he will ever get.

"The ticket price includes full cultural immersion into the future, including inflated meal costs and foods unavailable in our lifetime." The host's taut features betray his irritation.

"Whoa, dope."

"Thea." Ari tugs on my purse strap. "First thing I want to do after we eat is hire a taxi and see if we can find our houses."

"Oh, great idea." The Eastmoreland home where I rent a room is a couple of miles from here, and Giles's Sellwood townhome even closer. What would we discover today?

Zach scratches his beard. "How much you want to bet our houses won't be there?"

That nagging twinge returns, the one that's been hinting I might play God and find out if Mia's deadbeat mom ever cleans up and comes back. The future might really hold such records—*if* I can figure out how to access them. Imagine…

"My tummy's growling." Ari grabs her husband's elbow. "Let's go eat, Zachy. Thea, you and Giles too."

I've got hours for any research on Mia, and every experience will enhance this career-making article I so need. I nudge Ari's shoulder. "What's your food mood?"

"My food mood…" She plants her palm on her belly, closes her eyes, and hums a yoga chant. "Tummy is telling me…" She opens her eyes. "It wants a Reuben sandwich from Al's Deli."

"I doubt Al's is still around." Needing relief from the burning sun, I appease Ari with, "I'd like lunch too, but how about we change into our cooler clothes first."

I clutch Giles's hand and lead the way to the public toilets. Hordes of barely dressed, emaciated people shove past us, staring as though we're the aliens. I rise onto my toes, craning over them. Where are they all going and why do they look like they just emerged from a famine?

My stomach clenches, but not from hunger. They're heading to the vehicle we exited, apparently mesmerized by the apparition that materialized at the riverbank.

A child in a fuchsia shortie taps my hand. "Wut year yuh from?" I strain to understand her flattened words. Something about her looks familiar, but I can only glance back at her as Giles pulls me along the crowded sidewalk.

At the tall outbuilding resembling a silo, the lone door has no sign indicating gender. I raise a brow at Giles, then creep inside, ready to spin and flee if it turns out to be the men's side. Only three metal stalls are available, so why is the building so high? I lurch and nearly scream as a panel beside me moves. Then a shirtless man with a full beard emerges, brushing my shoulder, and I gasp out, "Excuse me, I meant to go to the ladies' room."

He gives me an odd look. "The wut?"

I backtrack to Giles's side. "The ladies' room."

Diversely-colored eyes—one brown, one blue—blink at me. "Uh, don' know wut you mean."

Giles steps forward and points to the panel. "What is this?"

"Not seen a elevator b'fore?"

"An elevator?" Giles frowns at the panel. Then his eyes widen, the truth dawning on him as it dawns on me. It's a lift for the upper floors. No wonder the building's so tall.

"How many stories?"

The man's feet swivel toward the exit. "Five."

Giles studies the ceiling, probably doing his own mental calculation. "For both men and women?"

He squints at us like we're imbeciles. "For anyone." He hurries away.

I put my mouth close to Giles's ear. "Does this mean there are no men's and women's restrooms anymore?"

"Looks that way," he whispers back. "We could see this coming in 2023."

"I guess."

If you go, be prepared to leave your gender identity behind.

Giles's head gesture tells me he wants to try the lift. Shaking off my trepidation, I grip his hand as the door slides open at our approach. We cram into the narrow enclosure, barely wide enough for both of us. His breath heats my neck. He bumps his shoulder to me. "These're meant to be used by one person at a time, huh?"

The lift ascends. But we didn't push any buttons. Where is it taking us?

Red buttons blink at each floor, and my dread rises in sync until it stops at the fourth floor and a disembodied voice states, "Stalls 4A and 4B available." So it knew there were two of us. Wow.

A surprised chuckle erupts. I enter stall 4B, and it slides closed. After hanging my bag on a hook, I exchange my leggings and T-shirt for shorts and a fuchsia tank top. Enclosed in a soundproof metal box with only a slit outlining the door,

I grit my teeth. I don't consider myself a claustrophobe, but this suffocating feeling must be what it's like.

At least there's relief from the cloying heat. After a deep breath and an antianxiety Scripture verse, I brush my long brown hair and apply a fresh coat of lipstick. My teeth need flossing also. The toilet lacks a flushing lever, but a button panel gleams above it. I touch one at random, and a sucking noise ensues. The water in the toilet sinks instead of flushes, similar to an airplane toilet. Huh. It must share plumbing with the stalls below.

Now how to exit this contraption? No way will I yell for help. Without a door lever, I feel around the door's edge. It whooshes open, and I nearly collapse. Giles's stall is empty. So where is he? Could he have left without me?

Outside the stall, three metal sinks line the wall, all without taps or faucets. How do people wash their hands? I'm reaching for the sink as if it can answer me, when a squirt of something moist slaps my hands. Then a gush of air sucks the moisture away.

Very cool contraption in a very cool building.

At least seven minutes have elapsed.

"Giles?" In this straightforward setup—three stalls, three sinks, four walls—where could he hide?

No answer. I palm my chest to still my thudding heart. He must be outside waiting. How dare he leave me alone here. Why didn't he wait, or at least tell me he was done?

The lift opens and I stumble out. On the ground floor, Ari and Zach hesitate outside the entrance. "Isn't there a ladies' room?"

"No, it's unisex." I point as someone enters the lift I vacated. "You have to try the smart elevator. It even tells you which stalls are free."

"Wait for me, 'kay?" Her eyes plead with me, revealing the misgivings I'm wrestling with.

"Sure. Did you see Giles?"

She shakes her head as Zach pulls her inside. I crane my neck every which way, but everyone's a stranger. I'm ready to give up when someone grabs my shoulders. I jump like a startled kangaroo. "Giles!" I force a laugh. "Where'd you go?"

He grins, his hazel eyes aglow. He waves in a wide sweep. "Just walked around, taking it all in."

I cross my arms. "I was worried. Why didn't you tell me you were ready to leave?"

He shuffles his feet, not meeting my eyes. "Sorry, love, just eager to explore. You're right, though. I should've said something." He drapes his arm over my shoulders while I veer between resentment and forgiveness. But still. His apology's almost…complacent. Is he sorry or appeasing me? Seriously, why he didn't realize I'd worry?

But I'd better work that out later. Right now, we're loitering in the boiling sun and surrounded by impossible details of a strange new landscape. Buildings worthy of a sci-fi movie set. *Jetsons* cars in an intensified sky.

"I've made a mental list of everything we need to check out today." His steps quicken, but he still won't look at me.

"Like what?"

He opens his mouth, but Ari and Zach hustle over. "Shall we go eat now?" she asks.

"Okay." I halt, and Giles finally looks at me. My turn to ignore him. "I'm surprised we're even thinking about food. Shouldn't our bodies still think it's the middle of the night?"

Ari stretches as if she just got out of bed. "You know me. I love me some midrats."

We walk with the crowd along paved paths that used to be carnival arcades next to multistory structures that must be apartments or condos.

"I'm with Ari." Giles slides his arm off my shoulders. It hangs limp at his side as if uncertain of its welcome on my person. "We should find food, then sightsee."

Zach snaps his fingers. "We should've asked the dude what time it'll be when we return. Will time have passed, or will it have stood still?"

Not sure how long the trip will be, I explained when I canceled my afternoon with Mia in case things ran late. My Little from Big Brothers Big Sisters has bad enough abandonment issues. I'd never risk her thinking I walked out on her too. I'll make it up to her during her recital Tuesday night.

Ellen and Sher stroll a few feet ahead, so we hurry to catch up. "We're going back to the capsule to leave our bags."

Sher swings hers off her shoulder. "Then how about we all go adventuring?"

"We were just talking about eating." I stride forward. Somebody has to lead the way. No way will I advertise how out of my depth I feel, particularly to Giles. He, Ellen, and Sher flank me. Zach and Ari tail us. "Has anyone tried using Mapamatics?"

"Let's worry about that later." Ellen shakes wispy blonde bangs back from her eyes. She sweeps her hand around like Giles did moments earlier. "Right now, I'm overwhelmed. I need to return to the capsule and chill."

Sounds great to me. I'm not sure what I think of this world of skin-and-bones citizens, bluer-than-blue sky, odd smells. Maybe we can talk McMurray into taking us back early. My editor might not understand, but my eagerness to leave outweighs my worry over my job. I'll make it up to her. I'll write the best feature story she's ever seen, as long as I can stay in 2023.

We elbow our way to the concrete pad where we left the time hopper. Giles pounds on the steel fence. Once, then twice. "Mr. McMurray?"

"Is he inside?" Ellen's voice rises in a screech. "Looks like he locked us out."

"I think he meant to lock the public out. He's not expecting us back for several hours." Giles taps his fingers on the gate, and it unexpectedly slides to the left.

"Wow, look at that. We're in."

I chuckle. "It knows you, love. The fence is your friend."

With all our gazes on him, he reaches for the capsule's door handle. The door clicks open. "It's on our holograms, remember?" he reminds us. Spinning around, he calls out to the surging crowd. "Sorry, we can't let you in."

Protests ring out, but he ducks inside and pulls me in behind him, followed by Arias.

"What the hey!" Giles shouts, blocking my view and lurching backward right onto my foot. "He's dead."

I gasp. "What? What do you mean?"

He steps aside. McMurray is slumped on the floor, his head propped against the seat I sat in less than a half hour ago, his torso bloody.

A wicked knife protrudes from his chest.

IN THE YEAR 2123

Don't faint, I command myself as I gawk at our host's lifeless body. My heart races like a runaway horse, and my foot throbs where Giles stomped on it. Our only hope of returning to the life we know is dead. "We're stranded here." Gasping for breath, I grip Giles's arm. "What do we do now?"

"We go tell the police." Grasping my shoulders, he spins me around where an open-mouthed Ari blocks my progress out the door.

"Let us out." I scoot past her. "We need to find the police."

But what are the logistics of law enforcement in 2123? Are they even called police now? Are they only accessible by hologram? If so, we're in deep trouble.

Even more troubling, if we can't get back to 2023, I can't contact my editor to tell her my article on Coltrane McMurray's time hopper is a bust before I've typed a single word. And to poor Mia, I'll be one more adult who's let her down.

If I never return, what will happen to my cats? This morning Grizabella and Rumpleteazer yowled at me even though I'd filled their food and water bowls. They'd sensed something up, so I gave them the extra loves they clamored for and reminded them, "Having food and shelter, with these you shall be content." What if I never get another chance to love on them, laugh at them, scold them with paraphrased Scripture?

My landlords will take them to a shelter. I shudder and try to pray, but I don't even have words. Still, I cling to the Bible's promise that Christ is interceding for me right now.

A peace overtakes me, a settled trust that God has this all under control, strange as it may seem.

The mob reminds me of the summer music festivals at Waterfront Park—wall-to-wall perspiring bodies. I keep brushing people, but Giles doesn't notice. He's checking each building we pass while I wipe sweat off my brow with my free wrist. Interesting that the prevailing building style consists of housing units anchored by cafés and other service businesses, a concept popular in my home year, now still the dominant style a century later. A real keeper of a concept. But the business names painted on the gunmetal-gray doors flanked by storage-unit-like walls are like nothing I'm familiar with. MedPac. JB Fundtax Avisors. Didn't anyone notice the misspelling? Finally, a dentist office, misspelled denist. Beyond those windows, children play at their seated parents' feet. Even in the next century, people need dentists. I hate going to the dentist, yet I feel a pull toward the door, comforted by its familiarity.

But Giles is on a mission. On the smooth expanse of 2123's equivalent to a street, helicopter-like vehicles land and take off.

Except they lack rotors and tails—the autopods McMurray mentioned. On the street's opposite side, a warehouse structure dominates the view. Tiny airplanes, like the remote-control toys of my childhood, fly in and out of its many oversized windows. CostWare according to the huge red letters across its beige expanse. The exiting planes are carrying packages. These must be drones delivering goods to consumers. Do brick-and-mortar stores exist anymore? I've seen no signs for retail establishments.

"Giles," I plead. Although our hands are linked, I'm a mere appendage on his single-minded journey. Does he even remember I'm still here? "Once we do find a police station, how will we explain who we are? Should we tell them the victim is from the year 2023?"

"Well, sure. Didn't McMurray say he'd already made some trips here? That's why the people were gawking. They already know about time travel. When we find the police, we tell them the truth."

My unspoken fear grows too big to ignore. "And how are we going to get b–back?" My voice breaks. "Are we just going to start a new life here?"

For the first time, Giles stops and looks at me. "Aw, Thea." His gaze darts around as Arias and the others catch up. "Someone here has to be familiar with time-travel technology and can help us get back."

As if reassured by his own matter-of-fact words, he turns again and leads us beside more commercial activities: A dance studio. State "goverment" offices. A café called BirdNest. The mouthwatering aromas of fresh-baked bread make my stomach growl, and my heart surges that maybe misspellings aren't as common as I fear. Or are we seeing the new standard—substandard?—English of 2123?

Roses bloom in strips of grass. Big, glorious roses in yellow and pink and orange. Portland is still the Rose City. Hanging baskets of pink petunias and red begonias draw my gaze to a wood-paneled door. "Can we stop in this café?" I ask. "They may know how to contact the police."

Giles stops and pulls the door open, and we enter a café that could have been transported from 2023. The cool temps bring relief. If only we could stay here all day. Decorative birdcages, sans birds, hang everywhere. No price tags. Maybe they're merely for looks, or maybe the prices show up on customers' hologram feed? Giles and I march to the counter, the others hesitating. Instead of ordering, Giles leans toward the woman manning it. Her two-toned eyes—one blue, one green—stare at us out of a face so stiff, it has to be plastic surgery. Nissi, says the embroidery on her mesh shirt's lapel. That is, if I've made it out right through a gap in her sculpted black hair shaped like an eagle's wings.

"We're trying to locate a police station. Can you direct us?"

Her face tightens even more than it already was. "A wut?" she deadpans.

Giles pauses, exhaling. "We need to discuss a matter with the police. How do we find one?"

She tilts her head. "The police?" She imitates his accent. "You need security?"

"No. We have a friend who's in a bit of a jam…"

Her quizzical look says she's never heard an Aussie accent and possibly even that expression. How much can the English language have changed in a hundred years? Her slurry yet rapid-fire accent is an odd mishmash of hillbilly and urban to my twenty-first-century ears, bringing to mind a rapper dressed in a plaid shirt and overalls. Does everyone here talk that way?

"Robot or hooman?" She rubs her nose, disturbing the smooth arrangement of her hair's eagle winglets.

"Uh…"

"Human, please," I interject.

"Get em from yer hullagram," she snaps in unconcealed irritation, no doubt wondering what kind of doofuses don't know the simplest tasks.

I wonder what word has replaced *doofus*. Do they still say dweeb or nerd? How about, nerdweebus? We're all of those and more as we look at the screens that've been hovering in midair near our right hands since we left the capsule. I have no clue how to "get em from my hullagram."

Ari's bewildered expression deepens my anxiety.

But Giles, the only one of us who heeded McMurray's tutorial, steps away. "C'mon, mates. Let's go sit down and get this done."

A birdlike metallic object zips past my head, and I jump back, stifling a scream. "What was that?"

I swear I hear Nissi snicker. "Wutch out for delivery drones," she calls. The Lord knows what she must think of us now. She freezes, eyes narrowing. "Wait...yull from that time sheen?"

Time sheen? Oh, time ma*chine*. I turn to her in relief. "Yes, we are."

"What year you from?" She says it in one word, *wuhyearyafrum*.

"Um, 2023. Listen, our driver is dead, and we can't get back to our home year. Someone killed our driver!" My voice rises toward hysteria as Giles places a reassuring arm around my shaking shoulders.

"Unforch. Unforch," Nissi keeps repeating and shaking her head. "Obvy yull not from here. Yull talk like robots." She squints at us. "But yull not robots."

Didn't she care about our dilemma? "Can you help us find someone to talk to?"

She pokes around on her hologram, and I hear a distant siren. "I grammed Pope, and they on their way."

"Pope?" Not *the* pope?

"Portland Police."

I let out a whoosh of breath. Aha, a name I recognize. An organization I know. Even a century later, the men and women in blue still patrol my city. Or are they robots? It wouldn't surprise me.

While we all wait for "Pope" at a booth near the door, Nissi serves us coffee on the house. I take a cautious sip. It has a more acidic and less bitter edge to it. She hovers, a spark of interest now aglow in her mismatched eyes. "Heh, what's life like in 2023?"

"A lot less crowded," offers Ari.

"Oh, marvy."

Giles holds up his cup. "Excellent brew. By the way, what's the population of Portland now?"

"Close to three milly."

"Three million people?" I feel my eyes grow big. "Is that just the city or the entire metro area?"

"City pop's three mil. Metro pop's near eight mil."

Giles's brows rise halfway to his hairline. "The Portland area has grown over five million people in a hundred years." It explains the massive high-rises popping up from every direction.

"That's insane," says Ellen. "Does Tacoma still exist?"

"Yeah, takes half hour to get there by MegaMax." Much quicker than Ellen's three-hour car drive. I visualize a Portland Max train car flying through the air at three hundred miles per hour.

Glancing at the door, I will the police to burst in and rescue us. Instead, the door flies open, and two adults of uncertain gender and a child walk in. Both adults wear pants resembling loincloths, matched with shiny striped tank tops. As they near, it's apparent their shorts are a twisted mishmash of fabrics. A twenty-second-century version of macramé, perhaps? The child, seven or eight, has long hair and wears a dark blue onesie. It's gotta be a boy with the way he struts. But I could be wrong. I crane my neck for a better look at the two following them inside. A tall, thin guy in a blue uniform peers around, his oddly plastic-like face as motionless as a Halloween mask. A robot? Accompanying him is a long-haired, thin young woman in a lighter blue uniform. Giles waves them over.

"You need to report a murder?" The robot sounds… human. His badge reads Zorius. He slides onto the bench beside us in one silent move, a hologram floating near his right hand, his left finger tracing figure eights above it. The screen flashes and then fills with words as Giles explains the situation, the thing recording us.

Ari twitches beside me, her mouth frozen in middrop, probably from sitting in such close proximity to a real-life robot. And this whole situation. Like me, she must feel she's been dropped into a sci-fi movie set.

"Take us to the murder site," the woman cop, whose name badge says Ruba, orders in the same flat, sloppy speech I'm starting to recognize. It's like everyone speaks with their mouths half open.

Ruba stops and stares at me, then says, "You again?"

My arms creep around my middle. Who does she believe I am? "Um, no, I don't think we've met before."

She narrows her eyes at me, then at Giles, as though we're already under suspicion. "You have a twin somewhere?"

I shake my head, and she blinks twice. "Yull not the couple whose autopod got stranded bout ten years ago?"

"No, this is our first visit. Must've been someone who looked like us."

But the implication hits me. If people in the future look like me and Giles, our descendants must still live in the area. Oh, how cool to meet and talk with them!

Ruba waves us on, and we all traipse out of the café. During the walk, she keeps sizing us up, then shaking her head.

I gulp, uneasy under her scrutiny, even though I get why she's doing it.

As we approach the capsule, more folks, many with two-toned eyes, crowd around. What is up with those eyes? The crowd has grown so large the cops have to push their way through, the six of us on their heels.

"Scuze us. Scuze us," the robot and the woman command. They clear a path to Midnight Rider, then order Giles to unlatch the door. Ruba gapes at the capsule, muttering under her breath a phrase that sounds like "not an autopod after all…time machine." She gives us another questioning look, then opens her mouth presumably to ask a question.

I turn away from her, tired of answering their questions. Here we are having to fend off more questions from the mob. I ignore them. Two more robots appear and consult with the cops. The forensic team, maybe?

"What happened?" asks a long-haired teen girl, dressed in a bikini, along with her two friends. None of the three shaved their legs.

A back-to-nature mindset will be prevalent in the next century.

"Why you here?" This is addressed to Giles from a preteen boy in purple sunglasses and loudly colored trunks. Don't these people ever get dressed? Yet the air is so warm, part of me identifies with them. I want to strip off my tank top too. And I probably could get away with it.

Climate change will become as dire as we've been warned.

Giles ignores the boy.

My companions and I crane our necks to see inside the capsule, but the woman cop's body blocks my view. I cling to Giles's arm. "How are we going to get back, love?" My breath quickens, and, despite the hundred-and-fifteen-degree temperature, my blood chills.

"I told you already. Someone here has got to know how to operate this thing," Giles nearly snaps. He's usually so calm and self-possessed. If he loses it, we're screwed. His chest expands as he takes a deep breath and turns to the crowd. "Hey, do any of you know how this thing works?"

The mob shouts louder. I can't make out what anyone is saying. But then a short blonde-haired woman elbows her way toward us. "I do. I know how to drive it." She's pulling a brown rolling suitcase.

A huge load I hadn't realized I carried lifts from my shoulders. I smile. "We'd be so grateful if you could get us back."

Sliding wire-rimmed glasses to her nose with her free hand as though trying to get a better look at us, she smiles back. Crinkles form around her blue eyes. She looks like a friendly down-to-earth mom of teenagers. So how'd she acquire her technical knowledge? "What's your name?"

"Penelope, but everyone calls me Penny."

Wait. That's twenty-first-century American speech. Not that slurry rural rap we've heard since we arrived. It explains the out-of-place eyeglasses, the first I've seen since we arrived.

At last, the two cops back out of the entry and close the door, leaving the two robots inside examining the body and surrounding area.

Giles steps forward. "As soon as the body is removed, we'd like to return home." He points to Penny. "This lady has offered to drive us back."

"Nobody is going anywhere," says the robot. "The man inside was stabbed five times. None of you will be allowed to leave until we find out who killed him."

IN THE YEAR 2123

Arias loses it. She stalks forward, elbows punching through human obstacles. "You can't do this to us. We all want to go home! My husband and I have a food cart that needs to be opened in the morning."

In one smooth motion, the robot plants his mechanical arm in front of her. While they argue, I take a closer look at Penny. Unlike the nearly nude women in the crowd, she wears a red sundress I'm almost positive I saw at Nordstrom Rack last month. Her purple-painted toes complement her blingy flip-flops.

"Cute dress," I say. "Are you from the twenty-first century like us?"

Her graying blonde hair, fastened atop her head with a tortoiseshell claw clip, sways with her nod. She sports a quintessential 2020s Portland look. "I am. I was supposed to return home with Colt. I've been here for a week, and I'm anxious to go home too. Like you."

Ellen and Sher appear beside me. "How fascinating." Sher tugs on her heavy chain-link necklace. "What were you doing here for a week?"

Penny's red fringe earrings sway. "Research. I'm Colt's assistant."

"Ah," says Ellen. "That's why you know how to get us home."

"Yes." Another nod, a friendly smile. Yet McMurray didn't mention an assistant. I open my mouth to ask what she was researching, but Robocop's hollering drowns me out. "Did any of you see someone enter this capsule?"

"No," shouts the crowd.

"So how did perp get inside?" the lady cop asks her colleague.

Robocop spins and eyes the six of us trembling before him. "Which of you discovered the body?" He points to Giles. "You?"

The lady cop lowers her brows and narrows her eyes as she tilts her head at Giles. I can already hear what she's thinking. *He found the body. How do we know he didn't stab the man?* My heart thuds. Do they suspect any of us? We all came back to the vehicle.

But only Giles, Ari, and I stepped all the way inside.

Giles nods at the cop's question. "I did."

Robocop blocks the surging, shouting crowd from breaching the open gate, so Ladycop resumes the interrogation. "See anyone else in pod? Or round it?"

"Nobody inside, ma'am, but lots of people were nearby." Giles leans against the capsule's fuselage, his arms crossed, forearm muscles bulging.

How can I be focusing on his brawny physique at a time like this?

"Any smashed windas? Or anythin else indicate how they got inside?"

"No, ma'am."

Her narrowed gaze rests on him a moment too long. She must not recognize the term *ma'am*. "Was door locked?"

"It was."

Robocop studies his screen where words are scrolling. Another recording? How many times will Giles need to repeat his story before they have enough?

Aha, I get it. He's comparing notes to see if Giles makes any contradictory statements. I clench my jaw. *Careful what you say, honey. Don't get rattled!* I reach my hand to Ari and clutch hers, the contact comforting.

But the interrogation of Giles is growing personal. "Why did you go inside in first place?"

"We needed a place to store our backpacks. We'd just changed into cooler clothes, and we came back to stash our stuff. Then we planned to go find something to eat."

It should be obvious none of us lingered, seeing as we're all still toting our bags.

Robocop's mechanical stare fastens on Giles. "How much time elapsed from when you first exited to your return?"

Giles ponders for more than five seconds, so Ari replies for him. "About twenty minutes."

"Twenty minutes." Robocop's attention, drawn away from the script, now fastens on Ari.

Don't say anything, I urge her silently.

"How did someone get inside during those twenty minutes without anyone seeing?" The two cops look at each other, one expressionless, one baffled.

"I think I know how they got inside." We all swivel to Penny while she rolls the suitcase in front of her and props one knee on it. "There's an emergency exit in the back. It's not hard to spot."

"And you know this, how?" asks Ladycop.

Penny braces her forearms on the pull handle and crosses them. Her long, pale hands hang there, displaying manicured nails like painted arrows. "Oh, well." She gestures at me. "As I was saying, I am—was—Colt's assistant. I planned to return to 2023 with him tonight." Her face flushes, and she blinks away a tear. "But with him gone, it's up to me now to get everyone back to their home year safely."

"Not till we solve this crime, you," Robocop reminds us.

Ladycop is already making her way round to the capsule's rear, and we follow her past a decorative shrub to an emergency exit akin to those on school buses. To the right and the left—all sides, actually—a fence far taller than I am blocks my view.

The cops mutter about how easy it would be to enter here undetected. They examine the latch, find it locked.

Then Robocop runs a finger along it. "It doesn't look like anyone tampered with this. But it seems plausible the perp got in this way."

"He probably let whoever it was inside." Penny raises her chin. "No need to tamper."

"Ah, so he recognized the person."

"Maybe not." She tosses Giles and me a glance, her thoughts evidently echoing mine. *The cops think it's one of us.* "Someone could have knocked, and he opened it to see who it was. Which means it could be anyone."

A nice attempt to deflect, but still my heart sinks. We might be here a long time.

I've never felt so homesick in my life.

IN THE YEAR 2123

Something Penny said caught the cops' attention. Now, they direct their suspicions at her. "You seem to know a lot about this vehicle. What did you say your name is? Penny?"

"Penelope Nichols. I know plenty about this vehicle. I helped McMurray design and build it."

Ari chuckles behind us. "Your name is Penny Nichols?"

The lady is gracious enough to grin. "My parents had a sense of humor. You should've heard the nicknames I got called as a kid. Like Moneybags. Or Penny Dollar. My favorite was Nickels and Dimes."

Robocop glares at them. "Quiet, please. We are going to need individual statements from each of you. Please accompany us to the interview room."

The interview room requires a trip in an official white police autopod. Bigger and quieter than a helicopter, it seats the seven of us and the two of them. We embark on a silent glide through an untroubled sky. Alongside us, other autopods navigate the skyways, some large enough to hold a family, others only big enough for one. Another layer of autopods fly below us, and several more above us.

Giles, his fascination evident from his scrutiny, crowds the robot operating the control panel. "Do these babies run on remote-control technology? Is that why no one's running into each other?"

"Correct," Robocop begins. "All autopods are equipped with radar and run on solar power. When they sense another pod nearby, they adjust accordingly. And they all go the same speed. With all the autopods 'talking' to each other, collisions and fatalities are rare." The cop launches into further technical explanation, but it goes over my head. If we ever make it home and I get to write the article, Giles will remember the details.

We're sailing high above Forest Park. Wildwood Trail snaking through the tall trees conjures up a year-old memory of the day I met fellow Aussie Giles Davies on a church singles' hike. Nudging him, I point to the spot of our first conversation, the Thurman Street trailhead, visible through the evergreens. How nice to see the city still places a high priority on preserving the unspoiled beauty of the nation's largest urban park. Giles grins at me and squeezes my hand, a twinkle in his hazel eyes. He must also be remembering that "kapow moment" of two soulmates meeting.

The autopod swoops to a five-story building's flat roof so abruptly I brace for a crash. Instead, it sinks as gracefully as an eagle to the paved surface. "Have you ridden in one of these yet?" I ask Penny, and she nods, her awestruck countenance answer enough.

We follow the cops to an elevator-type structure, and it lowers us to the first floor. We exit into a bustling lobby lined with windows.

"Unbreakable glass." Penny clatters along, still hauling her ugly hand luggage. How annoying to be stuck with it as if she's on an airport layover. "See how the view outside is a bit distorted? All the buildings have plasticized glass now. Guess they got tired of crime gangs breaking windows."

She chuckles.

But seriously, what a great idea. We need to do the same.

The people outside seem to bend as they walk, like crooked toothpicks. Which reminds me, I need to ask Penny why everyone is so skinny. And if she would be willing to let me interview her for my article.

We tromp into a windowless interrogation room. Huh. Police stations haven't changed much in a hundred years. Designed for intimidation, not comfort. "What odd-looking lights." I point overhead. "They're mere strips in the ceiling."

"But powerful," Penny says. "Everything is solar-powered now."

After we're all fingerprinted, Robocop explains he will be interviewing us all at the same time, which doesn't sound possible. But this futuristic technology "hijacks" the speaking voice so it can't be heard by others.

He connects with each of us via hologram, and the interrogation begins.

So here we all are, answering questions together yet privately.

First question: "How long have you known the victim?"

"Less than two hours," I say.

Penny's still talking. A minute later, she finishes her answer.

"Where did you go after you left the victim?"

"I went to the public toilets to change my clothes."

Again, we wait for Penny, who gestures and punctuates her speech with her hands. I'm dying to know what she's saying. Several minutes pass.

"Who else was with you?"

"My fiancé, Giles." I indicate Giles, who speaks with no sound. With a roomful of silent moving mouths, this feels like some weird, futuristic, sci-fi TV show. Especially when the lights change from blue white to yellow white. What is the purpose? "Ari and Zach were there too. We met up with Sher and Ellen after we changed." Although I can hear myself, the others, through some amazing technological miracle, cannot.

We get more questions we answered earlier until I'm weary of repeating myself. Then they finish phase one. "We're takin two of you to nother room for further questins," Ladycop says. "Rest of you stay put."

Which two?

"Mx. Davies and Mx. Nichols, please come with us."

No, please, not Giles. I scrunch my face at the unfamiliar term of Mx. I'll ask Penny later. A wave of heat assaults me, and I droop. My body thinks it's 2:00 a.m. and should be sleeping. Instead, I'm sweating bullets in a boring room without even a smartphone to occupy myself. As Giles and Penny are led away, I move closer to Ari, whose bloodshot eyes and sniffles betray her anxiety. She takes a tissue from her bag and wipes her nose. Ellen and Sher are conducting a quiet conversation, all wringing hands and squeezing knees.

Fabulous irony. Giles, who pushed for us to get the police involved, is now their number one suspect.

GILES

Giles's heart skipped a beat when Zorius grabbed his arm and escorted him into another nearly identical room. Windowless, with the same snaky embedded ceiling lights, it held a handful of chairs and a desk. With those lights off, it would be as dark as inside a cave. And just as scary. The worry etching Thea's beautiful face surely mirrored his.

Sucking in a deep breath, he reminded himself the cops couldn't know why he signed up for this trip. Thea didn't even know. She'd be appalled he'd kept such a big secret.

Ruba sat Penny down next to him, and the two cops faced them. Penny's poise deserted her, shaky hands gripping the suitcase handle betraying her nerves.

Ruba's gaze raked over him. "Ever time travel in that thing before?"

He shook his head. "No, this was our first time."

"Boozlin how much your time chine looks like that stranded couple's autopod from ten years ago. Yull even talk like them."

Who knew what she was talking about. He could only shrug.

"We got robocam evidence of yull's movements today, both of you. But we want to hear it again."

Thea must be fretting in the next room, squirting sanitizer on her hands as if germ-free hands could keep misfortune, like viruses, far away. He squelched a huff, then reiterated the story he'd given twice before. "May I see the evidence, please?"

Zorius lifted Giles's arm to manipulate his hologram screen, tapping some strange icon. An image of a crowd appeared, as did the area where they'd exited McMurray's machine. "At 12:05 p.m." The robot tapped the image of the public toilets, and the crowd seemed to jump from the hologram and materialize before them as if the scene had been transported to this room.

Giles scrambled backward in his seat. How very *Star Trek*. This was holograph technology taken to the next level. Rather, the next stratosphere. Lifelike 3D images of himself and Thea approached the building and went inside. He suspected what came next.

"But here's the part you didn't tell us." Zorius maintained his mechanical monotone. "You left the building for five minutes." He tapped again. The scene transformed to focus on a young man—himself—striding toward the river, hands in pocket, gaze on the ground, before vanishing. Man, if only he'd known he was being filmed.

"Where did you go?"

Giles clenched his fists to keep his hands from trembling.

"You walkin like you had *desti*nation, not just wanderin aimless." The lady cop's eyes had grown hard.

He gulped. "I, uh, *was* just wandering around."

"What if we were to find a witness who told us you went to the murder site?"

Another gulp. He didn't dare reply. He'd wanted to chat with McMurray one-on-one and filch his own camera if possible. They wouldn't believe his intent was innocent. Besides, when he got to the machine and saw McMurray getting up from his seat, he'd chickened out. It must have been the moment before the murder. Yet Giles hadn't seen anyone else go inside before he returned to wait for Thea.

The same scene reset, and the robot's finger tapped the image of a young bald person in shorts and a bikini top walking behind Giles. In the blink of an eye, the holographic image stood before them. "Hello," said Zorius, Spock-like. "We need you to answer a question."

"Yeah." The squeaky voice revealed a scared young woman, her nervous fingers playing with her floral swim top's strap. Was the bald look on girls a thing now? Zorius moved his hologram in front of Giles, and her eyes widened. "Do you remember seeing this person a few minutes past noon near the river?" He replayed the scene in which she followed Giles.

"I, well, kindy. I want really payin attention."

"Do you remember where the person went after the cam lost sight of them?"

She shook her head, and Giles squelched a relieved exhale.

49

"No." Her head kept shaking. "Like said, weren't watchin em. I went to the café right after."

"Thank you."

The girl vanished. Wherever she was, she must've been seeing a holographic image of Zorius carrying on a conversation with her. Wow, what amazing leaps of technological prowess. Their twenty-first-century methods of electronic communication now seemed so obsolete.

But Zorius wasn't finished. "I want you to see what happened right around the time of the scene we just showed you."

A hologram appeared of McMurray going back inside Midnight Rider. Once again, the scene came alive around them. At 12:17, Giles saw the back of his own head and black tank top through the crowd, standing at the open gate. He held his breath, heart thudding. Would the cops recognize him? Thankful he'd happened to remove his telltale backpack and hold it in front of him in preparation for the thwarted camera grab, he forced his rigid shoulders to relax. He had nothing to worry about. Right? *God, please blind their eyes. You know I did nothing wrong.*

The cop zoomed in on McMurray, and Giles exhaled as his own image dropped off. McMurray looked over his shoulder toward something unseen, rose and walked to the rear, then returned to his seat. Seconds later, he disappeared from view. No matter how close the robot zoomed in, they couldn't discern anyone else's presence.

"Let's looka the satellite," said Ruba.

After further hologram manipulation, Zorius succeeded in zooming in about ten feet above the street. Giles scanned the bodies for his own, but the parts blended into one mass of moving humanity. "Here's the time machine." The robot's tap thrust the top of the vehicle into view. At 12:17, someone approached the rear from the direction opposite the gate. A wide-brimmed straw hat obscured their face, clothing, and gender.

"There our killa." Ruba sighed. "How they get through the secure fence?"

She backed it up fifteen seconds. Another steel gate, invisible to a casual observer but identical to the one opposite, flung open. A figure stalked inside the fence. But how could anyone except McMurray open either gate?

"Why a second gate?"

"Oh," Penny answered. "Colt wanted a way to sneak back inside without being followed."

Ten seconds later, the capsule's rear door opened, and the person stepped inside.

"Back up and gram em."

Robot did so, tapping several times on the hat. "They disabled their hologram."

Ruba let loose a curse. "Frus that we can't see who it is. They smart enough to know how to access it. They must know they bein watched and how to boozle it. Wut a muff." The contempt accompanying the words indicated muff didn't convey a positive impression.

"I was right." Penny thrust the suitcase back and forth with her foot. "He got in from the back."

"Did McMurray let em in? Or they let themself in?"

Zorius lifted his chin, the closest he'd gotten thus far to human emotion. "Couldn't tell. The answer to that would help us narrow down the suspects."

"McMurray not gon let in a stranger."

The robot backed up the footage. "Let's check the breezeway cams."

Again, Ruba cursed. "The cams got disabled. Look. See how footage goes dark at 12:13?"

"Can you see the perp's face?"

"Course not. They too smart."

Giles's heart threatened to pound right out of his chest. He willed his voice to stay steady. "Well, see? How would I know how to disable robocams? I can tell you think I was involved. That's why I'm here, isn't it?"

Zorius reverted to his Spock-like self. "We think they knew where the cams were and stayed below window level."

"Obviously someone more familiar with this area than me. I wouldn't know a twenty-second-century cam if it stared me in the face. I don't have a straw hat, nor did I know about the rear entrance or the other gate." If that didn't convince them of his innocence, nothing would.

Penny edged in for a better look at the satellite view. The same straw hat emerged from the back door, dirty deed in the books, and the unknown perpetrator retraced their steps through the open gate to the riverside breezeway, disappearing beneath the solid wood frame. "Who in the world is that? Could there have been witnesses?"

Ruba manipulated the image to show the street cam's view. "The fence blocks the rear view. They snuck in on the river side where there no cams."

"It's someone who knows how to get through the gate. Let's get the Xcam on it."

But even an X-ray wouldn't penetrate the fence's heavy steel. Ruba's muttered curses echoed Giles's frustration.

"What about the knife?" Penny clamped her feet around her luggage. "Any way to trace it?"

"It a modern-style knife."

"Well then," she challenged, "how would any of McMurray's passengers have obtained such a weapon?"

Robot eyed her. "Valid point, Mx. Nichols. Where were you at 12:17 p.m.?"

"Eating lunch at the café down by the river."

"Show us."

Penny, who had already mastered hologram technology, straightened her shoulders and stilled her fidgeting. After locating the café's robocam, she showed them her image on the deck with her back to the camera. Although they couldn't see her face, she wore the same red sundress and hair clip. At 12:20, she got up and walked toward the café, the brown suitcase clattering behind her, revealing a glimpse of her profile obscured by sunglasses.

"From there," she explained, "I walked over to the public restroom."

He hadn't seen anyone in a red dress pulling a suitcase. He would've remembered. "You must've just missed us."

"Who besides you and McMurray would've known how to get through the security gate?"

"Nobody else that I know of. The sensor only recognizes preauthorized fingerprints."

Zorius touched the image, zoomed in on the guy behind the deli counter, and, like Giles's tailgater, the guy stood right in front of them.

"Help you?" The name stenciled on his lapel said Togg. The facial expression said startled.

Giles didn't blame him.

"Yes, Togg. We need you to identify someone for us."

"Yeah."

He moved the hologram in front of Penny. "Can you tell us if this customer came in around lunchtime today?"

"Oh, yeah, member them. But they wore shades."

"Do you remember what they ordered and where they sat?"

"Uh, sub sandwich, I think. Outside."

"Thank you." Zorius blanked out the screen. "Penny, do you know of any reason there'd be a drone inside McMurray's vehicle?"

"A drone? Really?"

Zorius nodded. "We found a drone on the floor."

"What's that mean?"

"We don't know. It was inactivated. Did McMurray use drones?"

Penny's hands clenched. "Not that I know of." But if McMurray was keeping secrets from his assistant, her chagrin made sense.

"You free to go," Ruba told Penny.

Penny's shoulders relaxed, and she flung back her head like she'd been released from prison.

"But you..." Ruba's hard look pinned Giles in place. "We have more questins for you, so stick by till you cleared."

IN THE YEAR 2123

Ari stuffs the tissue in her pocket, then grabs my hand, her grip sharp. "Who do you think killed the guy?"

I pry my hand from hers. Seriously? She doesn't even use hand sanitizer. "I have no idea. It's absurd they think any of us had anything to do with it."

Her vigorous nod shakes her pink hair. "Why are they questioning Giles and the lady?"

Zach leans in. "Isn't it obvious? Giles was the first one inside. Plus, only he knew how to gain access. And the lady knew the guy."

"Still." Ari's big blue eyes blink at the empty wall. "Giles has no motive. Why would he kill the only person who can get us back? I mean, I know Penny can too, but Giles didn't know that."

I wipe my palm on my shorts, mystified myself by the law enforcement's thought processes.

Then Giles and Penny reenter the room with Robocop and Ladycop. Giles beelines right to my side, latching onto my gaze, but Ladycop interrupts our loving reunion. "We checked all your alibis, and most of em check out."

But she fails to specify which of them don't check out.

"However, yull need to be available for further questins as we conduct investigation. McMurray's vehicle bein guarded so don start thinkin you get go home yet."

I send a prayer heavenward that they find the culprit soon. The thought of my comfy queen bed warms my senses but also makes me wonder if any time has elapsed at home. Are we stuck in a time warp here while the clock is frozen at midnight in 2023?

The only person who would know the answer is dead.

Penny utters the sentiment I'm already thinking. "Can you take us back, please? I'd like to return to my B & B. Hopefully, they'll let me stay an extra day…or more."

As the cops escort us all to the autopod, I ask Giles what went on in that second interrogation. We follow the cops into the cooled interior, and I grab a window seat while the others clamber in around us. The pod climbs into the humid blue sky like a hot-air balloon. Somewhere above us, the bright sun beats down.

Giles's face animates as he narrates. "They consulted the public robocams which take round-the-clock images of everything. I thought I was in a *Star Trek* episode." He describes how the scene was recreated, leaving me in awe. While the two cops in front focus on their holograms and the pod drives itself, he continues. "They showed a satellite view of McMurray opening the rear door and letting someone inside."

"Could you tell anything about the person?"

"No, they were hiding under a big straw hat."

"Whoever it was didn't wait very long, did they?"

Our host died at the hand of an unknown killer in a big hat, stranding us a hundred years in the future, our own futures uncertain.

"So, love, why did they want to question you again?"

Giles pauses before speaking, a hiatus pulsing with potential calamity. "They caught me on camera walking around, and it made them suspicious."

My heart clenches at his tight-voiced delivery so unlike his usual self-assurance. Could there be more to the story he doesn't want me to know?

"When were you walking around?"

"While you were in the toilets changing."

Right, the empty stall, the leap of fear. Of course, Giles had nothing to do with the murder. But his alibi is shaky, or they wouldn't be keeping such tight tabs on him.

"Well, as long as you weren't anywhere near the time machine, you shouldn't have anything to worry about."

His pointed lack of a reply, his quickened breathing, frightens me more than if he were to come right out and declare his guilt.

"Right?" I prod.

He halts me with a big-eyed plea, inclining his head toward the watchful cops. Then he leans into my ear and whispers, "Talk later, okay?"

Unable to do anything but nod, I wipe my palms on my shorts. What is he hiding?

Still twitchy, I crane around my fiancé. "Penny, what about you? What was your alibi?" As a journalist, I'm used to asking probing questions. The recipients react either in defensive or with great relish…depending on what their answer is going to be. And how much they enjoy talking about themselves.

Penny is in the second category. "I was enjoying lunch by the river before heading over to meet McMurray." Her blue eyes gleam, her love of the limelight showing. "The café's robocam showed me sitting on the deck, then getting up to leave at 12:20."

"Speaking of time, anybody got it?" Ari calls from behind.

Penny checks her old-fashioned analog watch. "It's a few minutes past two." She taps the off-white vinyl strap. "So thankful I remembered to bring this with me."

Death has a funny way of interrupting life's plans. When we get back—*if* we get back—my article is going to raise more questions than it will answer. Will the readers react with sympathy for McMurray, with empathy for our plight? Or will they somehow blame me for capitalizing on a tragedy?

This could be the catapult to my career I've been waiting for…or the death of it.

IN THE YEAR 2123

We land feet from the murder site, and Ladycop forbids us from exiting until she updates us. "We gon put yull in dorm so yull have place sleep tonight. Jussit tight."

Outside, the crowd is still milling around. Men, women, and children study their personal holograms with the same studious attention we pay our smartphones. A few sport oddly stoic faces. They're either robots or surgically altered humans. Others look like twenty-first-century transgenders. Clearly human, but neither man nor woman. Several possess elaborate hairdos like Nissi, some have bald heads and loincloths, and most are the same skin color—a medium olive shade. I cannot distinguish any racial characteristics.

Outwardly, everybody looks the same.

Racial and gender disparities and tensions will largely disappear. The people live in uniformity and harmony.

"But we'll need clothes and food," Ari reminds our guards.

"We provide em." Ladycop exits the autopod. She and her partner work their way through bodies determined to hold up their approach to McMurray's machine. Cops scurry in and out, and police tape blocks access.

"They're providing clothes for us?" Ellen echoes. "But they don't know our sizes."

"Don't worry about sizes," Penny begins.

Sher snorts. "They're going to be way too small. Everyone here is super skinny." She points outside. "Do you see any large people out there?"

Ellen shakes her head. "Penny, why is everyone so skinny? It's like nobody has any body fat at all."

Go, girl! About time someone asked.

Penny gives a wry smile. "Drugs, my dear. Prescription drugs."

Ari clears her throat. "You mean, like, skinnifying drugs? The kind that keep you up all night?"

"Yes and no. Yes, they make you skinny, and no, they aren't stimulants. They've been perfected to have no side effects. They turn you into a lean calorie-burning machine. You get to eat to your heart's content and not gain an ounce."

Sher whoops and pats her denim-clad thigh. "Okay, I'm taking them drugs home with me. How do I get some?"

We laugh, a splash of sound, a welcome release of tension.

I twist in my seat to better view the murder site, then nudge Giles. "Look, they're taking the body away."

The body-shaped lump under a shroud is being pushed into an autopod with flashing lights. A futuristic ambulance?

"How is McMurray's family going to be informed if we're stuck here for a while?"

"I suppose, when he fails to return, they'll assume the worst."

"And never get closure."

"Penny, do you know who his closest relative would be?"

"Well…" She squeezes her chin as if it holds the answer. "I guess it would be his son."

"Do you know his son?"

Her gaze is far away. "I may have met him once. But…"

"We'll need to take his body back with us." Giles straightens his shoulders, thwarting Penny's chance to satiate my curiosity. "Then the first thing we need to do when we return is track down his family and tell them." He falls silent, unable to utter the terrible truth. "Say, Penny." He braces an ankle on knee. "Is time standing still in 2023 while we are here? In other words, when we return, will it still be midnight, June 3, 2023? Or will time have elapsed there too?"

A keen light glows in her eye. "Time is elapsing there the same as it is here. Like being on vacation. However, for the return trip, the operator can set the time to whatever he likes."

This was feeling less and less like a vacation by the minute. "I'm screwed if I miss more than a day. My boss'll be frantic if I don't show up for work." Not to mention poor Mia.

"And our food cart people are gonna think we joined the alien pod," says Zach.

"Now why would they think that?" Penny casts another of her wry grins over her shoulder.

"Only because he constantly threatens to hijack the next UFO he sees," Ari retorts.

No surprise Zach's weed-saturated brain would conjure up such a scenario.

Ellen doesn't hide her eye roll.

"You ought to be a writer, Zach." Penny sniggers, her high spirits infectious. "You guys, I can't wait to show you around. You will be amazed by life in the twenty-second century. The clothes, the food, the people…"

Weary after the release of tension, I rest my head against the window and catch the eye of a child watching me. She looks about six, maybe. Her shoulder-length brunette hair turns auburn where the sun touches it. It's the little girl in the fuchsia shortie who asked me what year we were from, whose face I knew yet couldn't place. She clutches the hand of a woman with similar almond-shaped eyes, one lighter than the other. White sunsuit, taut skin stretched over high cheekbones, pixie-cut platinum hair. Probably about ten years older than me.

But I clutch Giles's thigh. The girl looks like me.

She smiles and waves. I smile back. Her guardian notices and stiffens, her gaze glued to mine. Then she clutches at her heart as though overcome. Something like a spark of recognition flashes in her eyes. Yet that's impossible. Unless this woman and her daughter are my descendants. Do I resemble a relative of theirs they weren't expecting to see? My leg twitches at my urge to flee this pod and go talk to them. But maybe we can interact through the window. Nope, the windows are fixed. Wouldn't it be fabulous to know what the future holds for Giles and me? Will we have kids, and are these two the offspring from two or three generations out? Or, God forbid, are they descended from me and some other husband? For sure, these two have the answers, but the woman tugs the child's hand. Then they vanish into the crowd.

How will I find those two possible relations again?

The two cops stomp back to inform us of our next destination. "We're takin yull to dorm now."

We lift off again, and the crowd grows smaller below, leaving no sign of the woman and daughter.

"Can't you take me back to my B & B?" Penny pleads.

"No, yull got stay together." A siren cuts her off, and lights flash all around. Robocop utters a word that sounds like a curse, but that can't be, can it? "Another body? We need to change direction."

The autopod veers toward the riverbank, and we land a hundred yards downriver from McMurray's capsule, the cops discussing between themselves as if we aren't here. "A body was found on the shore. It was in the water for only a short time. Looks like drowning, but then the body didn't drift into the deeper water."

"Who found em?"

"A couple walking the path. They saw hair floating on the surface, went to investigate, then grammed us."

Ladycop turns to face us. "We takin a detour, folk. Got nother dead body on our hands."

"Why don't you take us to our dorm so we can relax?" Penny huffs. "Would be nice to put our feet up."

"Yeah," Ari agrees. "I could use a nap."

I nod. "Me too." I'd crashed for about five dream-filled hours after dinner last night, then got up at eleven to wait for Giles to pick me up for our long-anticipated Midnight Rider excursion. Ari hadn't slept at all. The lack of sleep was getting to all of us.

But we hadn't dreamed of anything like this.

THE GIRL

"Parent, why that person look like you?" I watch the funny grown-up get in the traption. At first, I thought it was Parent cept wider and with different hair. But Parent stands next to me holding my hand. "Why do them wear weird clothes?"

Parent pulls me away from the crowd, blocking my view of the strange grown-ups. "They from nother time."

"I axed em what year they from, but they dint tell me. They dresses and talks funny."

Parent tells me they speak Ar-kay-ick, whatever that is. They sound kinda robot to me, but weirder. Like the way Parent talk only at home. But in public, Parent talk like everyone else. They try to make me talk robot too. Even after I splained my school friends laugh at me when I do. My teacher says students not sposed to act like robots.

Parent doesn't know why the long-haired grown-up look like them. "I heard everybody has a twin somewhere."

"Where is my twin?"

An autopod lands on the dirt street, its hum blocking out Parent's words. "Wut?" I ask.

"You may not have met em yet."

"Oh. Does my twin look like me?"

"They does."

But then Parent waves down a robocop and asks about a dead person. Even though I like the robots, the way they talk and walk, all stiff and precise like the traption people, I don't wan act or sound or look like one.

Parent questions the robocop. "You know yet how they died?"

"We are working on the investigation," says the robocop in their machine voice. "We will release more details when we discover them."

"But..." Parent clutches Robocop's stiff arm. "But you have any suspects?"

"I cannot reveal that information."

Parent tugs me toward our partment, muttering the entire way and ignoring all my questions bout the dead person. Parent usually tries their best to answer my questions, so their behavior scares me.

Something must be awful wrong for Parent to forget I'm here. I know what'll get their attention. I grab my Treebotter Bots from my bedroom shelf and adjust their volume to its highest setting. Parent hates their high-pitched hum and makes me keep them down. "Zzzz-zzzzzz-zz!" I swing the biggest bot through the air like it's an autopod, its arms making such rapid circles I can't see anything but a blur. This is my favorite part.

"Hey!" There's Parent at the door, just as I thought. "Keep those down!"

"Kay." I smile and obey. At least I know they hant forgotten bout me, after all. But their eyes still look through me when they're not looking out the window at some unseen threat.

I shiver. Ever since that traption thing got here, everything is different.

IN THE YEAR 2123

The cops refuse to change course. Once again, they order us to stay before embarking. They pick their way over driftwood and detritus and stony ground, then disappear beyond another police autopod, this one black. The water sways and laps at the bank's crushed stones, the river as peaceful as the cloudless blue sky.

I wipe my palms on my thighs. "Penny, why did the cops call you and Giles by the title of Mix?"

She tugs her sundress hem over her knees. "They don't use Mr. or Ms. or Mrs. anymore. Everyone is Mx. The gender-neutral thing is big now. For those who still identify as male or female, it's either X or Y."

A conglomeration of opinions launch toward her, and we pass the wait arguing the pros and cons of gender neutrality. Three in favor, three against. I believe God knew what He was doing when He assigned us our genders. But Ellen, Sher, and Zach disagree. They believe gender is self-determined, that nondistinction equals nondiscrimination.

The six of us are never going to be on the same page, so I return to my people-watching, half hoping, half dreading spotting more possible descendants. How many progeny am I responsible for?

Someone shouts. Our group crowds to the windows on the river's side.

"They're hauling the body away," Zach says.

I crane to see. But the body on the stretcher lies beneath a white shroud, and my fellow travelers groan. The stretcher is loaded into another ambulance.

Five minutes later, the cops return. They won't share details, no matter how much we plead. "Nothin to tell yet." They lift us to our next destination a few miles east—a nondescript dorm room they expect us to share for an untold number of days and nights. Four sets of single bunk beds mean the couples are separated, but the men and women are not.

I crowd beside Giles in the doorway. Who knows, maybe we'll recognize the neighborhood. A six-hundred-foot-high wooded peak rises to the north. "Recognize that?" I point. "We're at Mount Tabor's southern base."

My arms creep around my middle and squeeze against the sinking sensation over the rest of what's around us. This used to be single-family bungalows, safe and friendly. Homes filled with doctors and teachers, restaurant owners and nonprofit managers. Giles and I enjoyed trekking tidy sidewalks alongside community gardens and landscaped yards, around the reservoirs, to admire the city view from Tabor's lofty top. Now obscene apartment buildings shine in the sun as far as the eye can see.

Back inside the dorm room, excitement vibrates around Penny. The other four surround her as she holds up her hologram. A newscaster is facing the camera. To his right and left are two still shots: one of McMurray and the other of a fair-haired woman. The words *a second death today* scroll beneath them.

I'd put the other victim around fifty-odd years of age. Graying hair, nondescript features. Two gray eyes. Thin twenty-second-century face obscured by a big straw hat.

"I knew her," Penny emotes over and over, emphasized with sharp hand gestures. "She frequented the same coffee shop I did. In fact, just this morning, I chatted with her and a friend of hers. Her name is—*was*—TigerLily. Such a nice person too. Such a shame."

My arms are strangling my middle, so I let them loose. "Do they know how she died?"

"Shush," snaps Ellen. "Penny, can you back it up to where the guy is explaining that?" Ellen gives me a pointed look. I'd glare back, but she's already turned away.

Penny replays the last moments. A robotic newscaster stares at us with somber face and expressionless eyes. "A body was found in the Willamette River an hour after the time-traveler Coltrane McMurray was found stabbed in his time machine. Police believe they'd only been dead a few hours at most but cannot specify a time or cause of death until further investigation. Identification is being withheld until the person's family has been notified. If anyone witnessed anything related to their death, please gram the police."

"There ya go, Penny," drolls Ellen. "Your chance for the limelight."

Penny tsks but adds a wry chuckle. "So that's what you think of me."

"Seriously, though." Ellen wags her ringed index finger under Penny's nose. "You need to, what'd he say? Gram the police?"

"Yeah, nobody calls anyone anymore. Everything is done by hologram. Anyway, I know nothing about her drowning."

"They didn't say she drowned," I remind her.

"You're right. I just made a you-know-what out of you and me by assuming."

The newscast keeps playing but gives us nothing new. The same images of McMurray's murder and Penny's friend repeat themselves until it moves on to something new.

Beside me, Ari makes a strangled sound as she tries to stifle a yawn. "I'm gonna lie down." She plops on the nearest bed.

Zach claims the bunk above her, and, as if Ari's sleepiness is a contagious virus, I find myself yawning and looking for a bed. I'm not picky. Plus, they all look alike in their cream-colored sheets. I settle on a bottom bunk, my backpack at my feet, and pull a brown blanket over my toes, shielding them from the cool AC. Soon, I've drifted off to sleep.

I come awake slowly. Golden daylight filters through the multipaned picture window, and I estimate the time at late afternoon or early evening. Sunset at this time of year still falls around 9:00 p.m., unless the earth's axis has shifted in the past century. I have no way of knowing. But Penny, snoring softly on the bed across from me, has a watch. It lies on the mattress next to her, so I creep over to check the time—5:55 p.m. I took a decent nap. But I'm refreshed and ready to get out and explore. Ari is stirring, her eyelids fluttering like something is trying to escape.

My whispered conversation with Ari wakes the others. Zach rolls over and groans. "What are you two plotting now?"

Ellen and Sher, next to the window, sit up and rub their half-closed eyes. Giles hops down from the bunk above me, settling beside me, and Penny swings her legs over the sides of hers.

"Hey, everyone." Her cheery tone chases away any lingering lethargy. She seems to have stepped into a de facto leadership role. Fine by me. I sure have no desire to steer this crazy ship. "I have an idea," she says. "But first, let's eat."

Whoa. On the table, plates of sandwiches have somehow appeared.

"Yo, food." Zach lifts a wrapped sandwich from the dish. "Where'd this come from?"

Penny helps herself. "I'm guessing the guard outside our door brought them in while we slept."

A curse bursts from Sher as she grabs meals for her and Ellen. "There's a flippin' guard out there? You'd think we were criminals or something."

"She's a robot," Penny clarifies.

"She?" Arching a brow, Ellen opens the paper wrap. "I thought this was a genderless world."

"How do you tell a boy robot from a girl robot?" Sher's laughter echoes, and her mirth, mingled with Ellen's, rubs off on the rest of us until I fear our chortles will bring said guard in to check on us.

Penny's mouth quirks. "Girl robots wear sundresses?"

I envision a softened yet still stiff robotic face peering in at us, wondering what kind of maniacs laugh during their "imprisonment." For that's what this is, despite our attempts at levity.

We're not going to be allowed out of here until they solve McMurray's murder.

GILES

Giles shifted on the hard mattress, enjoying the first bite of his savory ham and Swiss sandwich. He'd have relished it more if he were eating it with Thea in his sun-dappled dinette overlooking the Sellwood Bridge and the West Hills beyond. About as basic as they came, this room offered no artwork, merely a table and four chairs surrounded by the bunks and a sofa under the window. A kitchen filled with shiny gadgets he could figure out how to use in a pinch. The bathroom held three stalls and three showers, but he'd be danged if he'd share the facilities with any female strangers.

This layout must be replicated all the way to the top of the multistory building. What sort of people occupied dorm rooms these days? Singles with no families? It had the feel of temporary or overflow housing. No way could a couple like him and Thea raise a family in such an environment.

At least he had Thea, the prettiest girl in the room, by far, to eat with and hold hands with. She nibbled a ladylike bite of her sandwich. Early in their relationship, when he'd awaken thinking about her, he'd pinch himself, hardly daring to believe such an exquisite specimen belonged to him. For life. Yet her beauty was matched by her offbeat humor and sharp mind. A complete package. Not only that, she had the cleanest hands in Portland.

He took a second bite of the makeshift dinner. The meat's texture didn't resemble any ham he was used to. Lifting a corner of the bread, he examined the meat. It looked more like a slab of spam. Was it fake? Did pig farmers still exist, or was meat all produced in factories now? Oh well, he was too hungry to question it, and it tasted delicious.

Penny clapped, arresting everyone's attention. "Okay, you crazy kids, since we're stuck here for who knows how long, let's take our minds off our problem. I suggest we play a get-to-know-you game I learned in college. It's really fun." She silenced Zach's groan with a look. "We sit in a circle, and one person at a time tells an interesting fact about themselves that they don't think is true for anyone else in the room. Then one person is allowed to ask a further question on what you just shared. But only one question. Got it?"

Normally Giles tolerated such games, but this time, his unique fact would invite unwanted questions. He brushed Thea's thigh, then slipped his arm around her waist. She plopped her head on his shoulder and met his gaze.

He'd rather sit here and lose himself in her splendid eyes than answer risky questions. How he loved her, his Thea, the only woman—the only person—he knew who quoted Scripture to her cats. Watching her shaking her finger at them while spouting mangled Bible verses reminded him of a pretty televangelist and always made him laugh. Life with her would never get boring.

Thea, still holding his gaze, shifted him back to the present. And his predicament. Even though just one person would be allowed to question each sharer, it wouldn't stop anyone from bombarding him later with all sorts of queries he couldn't—wouldn't—answer.

They all perched on the lower bunks as Penny spoke. "I'll start. Then I'll choose the next person. Okay!" She crossed her legs and propped both hands on her upraised knee as if telling them a bedtime story. "My unique fact: I was born on May 18, 1980. Do any of you remember what huge geological event happened that day?"

Ari's hand shot up. "Mount St. Helens erupted."

Penny chuckled. "That's right. Now one of you may ask me a related question about my unique fact."

Giles raised his hand. "Were you born anywhere near the eruption?"

"Good question, Giles." Penny's eyes glowed, saying "attaboy" like she was his life coach at a mindfulness retreat. "I was born in Ellensburg, Washington, right in the path of the ash cloud. While my mom was in labor, the sky went dark and ash fell everywhere. She has some real hair-raising stories from that day."

"Can you tell us one?" asked Sher.

"Sorry, one question per turn. In fact, why don't you go next, Sher. Tell us something unusual about yourself."

Sher struggled against the smile tugging the corners of her mouth. She looked to Ellen as if her friend could rescue her. "Ah, you put me on the spot," she joked. "Maybe I am boring and have nothing unique to offer."

Ellen's vigorous headshake jostled her blond bangs. "Girlfriend, you know that's not true. You could tell them about—"

"Hey! Shush, you." Sher frowned at the floor, her fingers kneading her temples. Then she straightened her shoulders and lifted her chin. "Okay, here's my claim to uniqueness. I was born on the same day as Ariana Grande. June 26, 1993." She exhaled as though she'd bared her soul and was thankful it was over.

Giles would've pegged her as older than thirty. Sher gazed upon the world with the gray, thoughtful eyes of a Yoda. Younger than Ellen in years, yet the elder in soul age. Again, he suspected Ellen and Sher were more than best friends.

"Can you sing?" asked Thea.

"Trust me, I am no Ariana Grande."

His sister's obsession and constant playing of Grande's album *Yours Truly* on her iTunes made communication with her nearly impossible. And hearing Ariana at the gym and the supermarket and everywhere else soured him on the artist.

"That's interesting and cool, Sher."

Thea was only trying to be kind. He'd deem a shared birthday with a volcanic eruption far more exciting than sharing a birthday with an overrated diva. And Thea would agree.

His wandering thoughts teetered, then righted themselves as Ellen took her turn. "My claim to fame? My parents named me after a Beatles song. Grand prize to the first one of you who guesses the song."

"'Eleanor Rigby,'" Zach blurted, surprising Giles and probably everyone else. "*Revolver.*"

Ellen's brows rose to her hairline. "Wouldn'ta pegged you for a Beatles' fan, Mr. Hipster."

"Everyone knows the Beatles." Defensiveness laced his tone. "And I'm not hipster. I'm counterculture."

"Mr. Counterculture who's intimately familiar with the names of the Beatles' albums."

"Well, y'know"—he drew out his words in a mock drawl— "I spent a lotta time with my grandparents growing up and heard all the classic rock bands, 'specially from the British Invasion era."

"They sound like your typical cool-old-hippy grandparents."

"Way cooler than yours." Zach added the sharpened tone he reserved for special moments when people underestimated him. Apparently, he held Ellen with the same level of disdain she held for him.

Before the bad vibes erupted into something more toxic, Penny clapped again. "Stop, both of you." She scanned the room during the tense quiet, and Giles pretended to study the view outside lest she rope him in. The longer it took for his turn, the more time to prepare his answers for any questions they might throw at him.

"Ari, how about you go next?"

Giles slumped in relief and barely heard Ari announce her special talent.

"I paint rocks."

Silence, then a snort from Zach. "That's why she's known far and wide as Arias Rocks."

Ari stuck out her tongue at her husband. "Well, yeah, I've also been known to rock, and my website is Arias Rocks dot com, if you're interested in seeing my work."

And her painted rocks were spectacular. Thea had several in her apartment on which Ari had painted flowers or adorned with pine cones and ferns. Giles himself had one of her golden retriever puppy rocks in his living room, the closest he'd come to an actual pet.

"Just to clarify, I paint rocks in my spare time. My husband and I also own and run a food cart called Crazy A Z."

"Tell us more, Ari." Penny's warm eyes exuded interest. "Are the rocks a hobby or a second business?"

Ari grinned at Zach, who smiled with keen affection. Only Zach and Ari seemed to enjoy this game. Well, and Penny too.

"It started as a hobby." Ari swung her Converse-clad foot forward and back, forward and back, like an overeager metronome. "It turned into a business. I have customers from all over the country. The problem is, rocks, even small ones, are heavy to ship. So I switched to a lightweight composite material with the look and feel of smooth stones in order to make shipping more feasible."

Thea leaned in toward her friend. "Tell them who your first customer was, Ari."

Dear Thea. Giles could've applauded her for keeping the attention away from him. Perhaps the game would run out of steam before his turn. Or the guard would enter and declare the murderer had been found, and they'd be set free from their prison.

Fat chance of that.

Ari's lower leg gained steam as if it were dying to launch and flee. As, no doubt, they all were. "My first customer." She beamed a broad, infectious smile. "I had some of my rocks decorating the outside of our food cart—this was a couple years ago or so. One day this gorgeous stylish woman with one-hundred-dollar hair, all dressed like she shopped at Saks, came up to the window and ordered a salad wrap. She complimented me on my rocks and asked if I sold them. I said no, but if she'd like one, she could take one home. She said sure and put it in her purse. 'You sure you don't mind?' she kept asking, and I assured her it was fine. Then she went to a bench and sat next to a hulking guy who looked familiar. Finally, it dawned on me. It was Juwan Buckner, the Trail Blazer, and his wife! Anyway, turns out Mrs. Buckner wanted more rocks for her yard. I painted them, and she paid me and told her friends about me." She threw out a hand in a dramatic flourish. "And that's how it all started."

Zach elbowed her. "I keep telling her she needs to teach art."

Ari snorted. "Trust me, you don't want me anywhere near a classroom. I'd join the kids in their mischief and get fired on day one."

Penny's eyes gleamed. She must want to know more—they all did—but she abided by her protocol and called on Zach.

"Yo, what? You want to know something *you*-nique about *moi*?"

"*Oui*. Something uniquely true about *tu*."

"Okay, well, uh…" He looked to Ari for inspiration, but she only lifted her brows. With their profuse tattoos and nose rings, you couldn't find a more cliché Portland couple than Arias and Zach Adams. Her: short and round and streaky-haired. Him: pierced and wiry and black-clad. Them: the kind of young couple you see window-shopping on Hawthorne Boulevard, browsing in Powell's Books, buying organic produce at New Seasons. "Hmm. My birthday's nothin' special. Wasn't born on a vol-can-ic holiday."

Giles was never sure if Zach's disjointed speech was put on for effect or if his brain randomly misfired after years of heavy substance use.

"Hey, I know. I bet I'm the only one who knows that if you move one letter in Elvis, you get Evils." As the others waited for more, he drumrolled Ari on the head like she was his personal punchline-announcing timpani. Uncertain chuckles joined Ari's laughter. When she elbowed her husband's ribs, he parried with a couple side jabs. It might've turned into one of their playful mock tussles if Penny hadn't intervened.

"Zach wins the prize for most creative answer!"

"Uh, wait." Ari straightened and waved her hand. "He's got an even better answer. Don't you, Hacky-Zach?"

"Oh, you mean *Grimm*?"

"Yeah, I mean *Grimm*."

"'Kay." He drummed his fingers on the mattress. "I was an extra on *Grimm*. Got to meet the two stars and got their siggys. Bet none of you can say the same."

Several heads moved side to side.

"Auditioned for a small role as a monster, but didn't get it. Just couldn't muster up that inner monster, I s'pose." He scratched his bearded chin, his gaze distant. "Gonna have to work on that."

Ari wrapped his neck in an elbow hug as they all laughed. "But we're still proud of him. He made a great crowd bystander!"

"Woulda made an even awesomer monster."

Penny clapped. "I love it. How interesting! How long have you two been married?"

"Couple o' years, give or take." Ari landed more light punches on his ribs while Zach kept patting a rhythm on top of her pink-streaked hair. Ari's giggles escalated to excited shrieks when he captured her in a bear hug, and they fell to the mattress.

"Hey, you two." Sher's droll tone stopped them all. "Get a room."

Laughter rang out as the couple sat up, engrossed in their private world as though everyone else had intruded upon the scene. Minutes passed before everyone had calmed enough to move on.

Uh-oh. Penny was watching him.

"Giles."

His heart thudded as if it hadn't been overstressed enough today already.

"Your turn. What's your one-of-a-kind fact?"

He gazed at each face and stopped when he reached Thea's. Should he make something up? But no, she'd know and confront him on it later. If only the secret he was about to share wouldn't open so many cans of worms. And snakes and spiders, to boot.

He took a deep breath and launched a silent prayer, then searched Thea's deep-blue gaze as if he were speaking only to her. Love shone in the depths of her beautiful eyes, encouraging him on. "Most of you don't know this about me. I was adopted."

Thea smiled her approval for his honesty. His bravery. Holding his breath, he waited for the inevitable questions.

Naturally, Ari went first. "Wow, I had no idea. Thea never said a word. Do you know who your birth parents are, and have you ever met them?"

"That's two questions," he reminded her. "Maybe yes, maybe no. You'll just have to wonder."

Penny hadn't said they were required to answer the follow-up questions, only that they were limited to one. He owed nobody but Thea any explanations about his parentage.

And, when the proverbial time was right, he'd tell her.

IN THE YEAR 2123

Giles must've been so reluctant to open up old wounds. It took courage for him to bare his soul. The stress of his revelation has etched deep lines on his brow. Of course, there's more to the story, but the part he shared was huge. The subject has been fraught with pain ever since his mother admitted the truth while he was in high school. The search for his birth parents brought him here to the States. To Oregon. Now, he might be getting close to finding answers. "Thea, if I'm on the right track," he told me in our last conversation about it, all smiles and hopeful eyes, "my birth father is somewhere here in Oregon."

We left it at that, two days ago. He'd decided to reach out to his birth father after we return from this trip. But now…

But now Penny's calling my name, and I'm going to tell them all about…

"When I was in high school in Australia"—my chest swells—"my oztag team won every competition for four years straight."

Yep, blank looks. I need to explain oztag. Sometimes I forget the vast cultural differences between this country and my native land.

"Oztag is a type of rugby but not as rough. I guess the closest comparison in America would be flag football."

"Don't sound too exciting."

I glare at Zach. What gives him a right to judge? "It's not like you even watch sports anyway."

Ari jabs his ribs, and he doubles over in mock agony. "Be nice," she hisses.

The polite bland looks all round, save Giles's, tell me I erred in my choice. I rack my brain for something unique yet relatable but keep drawing a blank. Am I so boring after all?

Oh, wait. "I bet none of you are mildly dyslexic, like me. Sometimes I write my birth year as 1989, instead of 1998, making me nine years older than I am."

"I'm dyslexic too." Zach holds up a hand. "So you can't use that. How did you think I came up with Elvis/Evils?"

Point taken. And explains a lot about Zach. Nobody except Giles knows I'm here to write an article, and it's supposed to remain confidential. Not even Ari knows. But since we're stuck here, does it matter? After all, it's looking less likely the article will ever get finished.

My emotions swing back and forth.

Ellen, of all people, comes to my rescue. "How about sharing with us how you happened to move to the States?"

My heart clenches the way it does every time I recall that life-changing event. "It's kind of tough to talk about." Yet I sense a receptive audience, and maybe unburdening myself'll be cathartic. "I may need some tissue."

Ari disappears into the kitchen.

Huh. Not like her to abandon me at such a profound moment.

Then she's in front of me thrusting a paper towel into my hand. "Look what I found."

Gawking, I hardly dare believe ordinary old tissues are still available in the future. Thankful paper products haven't been done away with, I clutch it in my damp palm. Or is it paper? Although it looks familiar, it doesn't feel like the paper towels I'm used to. Its texture feels more like fabric. Must be made from a thin, soft cloth rather than paper.

"A few months after I graduated high school, my parents decided to stay the weekend at their favorite holiday spot, Phillip Island. You all would love that place. The terrain and the vegetation, even the houses, remind me of the southern Oregon Coast. However, I stayed home. I don't even remember why—probably had a date. Looking back, I will be forever grateful."

Tears start to burn, and I dab at my eyes. Sniffing, I steady my tone. "It'd been raining for days. There'd been warnings of possible flooding on Phillip Island for Sunday evening, so they planned to return to Melbourne on Sunday morning. The flood hit a day early. When the evacuation warnings came, they must've been caught unawares, then attempted a getaway in the dark, along with hundreds of others. But the water swept up over the road, and they were never seen again." Tears run down my cheeks, and Giles's arm squeezes tighter around me. Ari comes to sit beside me and hold my hand in both of hers. It takes a minute before I can continue.

"That night, I saw the news on the telly and tried over and over to call them. They never answered. The next morning, when they didn't return as planned, I knew…"

Silence, while the others absorbed the horror of the memory. "A childhood friend of mine had married an American from Eugene, Oregon. She persuaded me to come stay with her until I could get settled. I sold everything and fled to the States with my inheritance and life insurance settlement. I then enrolled at the University of Oregon and got my journalism degree. My friend's husband got transferred to Idaho. I wished her farewell and moved to Portland to work for the *Portlandia* newspaper." I sniff, feeling the tracks of my tears dry on my cheeks like gullies in the arid outback. "And here I am."

"Such a sad story," murmurs Penny. "I'm so sorry you had to experience such a tragedy."

I can only nod. They don't want to hear any evangelical platitudes such as, "But God knew what He was doing." Or, "If it hadn't been for my faith in God, I'm not sure I would've made it through." Many people, especially the unchurched, bristle at such sayings in the face of calamity. They believe God shouldn't allow anything terrible to happen to anyone. Such an unrealistic view of the Almighty. So I settle for, "Despite the tragedy, I can see now that something good came from it." I nestle into Giles. "I wouldn't have met this wonderful guy otherwise."

We've reached that awkward lull in which we've all said everything we're going to say to a roomful of relative strangers. The food is gone, and outside the uncovered windows, darkness has fallen. Somewhere, hidden lights have switched on, filling the room with a bluish glow. But I can't find the source. It seems to seep through the ceiling. A newer technology than lightstrips, then? I file the conundrum away to ask about later. Wondering if a cop still guards the door, I crane my neck to see, but the opaque night reveals nothing.

If we have to spend the night here, my clothes won't smell too good tomorrow morning. I glance around for the changes of clothes the cops promised us and spy a tall cupboard next to the kitchen. "Excuse me," I say into the expectant silence pulsing with an unspoken "What now, mates?" as I rise and step over to the double doors inviting me in.

Piles of gleamy fabric—forest green with the barest hint of gold, shiny jet black like a race car, paisley, and striped—greet me, but nothing looks like garments. Penny's voice reaches my ears. "There's enough clothing there for all of you. Isn't that nice?"

"These are clothes?" I wrest a blue and white patterned bundle off the top and hold it up. It billows into the shape of extra-large trousers.

"Oh, that one must be for me."

We chuckle at Sher, but Penny tells me to put them on over my shorts, that she has something cool to show me.

So I do.

Of course, the trousers hang off me, and I pull the waistband out to demonstrate, as if I were posing for a post-weight-loss photo. "Real nice, babe." Giles emphasizes it with a wolf whistle. My cheeks flame as I stick my tongue out at him.

"Thea." Penny stands inches from me. "Gather up the waist with your fist."

I do so, then jump when the fabric moves. Seconds later, the slacks have somehow shrunk to my usual size 6. But the fabric continues to twist and fold itself like a warm hug around my middle, and now I'm wearing a loincloth.

"Whoa, what just happened?"

Penny grins like a magician pulling a rabbit out of her shoe. "Pretty cool, huh? Fabric nowadays is made to shrink and expand, so now clothes come in only one size. Extra large."

Ellen snorts. "Yet there are no extra-large people anymore to wear them."

"That's true. Not many, anyway."

Clothes of the future are adjustable, obesity has been conquered, and Robocops keep watch everywhere.

"Thea, now pinch the fabric again."

I do so, and the strip between my fingers morphs from blue to red. Another pinch, and there's a purple stripe. Then orange.

So that's why some loincloths are so colorful. It's magic.

"Are these made in China?" Giles asks.

"Oh, there's no China anymore. The nations of China, Mongolia, Korea, Taiwan, and most of Southeast Asia consolidated into one entity called Asiatica."

As she educates us on the new configuration of nations—*Indopakistan will consist of the former Indian, Bangladeshi, and Pakistani nations*—the others help themselves to fabric swaths and play with the adjustable garments. "Is Australia still Australia?" I hold my breath, half afraid to hear the answer.

"Sorry, Thea, I'm not sure. But we can Cloud it." Penny holds up a garment that resembles a lumberjack shirt and then wraps it around herself. "What's interesting about this"—she pinches the shirt's seams, whipping it into shape—"is that adjustable fabric was being developed in China in our lifetime, in the early twenty-first century."

"While you're familiarizing us with this new world, Penny"—I exchange the striped garment for a solid-blue shift—"can you help us understand the new pronouns? For instance, nobody uses she or he anymore?"

"Correct. All pronouns are gender-neutral. Everybody is they/them."

I pinch the fabric, and it shrinks and molds to my body. "So if I say, 'They are coming to visit,' that means more than one, and if I say 'They is coming to visit,' that means just one?"

"Exactly. Awkward, isn't it?"

I roll my eyes. "Seems like it'd be simpler for everyone to acknowledge gender."

"I imagine when people switched from thee to you centuries ago, it took a while for them to adapt as well."

A knock on the composite wooden door hushes her, and we all freeze, looking at the door like prisoners awaiting our next meal.

Or freedom.

Penny opens it, and Robocop, followed by a smaller uniformed robot, steps inside. Still as stiff and stoic as ever, his uniform fresh and uncreased, yet is that a tiny smile on his compoplastic face?

"We believe we have solved McMurray's murder, so you all are free to depart."

Zach leads the whoops, Ari the cheers. The rest of us join in like kids on the Oaks Park roller coaster.

Giles is first to ask the question. "Who killed him?"

"We believe the person found in the river today killed the victim, then themself."

Penny tsked. "TigerLily Malone? That is preposterous. I knew her, and she never struck me as suicidal."

"We found a knife set in their living quarters with one of the knives missing. The knife that killed McMurray was the same style and pattern as the rest of the set. Then we found poison in the second victim's system, which at first suggested they'd been murdered—"

"What was the poison?" Penny's gaze could bore holes through his plastic head all the way into his metal brains, if that were possible.

"Noressic. We found a supply of it in their rooms with five doses missing. Five doses are enough to kill two people. Their blood count of Noressic was ten times the safety limit."

I gasp. *Ten* times? "The murderer was wearing a big straw hat like hers, remember?"

"But…but…" First time I've seen Penny at a loss for words. "Why in the world would she do that? She knew I was here working on a project for McMurray, but she never once asked me about him. Much less admitted that she knew him." She shakes her head, back and forth.

Inside, I'm shaking mine too. The mystery, although allegedly solved, has only deepened.

"What about the drone you found in the time hopper?" Penny adjusts her glasses more tightly on her nose. "Was it hers?"

First I've heard of a drone. I zero in on Robocop's reply.

"The drone was wiped of data and prints, but she could've used it to track him. However, we have enough other evidence to conclude our investigation."

How would a drone get inside McMurray's time machine? Part of his experiments? Or something more sinister? Who was TigerLily Malone? And why would she arrange such an obvious murder-suicide? Did she not care if anyone figured out what she'd done? My inner investigative reporter is dying to delve into it.

Penny answers my questions with her next words. "The only thing that seemed to be troubling her had to do with her daughter. She hadn't heard from her for a few days, and she couldn't bring her up via gram." She paces to the window and gazes out as if it holds answers. Her voice dips, and I strain to hear. "She and her daughter had been estranged for a while. Then her daughter contacted her, and they were back on speaking terms. Then…poof. Gone." She snaps her fingers and retraces her steps to the cop. "Lily thought it might have had something to do with the young man she'd been seeing. She thought he had a bad influence on her."

Robocop is recording her, but she isn't shedding any further light on the case. He ushers us to the police pod, and I keep the loincloth on as we're flown to McMurray's vehicle. The shorts are softer than anything I've ever worn. Colorful and attractive, they'll fit right into quirky twenty-first-century Portland.

We soar over the city. Could TigerLily have learned her daughter was dead, that McMurray was responsible for her death, therefore she had nothing to lose by exacting revenge, then offing herself? If he and TigerLily knew each other from one of his previous trips, is this scenario all that far-fetched?

The full moon glows as brightly as last night when we launched a mere nine hours ago. Only nine hours ago? It feels like twenty-nine. The crowds have disappeared from the vicinity, but my little clone still haunts me. If I go back to my home year, I'll never see her again or find out who she is.

And I will never know TigerLily's motive for murdering McMurray. Unless he had something to do with her daughter's disappearance? But no, that's preposterous. It wouldn't be reason to commit suicide.

As the cops load McMurray's shrouded body into the rear of the time hopper, they extract a promise from Penny that she will enlist the Portland Police Bureau's assistance once we land. I'm thankful I'm not the one who will need to transfer the body, inform the family, all those messy, tragic details.

Penny sits in McMurray's seat, and I stare at a blood spot someone missed on the floor. Other than the body in the back, it's the only evidence of today's tragedy.

The stars are spinning due to my addled brain. I need to get my mind off the subject. "Penny?" I scoot forward. "I see we're returning under a full moon, just like we did last night. How did McMurray know what day the full moon would happen in a hundred years?"

Giles squeezes my hand. "Apps can calculate full moons for the indefinite future."

"Really? I didn't know that."

She glances over her shoulder, her round mouth open in a silent chuckle. "Oh, don't believe that full-moon nonsense. I mean, think about it. Wouldn't that defy the laws of physics?"

"Time travel itself defies the laws of physics."

She tilts her head. "He respected the laws of physics and knew how to work with them to accomplish his goals. But he also loved romanticizing the process. If he'd explained the technicalities of time travel, it would've put you to sleep."

"Not for me," Giles continues. "I'd love to know what makes this work. Will you explain, please?"

"Oh, okay, for you, I will. I can't reveal McMurray's proprietary secrets, but I can give you an overview." She fiddles with the instrument panel and launches into a demonstration of quantum physics, filled with terminology I'm unfamiliar with. Just in time, I remember my cell phone—still with no bars showing, but with a working camera—and start recording.

Penny halts her demo. "Thea?" The hardness in her eyes, her not-quite-harsh tone, reveal a side of Penny I didn't know existed. I would've lurched backward if I weren't sitting down. "Didn't you sign an agreement? No photos or recordings?"

"Well…" I gulp. "McMurray isn't here anymore."

"The agreement still stands."

She turns to the panel, and, still taken aback, I whisper to Giles, "Did you catch all that?" At his nod, I continue. "Can you remember it for my article?"

"Here we are," Penny interrupts. "Home sweet home." Just like the first leg, the return trip took mere seconds.

The window reveals a blanket of nothingness dotted with tiny holes through which piercing eyes seem to watch us. I shiver, unable to tell the difference between the future and the present. Until my cell phone, lying on my lap, pings.

Hooray! It's a spam text, but grateful for this tiny anchor to real life, I nearly kiss the screen.

Ari and Zach scramble to their feet, wrestle on their backpacks, and practically jump from the steps. "Hurry, Thea!" Ari calls out. "We wanna get home."

We exchange farewell-and-nice-to-meet-yous with Ellen and Sher as they disappear out the exit, while I sit frozen, reluctant to move. My eyes plead with Giles, but he only scrunches his face at me. He can't read my mind.

I turn my yearning gaze to Penny. "Take us back. Please?"

Jaw dropped, Penny gawks. "Take you back? Why?"

"There's a story there. I feel it. A big one." I lean in, transferring all my longing to my face. "I need to find out why TigerLily killed McMurray. Can't you understand? I'm a newspaper reporter. I know the who, the what, the where, and the how. But I won't have an article until I know the why."

NEL

I didn't see Nel again until my freshman year of high school. At first, we didn't recognize each other. Her shocking blue hair drew attention away from her features. But as we passed in the hall, she scrutinized me as closely as I did her, wondering why she seemed familiar.

Then she called my name. Recognition punched me in the chin and sent a tremor down to my toes. "Nel? Oh, wow, Nel!" I managed to stammer out a "how are you and what are you doing here?"

"Same thing as you!" You'd never know she was a sociopath when she grinned that disarming grin at you. "Doing time until we can get out of here and out into the real world." Like in fifth grade, she attracted attention the moment she opened her mouth. The passing crowd gaped, whether at her loud declaration or hair, I couldn't be sure. They didn't know her true colors, didn't yet know they fed her outsized need for validation by their staring. Hadn't yet learned they were better off paying no attention to her.

With Nel's mom's warnings still ringing in my ears after three years, I wondered how I could avoid Nel without her noticing. And retaliating. Was it even possible?

Turned out, she was in two of my classes, Freshman Science and History. Even worse, science teacher Mr. Putnam acquiesced to Nel's sweetly worded request that she and I be lab partners.

I didn't dare object. But I did send a silent, desperate prayer to the God I wasn't sure I believed in.

"Where've you been the last few years?" I kept my tone nonchalant when she stuck to my side after history class.

"Foster homes." Curses spewed from her twisted-up mouth over her newest foster family. "They practically put me in chains. They're so flippin' strict."

"Do you miss your mom, though?"

"No way. Only the worst kind of mom accuses her daughter of lying."

But what if it's true? I wanted to say.

"And I hope my dad rots in prison for the rest of his life," she added.

Despite his numerous claims that he'd never touched his daughter, and after two appeals, her dad remained incarcerated in the state penitentiary fifty miles to the south. Nel's mom, believing in her husband's innocence, headed up a grassroots advocacy group with other family members of the falsely accused, working with the state legislature and writing letters to editors. And how did I know all this? Obsessive curiosity. Because once Nel digs her claws into your psyche, you're never free of her.

I zipped my lip to keep from saying the wrong thing, and we parted. A weight lay upon my shoulders. A burden I expected to carry as long as Nel stayed in my orbit.

Looked like I would never be free of her.

GILES

Giles couldn't believe Thea wanted to return to the future. Neither could Penny, judging by her slack jaw and piercing gaze. "Good grief, Thea. I can't take you back." She gestured toward the shroud in back. "I have all kinds of things to deal with, what with the police and all." Her grayish-blonde bangs swished across her forehead as she palmed her hair with agitated swipes. "Did something about the crime unsettle you?"

Thea opened her mouth, then closed it, appealing to him with her eyes. He needed to talk her out of this crazy idea. "Thea, your editor will love your article the way it is."

"But it'll be so much better for the readers if there's closure."

"Closure isn't likely, love, even if we could hop back to the future. Our lives are here."

She nodded, then eased her bag onto her shoulder, reluctant to leave.

He hit the point home. "We'd need a good supply of future currency just for a single day of food and lodging."

"We didn't spend any of the currency we had," she reminded him. "We never got the chance."

"C'mon, Thea." He gripped her elbow and eased her to her feet. "Penny has a lot to take care of. We can talk about this at home."

She seemed to see the sense of this, still nodding. "All right. Penny, how do we get in touch with you?"

Penny was feeling around under the seat as if looking for something. "It's on the web. On Coltrane's page." She turned her back to them and continued her search.

He set his business card on the dash. "If there's anything we can do to help, let me know. If the police need to talk to us, here's my cell."

Penny stopped her exploration long enough to wish them farewell.

Thea sank into a subdued silence on the drive home while Ari and Zach did all the chatting. "You guys, it's only a few minutes past midnight. We probably got back a second after we left!"

"Yo, that's trippy."

"I'm thinking about a new theme for my rocks, Zachy. How about 'I traveled to the future and lived to tell about it'?"

Giles understood how Thea felt. Her journalistic instincts steered her to the most compelling stories. Little wonder her editor trusted her with this one. Thea must be as curious about the woman's motives as he was.

But maybe there was a better way.

All the air whooshed from his lungs when he pulled up beside Zach and Ari's Hawthorne bungalow and the other couple said goodbye. With Ari's chattering mouth silenced, he and Thea could discuss it in private. He took a left on Hawthorne and retraced their route back to Sellwood. "I have some ideas. Why don't we go to my place and do some digging? Unless you're tired."

His adrenaline level had spiked as though he'd consumed two cappuccinos. The afternoon nap, the surreal conclusion to their adventure, had left him with an elevated heart rate and bedtime the last thing on his mind.

But it may have drained Thea.

The darkness veiled her eyes, but was that hope or curiosity radiating? Maybe both. "I'm not that tired. But I am curious about where you went when I was in the toilet."

"Yeah, I've been wanting an opportunity to tell you." He glanced at her shadowed face, unable to discern what emotion hid there. But he trusted her with the truth. He rolled his taut neck side to side, but couldn't loosen it or his inched-up shoulders. "I did go back to the time hopper. I thought it would be interesting to chat with McMurray one-on-one, but I also hoped for an opportunity to grab my camera while he wasn't looking."

"Did you tell the cops?"

"I didn't dare. They were already suspicious of me. The cam showed me heading in that direction, but it didn't show me going in."

Her intake of breath told him he could've chosen better words. "I didn't go in, if that's what you're wondering. I saw him get up and head to the back. Then, I don't know, just thought better of it. I felt like I was being watched."

"Of course you did. There were cameras everywhere."

"Drones too. There was a little drone flying around near me, and, I don't know, something made me stop and rethink. Figured I could talk to McMurray later."

"Really?" Her fists clenched in her lap. "You got a check in your spirit?"

"I suppose." He tightened his grip on the wheel as he braked at Holgate Boulevard. "Yet I don't know why the Lord would urge me to turn around. I might've interrupted the murderer. Maybe even stopped her. Why wouldn't the Lord want that?"

"Good question." Her soft voice grew husky as he drove through the intersection. Few cars were out this late. "And we wouldn't be sitting here wondering why TigerLily killed him."

"Among other questions."

"Right. Let's say something happened between TigerLily and McMurray that enraged her. For instance, she found out he was responsible for her daughter's disappearance. Although I'm skeptical. There's got to be more to the story than what we know. It could explain why she befriended Penny and said nothing about knowing McMurray." Thea held up her phone with Facebook open on it. "Still, if Penny worked with McMurray, wouldn't she know if he knew TigerLily?"

"Only if he chose to tell her."

"I'm going to send Penny a friend request right now and ask her what else she knows."

As he drove south on Milwaukie Avenue, the familiar homes, stately ones and cute ones, with their tidy yards and glowing porch lights grounded him. He and Thea loved the vibe here where kids ran through sprinklers in summer and built snow forts in winter. Where college students crammed for finals in their parents' basements and young parents bought row homes and strolled their babies alongside boutiques and pizza joints and hardware stores. Thea studied her phone, oblivious to the signs of home. "It just occurred to me—the cops didn't identify her. The only reason we know her name is because Penny told us." Her head swiveled toward him. "I found Penny. Her profile photo is at least ten years old. She's not this young anymore."

The neon lights of Paddy O'Rourke's Alehouse came into view, the final landmark before his street. Music from a live band thumped, vibrating through the car and his teeth as he turned left. He'd never been so grateful to see the nightclub patrons gyrating and staggering on the corner. No longer annoying, now a sign of homecoming.

In a hundred years, all this would be gone, replaced by monster dormitories.

He pulled his car into the ground-level garage, and they ascended the stairs to his living room and sunk into his plush suede sofa. Giles logged onto the laptop he'd left on the ottoman. His hands hesitated over the screen. "Perhaps we should research Coltrane McMurray himself. We might find some hint as to why he got murdered."

The floral scent of her long hair tickled his nostrils as Thea leaned over his shoulder. "He admitted he'd already made some trips to the future. He probably met TigerLily on one." She snapped her fingers. "I wonder if they had an affair." But doubt laced her tone as if she knew it was a stretch. "Let's check his social media accounts."

He slid his laptop into her waiting hands. As Thea bent over the keyboard to log onto TikTok, he rubbed his scratchy eyes, exhaustion from the strange day now overpowering him. He was about to suggest they wait until tomorrow when Thea said, "Oh, if only we could Google the future."

The sleepy sensation fled. "What do you mean?"

"I saw a little girl and her mom today. Both of them resembled me, especially the little girl. I wish there was a way for Google to read the future and tell me who they were. I wish I could look the mom up on social media. What if she's my great-granddaughter?"

"I wish you could too." He squeezed her slender fingers. "If they're your descendants, then they must be mine too."

"Google can find anything from the past or present. But if they're so brilliant, they should be able to find anything in the future, as well."

Giles shook his head. She was treading the edge of delirium. "We both need a good night's sleep. How about you crash on my couch and we resume this tomorrow?"

A long sleep would do both of them a world of good. And he could wake up to a normal world again.

IN THE YEAR 2023

That night on Giles's couch, I dream of the little girl. She calls me Mummy, and I call her Zula. McMurray drives us around in his time machine. We visit the Roaring Twenties, and I dance in flapper dresses. Arias appears in a Fifties poodle dress and whisks Zula and me off to an Elvis show.

I awaken on Giles's sofa at 6:00 a.m. still tired, but kiss him goodbye, and catch an Uber back home. I'm still not comfortable driving on the right side of the street, so why own a car when I can leave the driving to others? Once at home, I reassure Grizzy and Rumple, who cast reproachful stares and meows at me. "I will never leave you or forsake you," I remind them.

When they've relaxed inside a sun puddle in the living room, I hop on my usual TriMet bus to work and settle at my Pearl District office desk by 7:59 a.m. Logging onto Word, I begin typing, thankful for autocorrect which makes Word dyslexic-proof, though I need to be careful with numbers such as dates and amounts.

I'm well into page three when my editor, Stefanie, pokes her head in. She slides into the opposite chair as I fill her in. Afterward, she sits mute, her wide eyes staring. Then she straightens her shoulders. "You must learn more about McMurray if you want to make your story as rich and full as possible. Finding out why he was killed would be icing on the cake."

She sends me off to my interviews, but before I leave the lot, I text Mia. *Mornin', girlfriend. Here's wishing you a fabulous day!*

She's probably on the school bus, so I wait in my car for her reply.

A minute later, my phone pings. *Still coming to my recital tmrw nite?*

Absolutely! I wouldn't miss it for anything. Ur an amazing dancer!

No reply, so I start the engine. Forty minutes later, I'm standing outside an off-white Happy Valley townhouse smack in a row of identical 2000s-era homes. A fresh-mowed-grass scent wafts from the mower an older gentleman pushes along next door. Some residents attempt variety with porch furniture or colorful shrubbery. Otherwise, you'd be hard-pressed to find the right home in the dark.

I give the doorbell a hesitant tap, then jump at the chime from inside. The door opens, and a faded version of McMurray's estranged wife blinks at me. She's several years older than her social media photo. Per the Portland Police, she was given the news just this morning, so I'm intruding on her grief. Maybe I should've waited.

Too late now. "Marilyn McMurray?"

"Are you Thea?" Her rough voice scrapes against her throat like she'd just gargled with battery acid.

I show her my media badge as I search her face for traces of resentment. "Yes, Thea Daniels of the *Portlandia*. Thanks for agreeing to meet with me."

"Well"—she sniffs—"don't know how much help I can be. I haven't had any contact with Colt for months. Our divorce was going to be final next month."

She opens the door wide to let me into a narrow living room, and I sniff the sharp aroma of fresh-cut flowers. A vase of bright red rhododendron blooms, obviously culled from the shrub out front, sits on a round side table.

Marilyn gestures me to a gray suede armchair. "Can I get you some water? Soda?"

"No thanks." This woman doesn't appear to be grieving her estranged husband, but she knew him better than almost anyone else did. I turn on the recording app. "As I mentioned on the phone, I will be recording this interview."

"Okay." She settles across from me in a similar armchair. "What can I do for you?"

I hesitate, tongue-tied about where to start. Mustering courage from experience, I plow on. "We want to do a feature story on your husband, as he was a trailblazer in an area of travel nobody has ever done before." The script I'd practiced in the car kicks in and pours from my mouth. "Not only that, his death raises many questions, and, although we have no way to investigate it in our timeline, we are hoping to discover answers on why someone would do such a thing."

"Well, I have no idea."

"Did you know TigerLily Malone?"

She snorts. "Sounds like a stripper name."

I press my lips tight, stifling a giggle. "She was identified as the culprit in your husband's death. Do you know what your husband's connection to her might be?"

"I can make a pretty good guess, seeing as he made several trips to the future."

"So is your conclusion his death was the result of a lovers' quarrel?"

"Yyyep. What other reason would there be?"

The dead woman's image teased my memory. She'd looked at least ten years older than McMurray. No longer a young woman, nor a woman who'd garner a second look when she passed you by.

Wholesome. Not a woman who'd generate obsessive passion in a man's heart and not stripper material.

I shift the phone in my hand. "Did you hear about the police's theory that she committed suicide after she killed him?"

She leans forward, her hands squeezing her knees. "I did. Even more proof they were lovers."

"The police are looking through his belongings for anything he might have brought back that may have been hers."

"Interesting. A memento from the future. I hope they find something."

The pulsating record light on my phone twitches something in my brain. My thumb covers it. "How are the kids dealing with this?"

She heaves a heavy sigh and glances over her left shoulder. "Colt Jr. is not doing well. He's holed up in his room playing video games. If you were planning to interview him, don't bother. I'm not allowing the press access to him. He's only twelve, for cryin' out loud."

"I understand. You have custody of both kids?"

"We shared custody. Our daughter's fifteen and staying with my sister for the time being."

"I understand there's a grown son?" I skim my notes app. "Brendan. McMurray's son from his first marriage." An internet search had confirmed Penny's statement.

"My stepson lives with his wife and daughter in Hillsboro and is an engineer for Intel." She taps out a cadence with her flip-flops, still keeping her knees in a death grip. "Those scientific genes run in the McMurray side of the family."

"Would he be willing to talk to me, do you think?"

"He might. He was close to his dad, proud of him. He'll be grieving, but he's outgoing and might enjoy telling the world who his dad was."

✦◆✦

Brendan McMurray agrees to meet me for lunch the next day near the Intel campus, on the far west end of the metro area. He's on bereavement leave, he tells me, and he's free anytime.

A forty-minute drive lands me in a newer neighborhood of colorful five-floor apartment buildings anchored by upscale eateries and retail shops. I've never been to this part of Hillsboro, an area teeming with youthful, high-tech nerd types, a startling contrast to the old-money neighborhood where I rent a basement suite. It's as foreign to me as the Portland of the future. And bears a primitive resemblance. Curious how I can already see remnants of the future in the present, as if I'm standing inside the blueprint of a distant world.

Right away, I spot Brendan in the corner of the window-lit IntelliDeli. His face tightens when he sees me, and I search for traces of grief. A lot of his father shows in his features, but other than the frown lines marring the space between his brown eyes, he seems to be coping. With his dark-blond hair and steady gaze, he also reminds me a bit of Giles.

A young Asian woman takes our orders. After Brendan waves away my apology for intruding on his grief, he gives me permission to record. He talks about the time machine and his father promising him a trip someday. His face sags as he narrates how the timing never seemed to work out. "I work all week, and weekends are family time." His shoulders slump. "We kept putting it off. I assumed we had plenty of time. I mean, who would ever imagine such a thing?"

"Again, I'm so sorry about what happened to him." I then ask him the same questions I asked his stepmother. No, he's never heard of TigerLily Malone and has no clue of her connection to his father.

"We feel your dad's story isn't complete until we get all the details."

"I don't want his dirty laundry aired, though, if he had any. So whatever you find out, you'll need to run it by me first."

I hear the unspoken warning of possible future libel if we aren't careful.

"I can't imagine Dad carrying on with a woman known by a name like that, but for whatever reason she murdered him, I hope she burns for eternity." Some emotion peeks through those stoic features. "If she hadn't killed herself, I'd travel to the future and do her in myself."

I shrink away. Time to switch to a safer subject. "Speaking of, my readers will want to know if you plan to keep your dad's time-traveling legacy going." An idea is brewing in my mind. "Will you continue operating Midnight Rider?"

He tilts his head back and forth as if pondering the notion. The server plops a glass of 7-Up and a bagel sandwich overflowing with sprouts and avocados in front of him. Ignoring the food, he keeps his gaze on me. "Eventually. Maybe. But…"

A blueberry muffin appears before me, complete with sparkly sugar crystals, diamond-like in the window light. I sip ice water, then take a tentative bite. Is Brendan going to make me eat alone? He's not the least bit interested in food.

"Don't you think he'd want you to keep his dream alive?" My fork pries free a tasty bite of muffin. "Penny could teach you how to operate it."

"Oh, I'm pretty sure I know how to operate it." He picks up the bagel and eyes it, then runs his tongue along the bulge of avocado threatening to spill out. "Dad talked about it enough that I can envision how all the components work. He also said I'd inherit his half when he died, so if Penny has any ideas for it, she's gonna have to run them by me first."

I concentrate on chewing as pedestrians pass beyond the window. Businessmen in suits stride along beside moms with strollers and clumps of high schoolers lugging backpacks, all radiating energy and joie de vivre. The pulsating revving of newer-model sports cars accompanies them. But before I can screw up my courage to ask the biggest question on my mind, he cuts into my thoughts.

"My dad told me a lot about his trips to the future, and he made me swear not to tell. But now..." He twists his bagel around as if he can't decide whether to eat it. "Now, it doesn't matter. He's not here to object." He lifts his head, meets my gaze, his eyes alight for the first time since I sat. "I'm interested to know what you thought of our city in a hundred years."

"My article will be published in this week's issue. Be sure to read it. It will answer your question, including some you didn't ask."

"What stood out to you the most?"

"All the people! It was so crowded. Did your father tell you how the population will explode?"

"He did. I have to wonder where all those people came from. It's gotta be from immigration. I don't think our low US birth rate will lead to several million more people." He takes his long-awaited first bite of bagel. "What did you think of the integration pavilion?"

"Integration pavilion?" I set my fork on the plate. "I have no idea what that is. We didn't get to explore because the cops wouldn't let us leave. So what is an integration pavilion?"

"It's a huge camp where the homeless live." He chews, followed by another big bite, then washes it down with a gulp of soda. "Don't let the name fool you. They're for isolation, not integration. Take the drug addicts and the mentally ill we have today and multiply them a hundredfold. Then gather them all up and give them an area to live in separate from the rest of the city. In a gigantic tent. Build dorms inside the tent. Provide free medical care onsite which includes as much drugs as they want, protection from ODs, and three square meals a day. Everything is free." He's finishing off his sandwich, speaking with his mouth full as if to make his words more palatable. "They're in prison, but they don't know it. All they know is they can get high all day, eat and sleep whenever they want, and nobody holds them accountable."

My heart is shuddering. "But why? Why won't the homeless problem be solved by then? Why will the future leaders decide that's the solution?"

"Because the people getting rich off the drug trade and the homeless industrial complex don't want the problem solved." He pats his mouth with a napkin, and crumbs fall to his plate. A green smudge of avocado jiggles as he waves the napkin. "What would happen if we won the war on drugs or if we housed everyone and no longer needed the powerful organizations in charge of meeting their needs? A lot of people would lose their clout and jobs."

I nod as I down the last bite. The truth, though plain to see, is still hard to swallow.

Like the saying goes, follow the money. And this trail leads to an unpleasant reality.

My readers will want to know this.

"The county prison is housed there as well."

"May I quote you?"

"You sure can." Brendan drums his fingers on the table. "It's time to expose this scam for what it is."

I take a deep breath, then plunge right in. "My employer would like to make you an offer." At least, she will when I talk her into it. "If you're willing to transport my fiancé and me back to the future so we can investigate your father's murder, we'll negotiate a generous fee." Crossing my fingers, I can't believe my presumptuousness. If Stefanie refuses, I'm in deep trouble. I search Brendan's eyes. Will he agree?

The gleam in his eyes tells me I've hit the jackpot. "Okay. I'll do it."

I can't wait to tell Giles. And Stefanie.

IN THE YEAR 2023

Mia smiles only when she's told to, and Willow, her dance instructor, is a champion smiler. "Willow gives us smile awards, that's why I go along with it," Mia explained over lunch last weekend.

Had I ever been so closed-off at her age? "But, Mia, you have a beautiful smile. You should show it off more often. And not just when you dance. Didn't you win the smile award at your last recital?"

She nodded, her mouth contorted in a quasi-smirk, the kind kids display when a big toothy grin threatens but they don't want to set it free. It could jeopardize her cool quotient. My heart twisted along with her hidden grin. She hasn't had much to smile about in her ten short years of life.

The dance studio hums with proud chatting parents accompanied by bored kids only there to watch their older siblings flaunt their talent. As I scan the bleachers, memories of my fun but sometimes difficult outings with Mia run through my mind. Like when I took her to the zoo and she had a meltdown at closing time because she hadn't gotten to see the monkeys. We should've gone there first, but how was I to know?

Mr. and Mrs. Maceira, Mia's foster parents, wave to me, but Mia's mom is nowhere to be seen. No surprise. Vanessa Maceira greets me with a shoulder hug, her silky black hair brushing my cheek. "I saved you a seat." She pats the bleacher, and I sit, the cold of the metal seeping through my jeans.

When the nine girls file onto the stage, Mia meets my eyes and gives an almost indifferent wave. But the glow on her face and clamped lips belies her body language. Why does that girl refuse to exhibit pleasure? Could it be she fears it'll be taken away from her if she dares to show joy? Little Miss Grinchette.

In each of the five numbers, Mia shines, that glow transforming her sullen face. My favorite is the "Happy" dance, Pharrell Williams's big hit. I can't help but tap my toes, but I resist the urge to get up and boogie along.

Afterward, Mia stands statue-like as we hug her, her countenance stoic again. If her mother were here, would it wipe that frown away? "Hey, want to go get some ice cream?"

Her face lights up. "Salt and Straw?"

"Absolutely." I turn to Vanessa. "I'll have her home by seven thirty."

Vanessa tucks a lock of Mia's thick blonde hair behind her ear. I catch a slight flinch from Mia, but Vanessa doesn't seem to notice. "Perfect." Her modulated tone stretches out the word. "She has a math assignment due tomorrow. Mia, if I let you go with Thea, promise you'll do your math?"

Her nod is brief, and I assure Vanessa I'll back her up. Off we go to Salt and Straw, Portland's gourmet ice-cream establishment. We like to call it the Starbucks of ice cream, as the founders did for ice cream what Starbucks did for coffee. Adventurous Mia orders mango pie with chocolate sprinkles while I request my usual: the delectable cinnamon snickerdoodle.

Ice-cream cone in hand, she pounces. "How come you wouldn't tell me where you went on your trip?"

Tread softly. I concentrate on the action outside. A hand-holding fiftysomething couple emerges into view, heading to dinner at one of Division Street's trendy restaurants, I'll bet. The khaki-clad man can't keep his gaze off her. With her free hand, she primps her dyed-blonde hair. *Will Giles still look at me like that in thirty years?* A young mother pushing a stroller with one hand and gripping a five-year-old with the other shoves opens the door with her hip and proceeds to the end of the expanding queue.

"Looks like we beat the rush." I delay the inevitable.

Between licks of her cone, Mia rolls her eyes, hand on waist. If she were standing, she'd be in my face, tapping her toes and giving me the evil eye.

The little girl with the mother squeals and tries to drop to her knees, but the mom is having none of it. "You better knock it off right now if you want ice cream." Although I can't hear them, I see the words forming on her mouth. "I'll walk right out of here." The scowling preschooler settles for bouncing in place instead.

Mia clears her throat, loud and deliberate.

"I'm sorry, dear one." I run my tongue around the gooey sweetness, the cinnamon tingling. "I'd love to tell you where I went." I reach for her hand, but she pulls it back. "But I can't. My boss swore me to secrecy."

Her pout eases maybe a fraction.

"But when my boss gives the okay, you'll be the first to know all about it. Okay?"

"'Kay."

"In fact, I'm going on another secret trip tomorrow, but I shouldn't be gone long."

Mia turns her gaze from me and focuses on the wall. Message received. Time to try a new strategy from my bag of tricks.

"Have you ever been to Oaks Park?"

A spark lights her eyes. "Where that humongous roller coaster is?"

"That's the one. How about we go next weekend?"

Aha, a genuine grin, albeit quickly smothered. "Ha. Totes cool."

"You can ride that coaster until you throw up if you want."

Her cone is down to molehill size, and she levels it off with her next bite. "Better not bail on me, then."

I force a big grin back. "Who, moi? Why, my motto is, No Bail, No Fail."

A chill works its way up my spine at the idea of failing Mia. God forbid I should ever add to her life trauma.

GILES

Utilitarian was the word that came to Giles's mind whenever he hung out in Thea's basement apartment. Not that he didn't admire the colorful couch pillows and farmers market artwork attempting to brighten the monotonic vibe.

Still reeling from her news, he sniffed the fresh blooms purchased from the Woodstock Boulevard flower vendor and now cheery and bright on the card-table-slash-dining-table. "You're going back to the future? Tomorrow?"

Her landlords, a retired Reed College professor and his wife, had updated their 1920s brick bungalow, tucked on a side street lined with Colonials and Cape Cods, two years ago. Thea made this space a home with fake plants and framed family photos, but with their upcoming wedding and hopes of buying their own home, she kept most of her earnings in an ever-growing savings account.

"Yes, isn't it awesome?" His fiancée clasped his hands and swung them back and forth as they waited for their Costco lasagna to finish cooking, her way of showing excitement. "I had to use my most potent powers of persuasion on Stefanie, though. She authorized only one visit, so we have to make it count."

"We?"

"Yes, we. I'm not going without you."

"What is your primary objective, love?"

"To learn the truth about why McMurray was killed." Her sigh, her drawn-out words, betrayed her exasperation. Did she think he doubted her? "Like I told Stefanie, I plan to interview TigerLily's friends and neighbors. And family members, if she has any. Somebody will know something."

Grizzy, Thea's gray cat, threaded through his legs, vibrating with purrs. Giles breathed in the aroma of cheese and marinara. It wasn't like he and Thea were professional detectives. He wouldn't know the first thing to do to find answers. "And you want me there because, why?"

"For moral support."

"But I have to work tomorrow."

"Don't you have some vacation time saved up?"

"Sure, but my boss would appreciate a little more notice."

Her penetrating look alone told him she knew he could work it out. How could he say no to that face? And another trip to the future?

"Plus, I think you and Brendan could hit it off. Maybe Brendan will let loose and reveal something he'd be reluctant to share with a reporter."

The quality in Thea he most loved was also the trait that made her such a great journalist. Her persistence.

Once she got a story idea, she had to see it through to the victorious end.

He wouldn't be surprised if she won the Pulitzer someday.

The oven timer beeped, and he grabbed an oven mitt and hot pad. Steam hit his face like a warm fist when he opened the oven door, then lifted the tray, and set it on the stove.

Rumple, Thea's all-black cat save for green eyes and pink tongue, sat on her haunches and stared at him, begging for a taste of the delicious-smelling dinner.

Thea tossed a handful of kibbles into their nearly full bowl, and both cats went running. "There you go, babies. Provisions from the Lord. Now, let Giles and me have some privacy, 'kay?"

"Because she hast ravaged mine heart with her eyes."

Laughter burst from her at his Song of Solomon reference. Her teeth gleamed as white as Solomon's lover's. "And thou hast ravaged mine." She winked and blew him a kiss.

He cleared his throat as her laughter subsided. "And now for something completely different…"

"Yes?"

"When are you planning to pick Penny's brain some more?"

Thea, serious again, brought her tray over and cut a square of lasagna, maneuvering it to her paper plate with care, then scooped a helping of Caesar salad into her paper bowl. She preferred paper dishes over the "clattery" kind. "After putting me off for a couple of days, she agreed to meet me for brunch Friday at Cadillac Café. But she warned me she doesn't know any more about TigerLily than what she already told us."

He helped himself to two rectangles of lasagna and some salad, then followed her to the green cloth-covered card table abutting the kitchenette. The dark-green leaves of the camellia trees in her landlord's side yard offset their vivid white blooms, reminding him of clumps of snow on a billiards table. "She might know something she doesn't know she knows."

"That's what I'm hoping."

He blew on the lasagna bite, and the steam veered and dissipated. He popped the bite in his mouth. *Mmm, just right.* He swallowed and patted his mouth with a paper napkin. "How well do you know Penny?"

She suspended her food-filled fork halfway to her mouth. "About as well as you do. Why do you ask?"

"She just doesn't seem like the type."

"What type?"

"The scientific type. She struck me as the motherly type. I could picture her with teenage daughters, not sitting behind the controls of a time machine."

Thea's eyes flashed sparks. "Now, Giles Davies. That sounds sexist."

"No, no." He hated having to explain himself. "I didn't mean it in a sexist way. I mean, I thought the same thing of McMurray. He didn't look the part either, with his slight paunch and his cargo pants. He looked...fatherly."

She waved her fork around, giving him a split-second urge to duck. "Yet your remark only pertained to the female half of the team." She popped the bite into her mouth and chewed.

"Because she was already the subject of conversation." A car door slammed outside, accentuating the tension. But it was merely Mr. Davenport leaving in his BMW.

Thea's half smile shot relief through him. She wasn't mad, just giving him a hard time.

She set her fork on her plate and dabbed her mouth with a napkin. "As a matter of fact, Penny does have two daughters, both in their twenties and living in California. So see, scientists can be parents too."

"Right." He hadn't meant to open this can of worms.

Her phone chimed with an incoming text. "Oh, speak of the devil. It's Penny." Thea stuffed the last bite into her mouth, chewed, and swallowed.

"What's she want?"

"I'll read it to you." She lifted her phone. "'Hey Thea, I'm going to have to cancel on you for brunch. So sorry.'" A crease popped out between her brows. "'It's been crazy with police interviews and media scrutiny. Plus, like I told you, I really didn't know TigerLily at all. I don't know if she had other family besides her daughter. I didn't know her friends. I won't be much help to you with your article. When things have settled, let's do get together.'"

Thea sighed and started typing. "Just going to let her know we're going back tomorrow." She finished the text and set her phone down.

He swirled his fork through marinara puddles where the lasagna had been. "Hey, we don't need Penny. Between the two of us, we have one great brain."

She reached for his hand, lacing her fingers through his. "And while we're there, I'm determined to find my little clone."

IN THE YEAR 2023

Brendan twists in his seat to catch our gazes. "Just gotta know before we take off. Do you want to arrive one day later?"

"What if we were to arrive the same day, only earlier?" Giles's excited grin infects me.

"Sorry." Brendan holds up a hand. "Not possible for this thing to be in the same place at two different times. Maybe someday my dad would've found a way, but for now…"

"Hey, it's okay." Giles waves away his apologies. Strange how they interact as if they haven't just met for the first time.

Brendan fumbles in his pocket for his glasses and sets them on his nose. "If we were to arrive before my dad on the same day, in the same spot, he wouldn't have been able to 'land.'"

This was, as Zach would say, getting trippier and trippier. I lean in for a better look at the controls. The flickering lights mean nothing to me, and awe surges at Brendan's ability to operate this thing. "If we were to try it, would it alter history in some way?"

"Okay, now you're getting in too deep for me." Chuckling, he swivels to the control panel. "How about I get you there one day later?"

"If we were to arrive the day before, maybe we could prevent the murder."

Brendan scrunches his face as though considering it, reminding me of Giles when his brain deep-dives. Brendan shrugs, then fingers the panel. "If we could've prevented the murder, we wouldn't be here, would we?"

Could he give up so easily? I mean, why not at least try? But maybe he knows something we didn't know. The idea of altering the past is appealing, but I don't think God created time to be alterable. Time is fixed, not fluid.

Or is it?

"I should have asked Penny more about this when I texted her."

Brendan jerks his shoulders back and whirls toward me. "You told Penny we were doing this?"

Whoa. I didn't expect such outrage. "Is that a problem?"

"Yes, it's a problem."

"She didn't say she'd join us." I can't keep out a defensive tone. "In fact, she didn't even reply."

Brendan cranes his head toward the parking lot where fragments of yellow caution tape still flutter in the breeze. The police finally removed it last night. "Is that her car turning in?"

"I don't know what she drives."

"Just in case, we're leaving now." He makes a mock vroom-vroom sound as he prepares to launch Giles and me back to June of 2123.

But now my excitement is dashed that I'd misstepped with that text.

The gray Toyota presumably belonging to Penny disappears as, with a hum and a buzz, we launch once again to the future, and I abandon my futile circular reasonings. We left in such a hurry, we didn't bother with masks and seat belts on our return trip or now. When I mention this to Brendan, he chuckles. "Those were for dramatic effect. You don't need them."

I didn't even have time to watch the landscape change. The hop takes seconds. What a contrast from last trip. No sweaty palms, no white-knuckling the seat. This time, a settled sense of purpose overpowers any anxiety.

"Where to first?" Brendan pushes a button, and the steel gate slides open.

I halt my ascent from the seat and plop back down. "Wait. Won't we need holograms?"

"Um, yes, you will." He scrutinizes the control panel while Giles and I wait and gawk. Without our holograms, we can't spend money. And although we ate hearty breakfasts, we'll need to eat.

"Here's the icon," Brendan announces.

A hologram appears above my left hand. Giles, who's left-handed, smiles at the hologram to his right.

The milling crowds aren't paying us any attention, and my little clone is nowhere to be seen. "The police station is too far," I muse. "Let's start at TigerLily's dorm building. Then we can figure out how to get to the station to see if they've learned anything new."

Giles takes my hand as we follow Brendan off the vehicle.

Brendan touches the gate, and it closes, leaving the time machine behind an impenetrable fortress. Or so McMurray intended. Brendan lengthens his steps. "Point the way."

I point to the imposing building to the north. "She lived in the pinkish building on the river's edge. And, Brendan, how do I introduce myself? I can't say I'm from the *Portlandia*. It no longer exists."

Either he didn't hear me, or he's ignoring me. He gapes around at our new world, his Adam's apple bobbing. I repeat the question, and he startles. "Oh, sorry. As much as my dad filled me in on all this…" He sweeps his hand in an arc. "It's still…amazing. Anyway, I'm not sure what they call the local news. Just tell them you're an investigator and hope they assume you're with the police."

I'll have to wing it and pray.

As we trek toward the building, Giles peppers Brendan with technical questions about Midnight Rider. Brendan's answers all land way over my head.

Giles's lifelong interest in the inner workings of things has always struck me as strange, considering he chose accounting as a profession. "My mother was an accountant," he told me once when I asked him, "so I felt a familiarity with it. But sometimes I wish I'd chosen engineering instead."

No wonder he and Brendan hit it off so well. Giles is Dogbert to Brendan's Dilbert.

Our destination looms ahead. But where to go once we get there? Ah, the café. They might know the names of TigerLily's connections. I beckon us forward, and we jostle our way to a sliding plasticized-glass door. Inside, sunshine streams through the windows, and the ceiling strips emit dim white light. Drumbeats pulsate through the room, but I can't find the source.

Oh. It's coming from the light strips. Is this what they call music here? But then a voice joins in, managing to sound guttural and high-pitched at the same time. Is it a human voice enhanced by technology? Or fully artificial? More music-like sounds add to the odd mixture, but I can't pinpoint the genre. It's the sound you might get when you put a good old American burger on a plate with Asian stir-fry.

Drones flit back and forth between counter and customers, delivering drinks and food. Robots appear and disappear through a doorway behind which they slap sandwiches together and prepare drinks. One human guy in a thin tank top hanging to midthigh hovers nearby, keeping watch over everything, but, as far as I can see, doing nothing else. Must be a boring job. As we near him, his name hologram glows. Togg, the same guy the police interviewed.

"Help you?"

"Hi." I put out my hand, and he looks at it as if he doesn't know what to do with it. I lower it. Apparently, people don't shake hands anymore. "My name is Thea, and I am…" He won't know what a reporter is. "I'm an investigator, following up on the death of a woman who lived in this building. Is there a person in charge of tenants I can talk to?"

He gestures to the ceiling. "Second floor. Office to right the lift."

Huh? He talks like a teenager sending a mangled talk-to-text message. When did mangled texts evolve into this mutilated form of the English language? Seriously, nobody tried to stop it?

Giles tugs my hand, and the three of us follow Togg's directions to a nearly invisible panel in the wall. I search for buttons, but the walls on both sides are smooth.

"Second floor," Brendan says, and the panel slides open. He catches my open-mouthed stare and chuckles. "Dad said the elevators are voice operated."

The panel closes behind us, then opens again before I realize we've moved. We emerge into a stone-floored hallway with the same slitted ceiling lights. To the right, a door with the mangled word *ofice* painted on it stands open. Is it a misspelling, or the new way to spell it?

Behind a counter of the shiny composite material you see everywhere sits what I think is a human person, but I can't tell if they're X or Y. The hologram nameplate doesn't help—Nogard Riden. The person's olive-ish complexion hides his or her cultural heritage, which seems to be the aim. Their shoulder-length hair is a nondescript beige on one side, purple on the other. One eye is dark, the other light. It's like God took two different faces and slapped them together on the same head.

Whoever this person is, they have erased whatever God designed them to be. "Help you?" they say in the now familiar vernacular. The voice could be a higher-pitched male voice or a low-pitched female. How sad when someone feels they have to hide who they are in order to eliminate gender distinctions.

I introduce myself and watch Nogard's face when I tell them why I'm here. "What can you tell me about TigerLily Malone? Did you know her well?"

Nogard shakes their head and leans forward, brow arched. "Yull not from here, are you?"

Why does everyone keep saying that? "I moved here from Australia a few years back."

"Australia still say him her?"

Ah. Too late, I realize my gaffe. "Sorry. Still getting used to the way things are done here." At least, he gave me a ready-made excuse. "We're digging into the murder-suicide from yesterday and would appreciate any help you can give us."

Nogard straightens, then stands. Whoa. Nogard's about six foot seven. They're wearing a long tank like Togg's, and the wiry legs below the hem sport dark hairs. If they were in my Portland, I'd peg this person as a basketball player.

"The murder eveeone's talkin bout?"

"Yes. May I ask you some questions?"

"Just a mo." He or she motions us around the counter to two plaid chairs with composite frames. Nogard's probably a

Y, a biological male, with the way he moves, lumbering rather than graceful. Makeup covers a dark shadow on his jaw. He grabs another chair of a tweedy-type fabric, and the three of us sit facing him. He braces his elbows on his slab desk and steeples his fingers under his chin as his odd eyes regard us.

I inhale a steadying stream of air. "Are you the building manager?"

"I'm the supe."

"How long had TigerLily lived here?"

Nogard tilts his long head. "Moved here December last year."

"Hmm, about seven months." I clutch the chair arm. Good thing Giles and Brendan are helping me commit this conversation to memory as I have no recording device.

"Did they have a lot of visitors? Family? Kids?"

"No idea. Don't keep track a residents comin goin."

"Where I come from, building mana...supes are required to have references and an emergency contact for their tenants. Are you able to release that information to us for TigerLily?"

Nogard consulted his hologram. "Yull from Pope, you said?"

"Not exactly."

His odd eyes pin me, insisting on an answer.

"I...I'm from the...media."

"The wut?"

"I work for the local news."

"Oh. Got autor-zation?"

"Of course. What do you need?" I clutch my purse strap. Nothing inside it will suffice, so I hold my breath, fearing he'll call my bluff.

Giles rescues me. "Look, their boss, Stef Curry, sent us here. You can gram them if you need confirmation."

I tighten my grip on my purse. Stefanie's put up with her share of teasing over her name, but it could be my undoing now. What if Nogard's familiar with ancient NBA history, recognizes the basketball player's name, and calls Giles's bluff?

But he doesn't react, just waves away the suggestion. "It's okay. I can help." After his search, a hologram name, Zedda Sander, floats in the air. "Here. Their mergency person."

I'm so hoping it's TigerLily's daughter.

He looks at us. "Their sib."

Great. A sib might know the daughter's whereabouts.

"Not gone to gram it?"

Oh. He wants me to add the name to my hologram, the way we add contacts at home. I touch my finger to the empty air where the image hovers. It adheres to my finger. I drag it to my hologram. Voilà. It's saved.

Wow.

"I'll gram em when we're done here," I tell him. "Thank you. Has Mx. Sander been notified?"

"Yeah. Far as I know, Pope told em."

"Did Mx. Malone have a job?"

"They was botting instructor at Northwest."

"Do you have the name of their supervisor?"

He provides me with another name—Kall Humfry, which sounds masculine. But in this culture, I can't be sure.

Crossing my legs, I brace myself for my next question. Great, I'm clutching Giles's hand. I don't even remember grabbing it.

I lean forward and meet Nogard's two-toned gaze. "I need to know if you have any idea how Mx. Malone and Mx. McMurray knew each other."

"Solutely none."

Time to contact the sib. I rise, and Giles and Brendan follow suit. "Thank you for your time. Have a nice day."

NEL

I remember the first time Nel killed someone. No evidence pointed to Nel, and the murder was never solved. But I knew it was her. The crime had her modus operandi all over it.

After high school, I enrolled at OSU, and she got a scholarship to OIT. She tried to persuade me to go to OIT, but I lied and told her my parents insisted on OSU, as my father was an alumnus. Off we went to our separate lives, me breathing a sigh of relief all the way to freshman orientation. No more Nel. I joined the Greeks and the heavy partying lifestyle. Despite that, I managed a 3.13 GPA as a freshman computer science major. Yay, me.

I heard the news during finals week of fall term.

The winter sun shone down on the Memorial Union lawn and the first snowstorm of the year. Six inches had fallen yesterday, but today, the deceptive blue sky messed with our heads. Laughter from students building snow sculptures, screams from the snowball fighters, warmed the freezing air as though yesterday's forced hibernation had exploded into ecstasy at today's freedom.

Inside Memorial Union, I tried to concentrate on my studying, but the activity outside and the TV on the wall kept breaking in. A newscaster's somber announcement pushed everything else from my head. "Today, the mystery of the missing OIT student has been resolved. The body of Maddie Kim, missing since last week, was found this morning by a sledder in a wooded area outside the small town of Oak Knoll."

A young Asian woman's smiling face filled the screen, and my heart lurched. So it wasn't Nel. I didn't know whether to be thankful or disappointed.

"An autopsy determined she had been strangled. A fellow engineering major has been identified as a person of interest and the last person to see the missing woman. This person was interviewed and released due to lack of evidence."

On a hunch, I opened my laptop and went to MySpace, the most popular social media site for college students. I typed Maddie Kim in the search bar and clicked the top option, Madeline Kim. Yep, it's her. I scrolled through her photos and videos in search of a particular face.

There. Under the caption "my besties and I at The Boss," a photo of the victim with four other young women. One of them was Nel, beer bottle in hand and half-drunk smile on her face. Was Nel the "person of interest"?

Why was this the first I'd heard of a missing OIT student? I thought back over the past week and the intense cramming sessions. I hadn't been near a TV, that's why. I did another search for the news reports. What I learned churned my gut. Maddie recently won a robotics competition in San Francisco. I searched for the competition's runners-up. No luck.

The following week, her roommate told the campus police Maddie didn't return to her dorm after a night at an underage bar. "I left before she did," the roommate explained, "because she was deep in conversation with some guy. When I got up the next morning, she wasn't in her bed. I wasn't too worried, figured she'd gone home with the guy. But she didn't answer any of my texts and never did return."

Maddie's roommate was Nel. That sealed it for me.

IN THE YEAR 2123

GILES

Giles looked around and up at the sky as they left the building.

"How are we supposed to get to Northwest Reser Court where this person lives?" Thea gave an exasperated grunt. "We could've thought this out a little better, right?"

He placed a reassuring arm over her shoulders before she spun off into one of her not-quite-panic modes. Then he lifted his free wrist and spoke to his hologram. "Direct us to 11235 NW Reser Court."

An autopod veered from a group of five traversing the sky and plummeted beside them. As Thea gaped and Giles mentally patted himself on the back, Brendan grinned an "attaboy" at him. What a learning experience, picking Brendan's engineer brain. The man was a fount of detailed information, not only from his father but also from his own brilliant intellect.

"Enter, please," said a disembodied female voice as the checkered taxi's door slid open. Speechless, they obeyed. Brendan took the front passenger seat, Giles and Thea in back. Giles squinted at the empty front seat as the voice spoke again, as though the vehicle were under the control of an invisible driver. "Destination 11235 NW Reser Court," the voice repeated like the Max Train's announcer. "Approaching Gateway Transit Center," she'd say. "Doors to my left."

But what about payment? Oh. A notification slid across Giles's hologram. *153.00 D has been deducted from your account.*

Their currency level was reset upon their return? Stunning, the efficiency of twenty-second-century technology. Taxis that showed up in seconds. Payments that withdrew themselves.

"Giles, did you notice that weird dude's name?"

He shifted to Brendan. "Nogard? Yeah, it's dragon spelled backward."

"Yep. Great name, isn't it?"

Grinning beside him, Thea shook her head. Her soft hand gripped his as they zipped over the city to the wooded northwest hills. In their Portland, this area was an enclave of upper-middle-class and wealthy homes. Here dwelt partners in long-standing attorney firms. CEOs and business owners. Rock stars and famous authors. Had they all been torn down and rebuilt as dorms, as Sellwood had been? But as they drew nearer, many single-family homes still nestled among the Douglas firs, this neighborhood spared the high-density development of the flatlands, the poorer neighborhoods. "You'd think, after a hundred years," he muttered to Thea, "we wouldn't still be sparing the rich folks at the expense of the poor."

"I know, right?" Up here in the hills, the homes didn't look all that different from the twenty-first century. Newer, of course, and made with materials he'd never seen. But opulent, just as heavy on the city views. He sighed. Some things never change. Money still talked. Brendan regaled them on the new climate-controlled processes in use for construction, and Giles had to wonder how much accounting rules had also changed. Was GAAP still in use? Spreadsheets must be obsolete, and tax rules altered. Did the IRS even still exist?

The taxi swooped them to the road before a house with a charcoal exterior. The plasticized-glass windows could pass for real glass. Thea breathed deep, the door slid open, and they got out. Giles, rotating his shoulders and neck, relished the cracks of released tension. They stepped across flagstones bisecting a manicured yard and knocked on the chrome-like front door.

Not a sound.

"Is there a doorbell?" Thea's voice dropped to a reverent hush.

"Summon residents?" A deep voice jerked Giles backward onto Brendan's foot, pulling an oath from the other man.

"Yes." Awe tinged his tone despite his best efforts. From the interior, a bell echoed, then scurrying footsteps. The door flew open, and a weary-eyed dark-haired woman stood there, two tiny X children clutching each knee. Two more children, an X and a Y, appeared behind her, holding toys and sucking thumbs, eyes wide and questioning. A nearby thud drew his attention to a drone dropping a package down a chute. So this was how they solved porch pirating. And likely shoplifting also. He hadn't seen a single brick-and-mortar store since their arrival. The sooner they adopted this in the twenty-first century, the sooner crime would decrease.

Another gawking Y child gathered, older than the others. You'd think they never got visitors. Why all the children, and was this woman who stared at them their mother?

Thea cleared her throat. "We're looking for Mx. Zedda Sander. Is she..." Another throat clearing. "Is they, um, available?"

"I'm Zedda. What you need?"

"Sorry if this is a bad time." Thea eyed the children as she introduced herself. "We're here about TigerLily Malone. I understand you were...sibs?"

"They dead." Zedda sniffed and wiped the moisture from beneath her eye. "Yesterday."

"Right. That's why we're here."

"Why not just gram me?"

For this, Thea had no answer. How to explain the cultural differences of a hundred years ago?

She deflected the question. "How are you holding up?"

And are all these children yours? Giles clamped down the question.

"I'm shockin." Zedda motioned to the children. "Tiger's grands too. Three mine, two theirs. Now all mine." A tear traced a path down her cheek and disappeared beneath her chin.

"Did the kids' parents live here with you and the grands, then?"

"No, Tiger and their pring was stranged. But Tiger and I grewed em and schooled em." Another sniff, another swipe at the eyes. But no inclination to invite them in.

"We'd like to talk to the…pring, if that's possible."

"No, they stranged, like I said. No idea where they is. But they left their two prings with Tiger one day, told them to raise em. We've not seen em since."

Kids were called prings now? And what about the supposed happy reunion between mother and daughter? Zedda gave no hint.

Thea must be dying to see the inside, judging by her neck cranes and subtle side-glances. "May I ask you some questions? We can talk out here if you'd like."

"Spose." Zedda grunted, then stepped to the porch, and eased the door barely open. Even though Thea didn't show disappointment—being the professional she was—Giles sensed her frustration that the lady hadn't taken the hint and invited her in.

"Will the kids be okay in there alone?"

"Course. Oldest is twelve. They'll watch em." For good measure, she called through the doorway, "Jink! Watch them kids for a few mints." She stood, feet inches apart, arms crossed.

Thea, uncowed by the resistant body language, plunged right in. "Did TigerLily ever mention knowing Coltrane McMurray?"

"Nope," Zedda snapped. "And she didn't kill him either. Don't know why Pope insisted she did."

A gust of wind blew Thea's hair into her face, and she wrestled it back. "It does seem odd, then, if she didn't know him, that the police would make that conclusion."

The wind, as warm as an Australian breeze, whipped the branches on a twisted oak tree shading the front yard, raining emerald-green leaves. "They needed someone to blame."

"Did Tiger leave any kind of note?"

Zedda grasped her flying hair and anchored it behind her head. "Leave wut?"

"Er, a message? That sh—that they planned to do what they did?"

"Like tell someone they gone to kill themself? No."

"What a terrible shock it must have been."

"Terrible. Couldn't see it comin."

Brendan, who'd been pacing around behind them, blurted, "Well, that makes no sense."

Zedda drew herself up to her full five-foot height. "Nope, doesn't." She glanced at the barely open door through which little eyes peeked out, then pulled it shut. "Don't want pring to hear, but I think they—my sib—got murdered."

"Murdered?" Thea gasped.

"Yep. Somebody killed em. But Pope think they solved it and don't want to know."

IN THE YEAR 2123

Wow. I didn't see that one coming. "Zedda, why do you think that?" I will my voice to stay steady. Because, like "Pope," I'd also thought it was a done deal and we were only lacking a motive. "I mean, the evidence…"

"Bah the evidence." The hard edge to her voice sends me back a step. "That stuff is easily planted. They was framed."

"Did sh—they have any enemies that you know of?"

"Nope, they was a popular friend with everyone."

Brendan taps his fingers together. "Still not making any sense, then."

Zedda shrugs, her nostrils flaring. "Boozlin for sure. Cram Pope for givin up so easily."

"Have you explained all this to them?"

"They closed the vestigation."

"In that case"—Brendan steps forward and pats her shoulder—"we'll go tell them to reopen it."

We trudge back to the street where the autotaxi awaits. "Well. Now what?" I ask Giles as we hover next to the taxi, reluctant to get in. "Do you buy her story?"

"Not sure."

"Of course she's going to believe what she wants to believe." Brendan adjusts his glasses. "Nobody wants to believe their sister committed murder."

I tighten my grip on my purse strap. "I'd like to interview her boss, but I'm not sure we'd learn anything new."

Brendan steps toward the taxi, and the door slides open. We all get in as Brendan reminds us we can "gram" the boss. "There's no need for face-to-face visits anymore."

As we fly back to the time hopper, I speak into the hologram. "Contact Kall Humfry."

"Contact unavailable," states a voice. "Estimated time of availability, ten minutes."

Brendan snorts. "Probably in the bathroom."

I request a gram in ten minutes. By the time we near our destination, Kall Humfry's holographic image flickers in front of us. The big blond guy gives off the vibe of an aging football player. Not what I expected.

"What can I do for you?"

"Hi." I scoot forward from the front passenger seat. I introduce myself, state the purpose of my contact, and watch his face change from baffled to intrigued.

"Yeah, TigerLily. Wut a shame. They was jit. We're all shockin."

Remember your pronouns. "Did you or the other instructors notice anything different in their work habits or the things they said or…"

147

Wait a minute. Everyone works remotely now. There must be little interaction between coworkers. But Humfry doesn't act like my question is odd. "I didn't notice anything. They had no enemies I know of, and can't see em killin anyone. They was a marvy person. Sorry I can't be more help."

"It's okay. I thank you for your time." I end the gram and nudge Giles.

"What did he mean, they was jit?"

"Legit," say Giles and Brendan in unison.

"The real deal," says Giles.

"Solid, no drama," adds Brendan.

Ah, so TigerLily was a grounded, authentic person. Jit. Funny that those two figured it out immediately, their brains seemingly working in tandem.

I need to take that word back home with me.

But now discouragement is setting in. Seems this trip, instead of closing in on the answers we sought, only opened more questions, as though we've walked through the wrong door. TigerLily was neither suicidal, despite the fallout with her daughter, nor the type to make enemies.

So what happened?

Maybe if I set the investigation aside for now and move onto my next purpose, I'll find peace, even if temporarily.

"Giles, I need to do something while we're here. Something jit." I remove a photograph of my six-year-old self I'd slipped into my pocket this morning. "I need to look for this little girl."

"But isn't that you?"

"Yes, but the girl I'm looking for…"

"Oh right, your clone." Giles studies the photo. "How do you propose to go about it? It'd be like looking for a needle in a haystack."

"Remember she was in the big crowd when we first arrived?" I rub my thumb along the glossy, faded image of my childhood face and my mother's smiling down at me. "That might mean she lives nearby. We can just ask around."

I ponder whether finding my mini-me would make up for the lack of answers. Torn between the two, I'm almost ready to give up on the investigation and make my time worthwhile by finding the girl. So we exit the taxi and set out on a different mission.

We start at Togg's café and show him the photo. No spark of recognition flashes in his eyes. We move on to the café in the neighboring building, with the same results. Then I remember the BirdNest, and we cover the four blocks in five minutes. Instead of Nissi, a different person stands behind the counter. I show them the photo. The head tilt gives me hope we're getting warm.

"Wut that?"

"A photo. It real old. Jus wondered if you seen this g—child."

"Why you lookin for em?"

"Sh—they my niece. But don't know where exactly they lives." The vernacular slides off my tongue as though I'd been speaking it all my life.

"They in trouble?"

"Oh no, not at all." Oops, my Australian accent is showing. "Just wantin to visit em."

"Seems if you jit you'd know where they lives."

I resist the urge to roll my eyes. But I can't blame him. I'd do the same in his place. These people watch over their kids with the same diligence we do.

As we're leaving, I scan the crowd for a glimpse of her. But even if I spot her, what would I do then? I haven't even prepared a possible script.

Hi, I'm Thea. What's your name?

But if her mother was the protective type, would she allow her daughter to talk to me?

Hi, I'm Thea, and I have a photo here that could be your daughter.

That would freak her out. I listen to the guys converse like old friends, talking about cars and electronics, two of Giles's favorite subjects. And apparently Brendan's, too. Unable to offer anything to the conversation, I trudge the sidewalk as if I'm the odd "man" out.

And then I see her. Up ahead, a woman—her mother—is holding her hand as they slow next to a sliding glass door. The girl gives me a sidelong look as she disappears through the entryway. I grip Giles's arm. "There they are."

He jerks his attention away from Brendan. "Where?"

I point. "They went into that building right there."

Giles stops. "Okay. I take it you want to go after them?"

"Of course I do."

"What will you say when you get there?"

But my attention is drawn to a window on the second floor, to a hint of movement behind a blind's slats. I sense, more than see, someone watching me.

"I don't know. But I need to know what our future holds. Don't you?" And I make my way to my little mini-me, my stride determined, my mind resolute.

THE GIRL

The funny people from the traption are back. I saw them watching me and Parent when we got home. Oh, now the long-haired one is watching my window. How did they know where I live? The two big ones are watching Hair. See, I told you they funny.

Parent's tugging my hand. "Get away from the winda."

"How come?"

"They'll see us."

"They already saw me."

Coparent sits at their desk and wonders wut we doin. Parent tells em not to answer door if bell ring. "I'll explain later." Parent makes that yukky noise in their throat and yanks on me, nearly dragging me to the bedroom. They pull off the bright wig, and their dark bun atop their head poofs up. Then they snaps the contact lens from their right eye, and their eyes are the same color again. They lunges at me and picks me up, squeezing me tight as if I could run away. As I choke back sobs, they pushes me through the back door to a dark hallway, imprisoning me against their chest. "Why can't I stay with coparent?" I wail.

They pinches me, hard, on my arm. "Shh! Don't you make a peep, lovey, you hear?" They back to talkin robot, but their voice softens as they soothes me. Again. "I already explained why I need them gone."

They did splain, but didn't make sense. "But why they lookin for us?"

"They want to know who we are."

Hate it when Parent don't answer questins.

Our robocam's loud voice announces visitors, and I lurch.

Parent puts a finger on my lips. "Shh. No talking."

They puts their hand on a panel behind us and pushes on it. A click and a whiff of stale air tells us it's opening. They sets me down, and we squeeze through to a dark passageway. The dim outline of stairs leads up to our rooftop podlot.

In the distance, I still hear the robocam repeating its question. "Open to visitors?"

"Even if robocam lets them in," Parent whispers, "they won't find us."

"I want my Treebotter Bots." How can I go anywhere without my favorite action dolls? "And my rainbow belt."

"We'll get them later. I promise we won't be long." They's still trompin up the stairs. Four more flights to go. Parent lets loose a big sigh and squeezes my hand, then stops to catch their breath. The ceiling lights flicker like them want to turn off but then keep gaspin for air. They tugs me up and up. My heart is poundin in my chest like it wants to leap right out onto the dark wooden stairs and lay there, quiverin.

They opens a door onto the rooftop podlot and, still squeezing my hand so hard it'll hurt if I try to escape it, veers to our autopod, but dint say where we goin. Then they makes me hide behind the seat in case anybody is watching. "I'll be back in forty-five minutes, but you stay here until then, okay? Play with your toy drones."

I nod.

"But, just in case I'm longer than forty-five minutes, gram Coparent. They'll come get you."

Another nod. Then they kisses me and disappears into the elevator.

Parent doesn't know I know how to operate real drones. I dyin to know wut they doin and why I can't come too. I grab a drone from Parent's box and send it after them, tracking their movements. I see Parent leave from the back side of the building, maybe to avoid the funny people. They stroll the sidewalk, all fast like, but…how strange. Parent's headed right to the traption, the time chine. Now, the gate's slidin open, and they goin inside. The drone follows em in, and they looks up at it and frowns.

Uh-oh, I been found out. Parent snatches the drone from the air and eyes it. Their huge face fills the screen, and I shrink back. "Baby, if this is you, you better have a good reason to be spying on me."

Then the screen goes dark.

IN THE YEAR 2123

Mini-Me eluded us once again. Now, I'm hungry. I persuade Giles and Brendan to return to the BirdNest for some sandwiches, where we enjoy a forty-five-minute respite. It's not like we're in any rush. I relish the chemical-free turkey sandwich, the pure flavors of authentic ingredients.

Back at the time hopper, I rest my hand on the steel gate, my hair tickling my outstretched arm as my head droops. As the gate slides open beneath my hand, I hop back and collide with Giles. His Adidas cologne wraps around my senses as he places steadying hands on my shoulders.

What a waste of a trip. I have none of the answers I came for. Only more questions.

"Whoa." Brendan's sharp breath intake hisses in my ear. "Did you see that?"

"See what?"

"The gate. It opened by itself. It's not supposed to do that. I didn't have a chance to touch the sensor."

"Weird." Not heeding him, I scan the crowd in hopes of seeing the girl again, but odd-looking strangers mill around outside the gate, eyeing us as we eye them. I can't shake the strong sense that the mother and daughter know who I am or think they know. But why take such pains to avoid me? When we stood at their door, noises inside and muffled, agitated voices couldn't hide the brutal truth. They were home, but we weren't welcome.

Brendan opens the capsule door, and we shuffle inside and plop to our seats, the perfect place for a regroup. Cut off from the world outside, he rests his back against the driver's seat, ankle on knee.

Giles and I twist fingers, bounce knees, and give away our frustration. "What now?" I ask. "Stay? Head back?"

Brendan sighs. "Staying here, trying to solve the murder-suicide, seems to be an exercise in futility. The only way you're going to learn what happened is to be there to witness it."

My heart leaps. "Is-is that possible?"

"To take you back to yesterday? Technically, yes, but I can't see it working, since Dad landed in this same spot at noon the same day."

Prickles inch across my scalp. "What if we were to leave before noon?"

Brendan stares out the window through the still-open gate. People are passing on the sidewalk and casting curious glances our way, but no crowd has gathered like yesterday. They must be used to this by now. "Okay. Well, I guess we can try." He turns his attention to the control panel. "I'll set it for yesterday at nine a.m. Then, Thea, you go stake out TigerLily's place, follow her if needed, and Giles and I will keep an eye out here." He pins me with a look. "But remember, you have to be back by eleven forty-five a.m. sharp. That's when we need to be out of here."

"What if we aren't?" I swallow hard, my thoughts racing ahead. "What would happen if this is still here when he arrives?"

Brendan's brow furrows. "I don't know."

"Would it prevent the murders?"

"Again, don't know. Would his machine land on top of ours? Would ours disintegrate? Because, remember, there's only one Midnight Rider. This is the same vehicle you arrived in yesterday. You know, it's better if we don't put your question to the test. Be back here at eleven forty-five, earlier if possible."

I nod, rubbing my dry palms. The control panel lights up. I have a vague awareness of something just out of my reach, but even though I attempt to grasp it with my mind, it floats away.

"Reset?" the control panel asks.

When Brendan curses, I'm not alarmed at first. Out the window, I expect to see blue sky. Instead, the solid metal fence still encloses us.

And a million stars twinkle in a pitch-black sky. Something else as well. Are they sparklers? Fireworks?

Oh! They're autopods, covered in tiny colored lights like those we put on our houses and trees at Christmas. Mesmerizing displays of color zip through the dark sky.

"What the…" My head jerks around to where Brendan is poking at the control panel, swearing and muttering.

"What's wrong, Brendan?" I smooth the edges of panic from my tone. Maybe it's nothing.

"This is saying we're in 2113." Brendan lurches to his feet and towers over us. "It's saying we went back ten years instead of one day."

"No way." I pinch myself. This has to be a dream. Which would explain the darkness outside. "Can't you fix it?"

"I'm trying! But it won't reset." He paces in the space, tugging his goatee. "If I didn't know better, I'd say someone sabotaged it. But that's impossible."

My heart stalls. How could this be happening? I reach into my backpack and grab my hand sanitizer, rubbing a dab over my palms as though it can get us out of this predicament.

Under the dim ceiling lights, Giles's brow creases. His fingers intertwine in thinking mode.

"Well…" I gulp, aware of my vast ignorance of the science behind this thing. "How do you get it to reset?"

Brendan points to the clear panel where numbers and lights are blinking. "It works by touch. It prompts me for the destination year, and I key it in on this number pad. My dad designed a backup app that can be used in the event of a malfunction. But that only applies in our home year. There are no cell phone towers here."

The intimidating lights blink over and over, as foreign to me as a jet cockpit. "So what part isn't working?"

"It's stuck on the year 2113, as if someone keyed it in. And whoever it was didn't set a time, so it reset to zero-zero."

"Midnight?" Giles scoots forward to study the panel. "Any way to tell by fingerprints who it was?"

"I have no materials to identify any prints."

"But the cops could." I snap my fingers. "Let's go find them and ask them to do a fingerprint test."

Both men look at me, no doubt evaluating the merit of my idea. But I don't see any other option. This had to be sabotage. That's why the gate opened. We need to find the person and…

Giles slaps his thigh. "But it wouldn't help, because if someone did this, it'd be someone from the year 2123. We won't find them here."

I droop. He's right. "Are…" I struggle to utter my worst fear. "Are we stuck here, then?"

Brendan pounds the panel. "Unless I can get this thing unstuck, then yeah, we're stuck here. At least for the near future."

After hours of futility, we have no choice but to sleep on the time hopper's floor. I settle my head atop my hard backpack, comforted by this tangible connection to my 2023 life. But nagging the corner of my awareness is the question of how long we'll be stranded here. A day or two would prove interesting, but it's not like Giles and I can build a new life here. If luck is on our side, this time might prove to be as short-lived as our last excursion.

"Better start praying," I whisper to Giles.

He holds my gaze in his stricken one, nodding. Clasping my hand, he launches into a fervent plea to God to get this machine going again.

Brendan tries again. Nothing.

"Kind of hard to get a god to act when he doesn't exist," he mutters, and my heart nose-dives. Why would he try to put a damper on Giles's and my relationship with the Lord? That won't promote peace and harmony. He probably already feels like the odd man out, being stuck in this cramped space with an engaged couple. Giles and I need to be considerate and not do anything to cause discomfort.

As the horizon starts to lighten, as the starlight begins to fade, we sleep.

⟶ ◦◦◦ ⟵

I open my eyes to bright sunshine streaming through. I sit up and dig through my pack for dental floss and breath freshener. Might as well refresh my Dried Rose lip gloss too. It dawns on me I don't know the day of the week or month or season we're in. But maybe the control panel will show it. Wrapping up my grooming routine, I slither forward so as not to wake Giles and peer at the dash. But the only display is the year 2113.

I remove my beige Kipling purse as if it carries a way to get me home. My wallet still contains my credit and debit cards, driver's license, and currency. Not sure why I even brought it, knowing none of it works here. My useless phone still sits in a pocket of my pack, an anchor to my old life, and I grip it like I'm drowning. In a way, I am. The display is still lit, and I tap my ebook app. Hey, I can still read a book. Splendid. The battery display shows 79 percent, so I have a few hours. I won't be able to recharge once it dies.

Absorbing myself in the latest from Australian author Kate Morton, I'm soon caught up in homesickness, not only for my old life in Portland but also my Aussie childhood. The white-robed gum trees, the grassy rolling hills, the billabongs in summer. My phone screen blurs, and I sniff. Then tears are running down my cheeks. I pull a tissue from my pack and dab my eyes and face. I dare not let Giles see my distress. It'll make this situation harder for him. *Stay strong, Thea.*

Soon the other two stir, and Giles, unaware of my emotional state, decides we need to get outside and check things out. We venture out into the sunshine, staying within the nine-foot-high fence, which fails to improve my mood. Brendan cranes at the sky. "I'm guessing we're in one of the autumn months."

I gape. "How do you know?"

"From the sun's angle." Pointing, he draws an arc with his finger, which means nothing to me. Geometry was never one of my strong subjects. "See how far up the sun is and its angle? It's gotta be midautumn, maybe October."

"You're right." I sneak a sidelong peek at my hologram, which sprang to life with a flash and steady glow. "It's

November 1, 2113." I force a grin at his wide-eyed expression. Way to bring Mr. Know-It-All off his pedestal. Did he also peek at his hologram before putting us through that fake demonstration, trying to impress us?

But now it's his turn to be impressed with Thea's down-to-earth practicality. He scans open the gate, and we venture out to the sidewalk. Curious looks greet us, but nobody bothers us. On the next block, the public toilets are in the same spot as before. Good. After a few hours sleeping in my clothes, I'm feeling grubby.

When Brendan decides to return to the vehicle to keep working on a fix, Giles shows me how to check my currency level on my hologram. My currency level hasn't diminished, which means we have funds to buy coffee and breakfast. Comfort food and strong caffeine—the best antidote for the glooms. "Hey, how about the BirdNest café?" I suggest. "Maybe it'll still be there."

He agrees, and we traipse the same route past the "denist" office, then arrive at the beveled wood door. But the door is locked, and a Clozed hologram sign floats over it. Through the window, we see tables and counters, but nobody moving about. The name above the door gleams: Gandy's Café—Lunch and Dinner. We won't be getting coffee here this morning.

Yet a rich coffee scent and bacon cooking wafts from somewhere nearby. Across the street, on the sidewalk in front of the CostWare building, sits an old TriMet bus. Hmm, that wasn't there in 2123. I want to shout for joy. The beautiful orange and blue behemoth makes me feel I'm already home.

"Lookie, love. TriMet is now in the coffee-and-brekkie business. C'mon, let's check it out."

Inside the old bus, instead of seats, a counter has been added at the rear, behind which two robots scurry about. Table and chair sets are scattered throughout. Giles walks me through the hologram-ordering process. I order a fifty-three-dollar cup of coffee and a ninety-nine-dollar breakfast bagel. My currency level won't last long. But I shove that worry aside. At least, I have Giles here to share this ordeal. And God won't make us stay here much longer, will He?

Neither of us wants to return to the time hopper, so we find an unoccupied table to wait for our food. Knowing Giles is feeling the nostalgia too, I pat the cushioned seat. "Aren't these chairs the original seats on TriMet buses?"

"I believe you're right, Love."

TriMet will repurpose their buses as restaurants.

My article hasn't been in the forefront of my mind since we got here.

That must mean the article isn't going to happen.

Which means we aren't going anywhere.

IN THE YEAR 2113

"I'm telling you, Thea, nothing's happening." A vein throbs in Brendan's temple. "Here, why don't you try it yourself if you think you know so much?"

Wow. All I'd suggested was that he try it again, and he's jumping all over me like a wallaby in a forest of fallen logs. The interior is heating up, and not just from the afternoon sunshine beating down. This better not be our new normal. We've only been here four hours, and nerves are already fraying. Giles sits silent, and I suspect he's praying. But Brendan keeps challenging me.

"Here, Thea." He gestures me to the empty driver's seat. "Sit."

I hesitate, then step forward, and sit as though the seat might electrocute me.

"See this keypad?" His voice pummels me. "Go ahead. Hit the reset button."

I do, and nothing happens. "See? Now punch in the year you want." I peer at the nine-digit keyboard, intending to key in 2023, but my hand trembles so hard it hits the 2 instead of the 3. Yet the result is the same—nothing. Studying the panel, I notice nothing amiss. It contains commands such as Go, Lock, Set Date.

I lean forward and squint. Abort? "What's this?" Too late, my finger touches it.

"No!" shouts Brendan. "Not that one."

"But it didn't do anything anyway. I just don't get it," I mutter. "You were able to work it before."

He jerks an impatient nod. "Yeah, but my dad didn't prepare me for a malfunction of this magnitude."

Whoever did this to us, I pray God makes them pay. If we're stranded here much longer, we're going to have to figure out a way to get food and lodging. No way can we keep sharing this tiny space night after night. There's scant floor space, no food or water or bathroom. The three of us sit in silence, ruminating. Are Giles and Brendan fighting as hard as I am to keep despair at bay? Despite my hand in Giles's, my pulse pounds, and I cannot shake the profound awareness that his and my entire future life together has flipped upside down and topsy-turvy.

Giles breaks the dark tension first. "Brendan, which years did your father visit?"

I think I know why he's asking. I move to the seat beside Giles.

Brendan flops into the driver's seat. "He hopped forward a decade between the years 2030 to 2130."

"Wow, eleven trips into the future?"

"Yeah. So we just have to wait until"—Brendan gazes at the ceiling, no doubt doing the math in his head—"the year 2120."

"Seven more years?" Giles rarely raises his voice this loud.

"If I can't get this thing moving, then yeah." Brendan pounds the panel again, followed by another more vigorous slam.

I feel the same. I'm too panicked to cry. I can barely sleep. All the prayers in the world aren't changing our circumstances.

When will I awaken from this nightmare? It better be a nightmare. It can't be reality. A whole different life, my cats, my job, and a scarred little girl awaits me at home. And if I let her down…

She'll never trust another adult as long as she lives.

———◆◇◆———

Claustrophobia kicks in on day two. "Please, can we keep the gate open?" I plead. The inability to see anything except a solid black fence makes me feel like I'm buried in a coffin.

"You realize we'll attract unwanted visitors."

"Any visitors, Brendan, welcome or unwelcome, will be better than this limbo. In fact, why don't you just show Giles and me how to open it."

He's reluctant but knows it's easier than my pestering him. So he scans our fingerprints, and I run my hand along the sensor. Voilà, the gate slides to the right. "There. You can open it from either side now."

But later that day, a pounding on the capsule door makes us jump as if we'd been struck by lightning. "Open up!"

Two heads peer through the embedded window, and I gasp, recognizing one of them. Ruba, our friendly neighborhood cop, but ten years younger and several pounds heavier. I hadn't known she was a natural redhead. An unfamiliar robot partner stands beside her.

"You can't park here," she says.

Brendan pushes the button that slides the door open. A current of humid air rushes in as if he'd opened an oven door. The aroma of river water and rich vegetation also intrudes. Sweat breaks out on my forehead, but I have no more layers to remove.

"We're aware of that, ma'am." I want to shush Brendan. They don't use that term here. "But our vehicle malfunctioned, and we're unable to move it."

She glances inside, meeting my gaze without recognition. "Autopods not allowed on riverbank. We can get it towed to a repair shop."

"No!" Brendan pushes himself to a sitting position. "I mean, nobody here will be able to repair it. It…my dad customized it. In fact, he owns this tiny piece of land. We were trying to take it to him when…when it died."

"Your dad? You mean coparent?"

Brendan looks back at us in bewilderment. I shrug and nod.

"Uh, yeah, my coparent. He…"

"Where yull from?"

Of course she doesn't recognize me.

"I'm from this area." An edge of defensiveness laces Brendan's tone. He thrusts a thumb in our direction. "But they're…"

"We're not from here," I blurt, pushing myself to a sitting position. "We're just visiting."

"Need your names, please."

Ruba's partner hasn't said a word so far, just inched his head from side to side as if scanning the interior. Is he recording everything we say and do with those weird eyes and fake ears of his?

"Brendan Murray."

Of course, Ruba wouldn't recognize Brendan. But her recognition of us in 2123 now makes sense. Prickles creep up my arms, and my breath quickens. Because Giles and I look the same as we did then.

She's looking at me, waiting for my name.

"I'm…Marie." I give her my middle name. "Marie Davies." I grab Giles's hand. "And this is my husband. Griffith."

"Griffith," scooting closer, squints at me, the same realization dawning in his eyes—the memories of Ladycop who will claim, ten years from now, to remember us. Unsure why I felt it necessary to give fake names, I make a what-else-could-I-do face at him.

It's official. The future has collided with the past. And the past with the future. Must be the crashing noise I hear.

"You obvy not from here. Stopped sayin husband wife long ago. It's just spouse. Where yull from?"

Giles beats me to it. "We're from the east coast of Canada." Ha. He's betting Ruba isn't familiar with that part of the world. "We still use those terms."

"Well, we need to haul this thing outta here, somehow. Gotta gram a tow." She plants her feet and eyes our "home," hands on hips. "They bring it to our discard yard."

"B–but," Brendan stutters, "this is private property. Check your records."

The two put their heads together and study the partner's hologram. I take advantage of the hiatus to get out and stretch my legs. Oh, how nice to make a circuit around the vehicle, even such a short distance.

"Do you have the owner's permission to occupy his property?"

"Um, it belongs to my fa—parent."

More perusal of their records. "Sorry," her partner says. "There's no record of any family members on the deed."

"Since the owner not here to ask, yull gotta move out."

Brendan makes a growling noise. "We're just trying to get home."

"Shouldn't be a problem. Check with Megamax or FlyPods."

But MegaMax or FlyPods won't get us home. I could explain, but if I tell her how we got here, she'd haul us off to the nearest mental health clinic. Or, even worse, what if she decides we're best off in the integration pavilion?

God, please, I beg. *Get us home.*

But God is silent. At least, He's not letting us in on His plan.

Giles crosses his legs and plops his elbows on his knees. "We're out of currency." I'm grateful he remembered the twenty-second-century term. "We don't have a way to pay for transportation or lodging or food." He gestures at us. "And my spouse and brother and I have no way to get any until we get home."

His brother? Okay, not such a stretch, considering their somewhat similar features and builds. As long as Ruba buys it.

"Yull got any other family round here?"

I shake my head, forcing a pleading tone. "None. Can you direct us to any places where we can eat and sleep until we can get our vehicle repaired?"

She tilts her head, studying us. "Possibly can help. Just sittight till we return."

They leave, and we breathe out a collective sigh of relief as Brendan slides the door shut. The air is still and dry, at least a minimal improvement over the hot, humid breeze.

Then I let loose the smile I've been holding back. "Your brother, huh?" I poke Giles. "Good job. She bought it."

But the look he rakes over me erases the smile. "It's time I tell you, Thea. You too, Brendan."

My heartbeat skips at his ominous tone. "Tell me what, love?"

He doesn't reply at first, just watches his fingers caressing mine. Then his intense gaze meets mine, and I hold my breath.

"Brendan *is* my brother. That is, my half brother. A few weeks ago, I found out my biological father's likely identity." He pierces the tension with his index finger. "Coltrane McMurray."

GILES

There. His secret was out. No more hiding, no more worrying if the cops would discover his relationship to the murdered man. Brendan jerked his head like he'd been punched, and Thea, gobsmacked, stood there with gaping mouth and trembling hands.

But the grief at losing his newfound father moments after meeting him...well, that would take a while to get over. He'd never have the father-son relationship he'd longed for.

Giles predicted Thea's next words, could've mouthed them in sync.

"Giles! Why didn't you tell me?"

"I *am* telling you." Effort kept the defensiveness away.

"But you've known for weeks?"

"I needed to be certain before I told you." He cast her his most apologetic look, and the hardness in her eyes eased.

"Whoa, bro!" At least Brendan seemed exuberant. "Who's your mom, and how did you find out?"

Giles launched into the story Thea already knew, the search for his biological father that brought him to the US and Oregon. "The ancestry database led me to my biological mum, a lady by the name of Nancy Bacon, who still lives in Sydney.

I reached out to her to see if she'd reveal my father's identity, and all she told me was that he was from Portland, Oregon."

"Dad never mentioned anyone named Nancy."

Did Brendan doubt him or need clarification? "She told me he returned to the States after she got pregnant. They didn't keep in touch."

Thea turned her wide gaze on him, reassuring him she didn't hold his secret-keeping against him. "Giles, tell Brendan what your bio mum is like."

"Oh, she's so funny. We met for lunch, and she kept me laughing. If she were here, she'd entertain us, get our minds off our problems. After she placed me for adoption, she eventually married and had two kids. I have a half brother and sister."

Brendan leaned back in the seat, relaxed, as if he had no doubt of the story's truthfulness. "Did you meet them?"

"No, Mum wasn't comfortable with the idea. But she did show me photos, and the boy looks sort of like me." Thea's animated, hanging-on-his-every-word face encouraged him to continue. "But I wanted to know who my father was. She wouldn't or couldn't tell me, so I moved here, got a job, met Thea, and kept researching my ancestry. When I discovered McMurray was likely my father, I had to meet him to know for sure."

He squeezed Thea's hand, hoping she missed the unfortunate conclusion that if he hadn't pushed her to land the McMurray article, they wouldn't be in this predicament. "Thea, remember when we arrived and he mentioned he'd spent time in Australia? That, plus the resemblance, made me certain he was my father. And the fact I've always been interested in technology."

Thea's voice softened. "You could've told me."

Weren't they past that? "But aren't you glad I didn't?" Perfect rebuttal, coming right up. She wouldn't find anything to argue with. "The cops were already suspicious of me. If they knew I was the murder victim's long-lost son, they would've had even more cause to detain me. And you would've felt compelled to protect me by keeping it a secret. Would you have wanted that burden?"

Her headshake told him she saw reason. But Brendan grinned wide. "Didn't know Dad was such a playboy. So how many years older are you?"

Before Giles could answer, the cops reappeared with the twenty-second-century equivalent of a tow truck. Part helicopter, part semi, it spanned the entire width of the packed-dirt road. Ladycop ordered the three of them out, and they complied. Once on the street, Thea slotted her hand into his and searched his face with a where-are-we-going-to-go look. She tugged on her thin white T-shirt, ruffling in the hot breeze.

He shrugged at her unspoken question. Where would they get food? Clothes? A place to sleep? He turned to the robot. "You need to understand we have no place to go. No currency and no way to get home. Are there any resources for stranded people?"

Surely, social services would've advanced enough by this time. The robot opened his mouth to reply, but Giles almost didn't want to hear it.

"We have emergency shelters with showers and beds."

He sighed. Didn't sound very appealing. "How long can we stay there?"

"As long as you need, but they expect you to follow the rules and work for your keep."

If the shelters were anything like the ones he'd heard of, they wouldn't last a week. "Okay, I guess if that's our best option, we'll take it."

Behind him, the tow "truck" was hooking a contraption to the stranded time machine. "Where is it taking our vehicle?"

Ruba tutted. "To the discard yard couple miles from here. They keep it for six months. Then, if yull don't pick it up, they part it out."

What would anyone here need with old helicopter and airplane parts?

Oh, who cared about that anyway. He could hardly bring himself to consider the real question. Would they ever get home again?

"What about my wife and daughter?" Brendan had it even worse. "If I never return, they're going to assume I'm dead."

Thea's eyes sparkled with unshed tears as the tow truck hauled away the only tie to their old life. "Stefanie is going to be frantic. And Mia...Ari...Wow, I can't even imagine."

Ruba and Robocop ignored them, barking orders to the tow operators.

All too soon, it was over. And their new life began.

PART II

IN THE YEAR 2120

I've been waiting seven long years for the time machine to return. I tighten my grip on Giles's hand as we wait at the riverbank where McMurray will hopefully appear. My husband has our daughter, Daisy Marie, settled in her little lavender pack, adjusting it on his back. Brendan wasn't sure it would be today, but "sometime in the summer" was as close as he could remember. From the corner of my eye, I see him shuffling his feet at Giles's other side.

"He never gave me a specific date," Brendan reiterates. "Just the years. I mean, if I'd known we'd be stuck here someday, gee, I would've asked him for an exact date."

Here in this land where humans and robots coexist in an easy affinity, I've waited for too long already. Seven interminable years of adapting to an alien way of life and doing not too bad of a job of it, if I do say so myself. I'm grateful to Penny for her tutorial on clothes and language.

Yet the desire to go home nags, like a toothache my tongue can't resist kneading. I no longer weep myself to sleep in Giles's arms at night or find unexpected tears on my cheeks during the long days. A few years ago, I stopped looking through my sole possessions from 2023, my charcoal-gray Portland Gear backpack and beige Kipling purse, now stashed away and out of sight behind my shoe caddy.

No longer do I catch Giles watching me with the troubled countenance I've grown to dread. I don't lament the loss of my old life anymore—morning lattes with Ari, the hum of busy newsgathering at work, my comfortable SleepNumber mattress. Instead, I've determined to be out here every day to watch for McMurray until summer ends. He's my only hope.

Except for the sharp, daily plague of homesickness, it hasn't been all bad. Giles, who goes by Griff now, and I married after that dreadful day we realized we weren't going anywhere until McMurray could rescue us. A trip to the courthouse, and we left as spouses. We abandoned our dream of a fancy church wedding. We wouldn't have had anyone to invite. Plus, nobody really does that anymore—the bar is set much lower now. People don't marry. They "couple." As long as we're considered husband and wife in God's eyes, we can't worry what the culture says.

We have a beautiful little girl, and she's saved my sanity and given me a reason to smile again. How can I focus on my old life when I'm so busy focusing on her? Eyes of blue, she has my nose and her grandpa McMurray's sly grin. My fierce love for her grows day by day. Giles and I thank the Lord for her. I also thank Him that Giles and Brendan were both smart enough to find jobs and navigate this strange new world we landed in. Overall, Giles adjusted much better than I did.

My big takeaway? God is the God of my future, as well as my past. He hasn't gone anywhere, even if I have.

I've kept my eyes open for my doppelgangers, but so far, nothing. No one else here looks like me. Either the mother and daughter hadn't been here long in 2123, or I just haven't crossed paths with them yet. How cool if I get the opportunity to meet them someday.

At the end of Giles's first workday almost seven years ago as an accountant for CostWare Distributing—the new Amazon—he swiveled his chair toward me. "The accounting rules are a bit different now." He didn't even need to leave our dorm room. "I'm going to have to brush up on the new standards. Plus, it's strange to do everything via hologram. Few people, other than those in the service industry, go to work anymore."

"Hmm." I glanced at him, my fingers tightening on a framed print of big white flowers trimmed in blue, green, and maroon. Removing the whimsical cat print from above our queen-sized bed, I replaced it with the white flowers. "Look, love, don't you think this looks better?"

Giles nodded, his focus still on his work.

"And this cat cartoon belongs better in the common area, don't you think?"

"As long as the dormmates don't object."

After Daisy was born, we assuaged our curiosity as to the fate of our respective homes from our old life. Before the taxipod launched its search over southeast Portland, I directed it to my old Eastmoreland address. "Address not found," the control panel's voice uttered. Infant Daisy slept in my arms, oblivious to our mission.

"Put in the nearest intersection," Giles instructed.

"Take us to Southeast Seventeenth and Horton Street."

I held my breath while the display flashed and emitted soft beeps, wondering what was taking it so long.

"Destination noted," it told us. It followed the curve of the river for about half a mile, then veered inland.

In another minute, we landed on a street lined with climate-proof composite-material buildings. But not a sign of any single-family homes.

I clutched Giles's arm. "It's gone. The Davenports' beautiful brick home got torn down for this?" I waved my free hand in a wide arc at the obscene monstrosity dominating the block, my heart quivering. How our old life had vanished. It was as though we never existed.

Shaking our heads, we directed the taxipod to Giles's old street. "There!" he said. "Can you believe it? It's still there!"

I craned my neck at the five-story townhome. "They added more floors to the original, love. Wow!"

"But otherwise, it looks pretty much the same."

"Oh, but look." I turned his attention to the corner. "There's the old Paddy O'Rourke's Alehouse!"

"The one all boarded up and covered with graffiti? That's Paddy's?"

"What used to be Paddy's." I wasn't sure whether to shed a nostalgic tear or rejoice that the club's annoying festivities ended.

"We should search the Cloud and see if we can find anything about ourselves."

"You mean, like our obituaries? Are you sure you want to know?" The idea had occurred to me, but I'd resisted going there. Did I want to know?

"Aren't you curious too? Think about it. If we live for another sixty years or so, our deaths will be listed in the Cloud somewhere. Assuming we make it back home."

Despite my best efforts, I couldn't dissuade him. He embarked on a search once we got home. Unable to watch, I went into Daisy's room and drank in the sight of her sweet sleeping face, ever conscious of my husband's endeavor in the other room. What would he find?

It didn't take long before he opened the door. "Got a moment?"

"Did you find anything?" My breath caught as he crossed to the crib.

"Nothing." His finger caressed Daisy's velvet-soft cheek. "Nothing at all on the cloud about you or me."

My jaw dropped. "What does that mean?"

"I think it means our deaths are still in the future. I think it means we're never going to make it back to our old lives."

My head buzzing like a chainsaw, I refused to believe it. We couldn't be stuck here for good. But from Giles's face, he believed it.

That night, I couldn't sleep. Giles's dire words circulated around and around in my head like my childhood hamster on its wheel. Beside me, he snored away, carefree and clueless. Whereas my brain composed scheme after scheme on how to get us home, each one more fantastical than the last. Until I gave up and fell into a restless sleep, visions of time machines and dreams of my old life taunting me until the morning sun chased them off.

GILES

Giles gawked at the building across Belmont as he exited Preston Denal Clinic after an early morning teeth cleaning.

Interesting. Thea would want to know about this. He mounted his blue-and-silver Schwinn-Giant bicycle and embarked on the seven-mile ride home, waving to other cyclists as he passed. He could almost be home in 2023 again riding along Belmont, save for the lack of cars. The old asphalt pavements had been torn up and replaced with a condensed dirt-based composite material perfect for cyclists, walkers, and joggers.

Just before 11:00 a.m., he arrived home. Daisy was watching a holocartoon, and Thea was exiting the shower, wrapped in a big red beach towel. "Love, want to go on a jaunt across town?"

Her smirk never failed to get to him. "May I get dressed first?"

"I wouldn't have it any other way."

Chuckling, she donned a sundress—her almost daily go-to outfit—and, with Daisy in tow, hopped in their autopod.

"Where are we going?"

"It's a surprise. I found something interesting after my dentist appointment this morning, wanted to share it with you." He tapped the control panel. "Destination Belmont and Thirty-Eighth Avenue."

"Really? Isn't that near where Ari and Zach lived?"

He smiled. "You'll see." Zipping around and over buildings and other autopods still thrilled him after all this time. Speeding a car in the fast lane paled in comparison, even seemed pedestrian. Almost made this forced futuristic detour worth it.

The building he sought—a three-story structure built with graffiti-resistant and climate-proof materials—neared, and he lowered the autopod to the street.

He pointed at the front. "See the sign over that huge front door?"

Thea gasped out the words. "Arias Adams Arts Academy. Oh my, she must have been rich and successful to have done this!"

"This was her bequest upon her death," Giles explained. "She and Zach did quite splendidly in the food-service industry. In 2030, they opened a chain of restaurants—The Craze—and they were a huge hit. The latest, ahem, Craze. By the time she died in 2080, their wealth was immense. But they had no kids to bequeath it to, so she started a trust for this art school. It got finished in 2090."

"Wow. What a story. What about Zach? When did he pass?"

"Ten years before her."

"I'm happy and relieved they stayed together." A tear snaked down her cheek. Sniffling, she scooted closer to Giles, who pulled her head onto his shoulder. "Good for them. I wasn't ever a hundred percent positive those two had staying power." She swiped a finger beneath her eye. "I sure do miss my Ari. My creative, talented bestie."

Giles stroked the short wig she'd worn today, the texture rough beneath his fingers. "Interesting, isn't it, they didn't have kids. Didn't Ari want them eventually?"

Thea shrugged and shifted out of his grasp. "It was never one of her life goals. She just wanted to find her niche and be successful at it. And I'm happy she got her wish."

"Remember those two ladies from Tacoma?"

"Ellen and Sher? Sure. Wonder whatever happened to them." Before she'd finished speaking, she'd found them on the Cloud. "Oh my. I found Ellen's obituary. It says she died in May 2067, survived by her life partner, Sheryl Stark. And Sher died just a few years later."

They fell silent, their memories too big to speak of. Thea fingered the plastiglass window, gazing at Arias's legacy. "If only we'd stayed home and not come back. We could've witnessed Arias's success for ourselves. We could've…"

"I know, love." No use ruing events beyond their control. "We need to get home now." He started up the autopod, wishing for a way to fix the unfixable, to reach the impossible.

"Wait." She glanced back at Daisy, who'd been so quiet he'd nearly forgotten she was there. Ah, yes. She was curled up on the floor, asleep. "Let's go in. I've got to see this place. We can say we're interested in signing up our pring for classes."

Daisy whined when Thea rousted her, but Thea pointed out the building. "Would you like to learn to draw and paint and make pretty things?"

Daisy's eyes grew wide. Nodding, she took Thea's hand without complaint, hopping ahead, tugging on her mother's arm. What an easy child Daisy had always been. Would she be so compliant as a teenager? He'd read somewhere the easier the child, the rougher the teen years. If that were true, they were in for some hard years. He himself had belied that claim. Never a rebel, he'd sailed through childhood and adolescence like a yacht cruising Sydney Harbor.

Inside the academy lobby, a framed portrait of Arias Adams hung over the reception desk, which was manned by two actual people. Had that been a stipulation of Ari's? Thea stopped as if she'd seen a ghost and stared at the image of her old friend. Ari must've been in her fifties, still with the same mischievous spark in her eye, the smirk that promised a good time if you were fortunate enough to tag along. "Oh my. Look at her."

Giles grabbed Daisy's other hand. "Same Ari, thirty years older." No more pink-streaked hair. Instead, the middle-aged Ari sported a smooth blonde do. Quite flattering. Nobody would claim Ari as beautiful, but she'd narrowed the gap in her older years.

A throat clearing jerked him to attention. One of the X people behind the counter narrowed her eyes at him.

Right, their conversation must sound…odd. He grinned and approached. "Hi there. We're interested in enrolling our pring in art classes." He placed his hands on Daisy's shoulders and eased her closer.

The woman named Robb per her nameplate offered them a tour. They ventured in and out of classrooms, sat at tables stained with splotches of paint and clay, and examined student art both amateur and adept. But he paid more attention to Thea's reactions than the boring lectures, particularly, her double takes at each monument to her friend's talent. "Oh, Giles. Look at this display of her rocks." A shelf held at least a dozen of Ari's specialties, many of which he'd seen before at her food cart. Ladybugs, mushrooms, forest creatures, Mount Hood. So pristine, they looked brand new. Had someone restored them to their original state? He picked Daisy up to eye level with the shelf and read the plaque above the shelf aloud. "'Mx. Adams started their art career by painting rocks. Here are some samples of their early works.'"

Thea pointed to the ladybug. "I remember that."

Robb stopped and gawked. "You talk like you knew Mx. Adams."

Thea jolted. "Oh, uh, she—*they*—was my…my aunt."

"Your aunt? Um, grandsib?"

"Um, yes. They was my grandsib." She met his gaze and rolled her eyes, probably thinking the same thing as him. Why go to such lengths to change the terminology we all know and use just to hide gender?

"They must have passed before you were born."

Ari would've been far too old to be Thea's aunt, but Robb didn't seem to compute that.

Thea smiled. "I've seen pho—um, *images* of her work, though."

She cast him a stricken look as if fearing the woman would pick up on her verbal miscues.

But Robb's chin dip told them they had nothing to worry about. "We can enroll Daisy today, if you like."

Daisy jumped at this. "Please, Parents? Want paint rocks."

Thea grinned, and Giles slipped an arm around her. Their daughter would carry on Ari's legacy. Whether or not she achieved Ari's astonishing level of talent and success remained to be seen.

IN THE YEAR 2120

Brendan and Giles have bonded like true brothers, yet the differences between them have become all too obvious. Brendan: self-centered, entitled, demanding. Giles: family man, godly, generous. I avoid Brendan as much as possible. Either Giles doesn't mind Brendan's character flaws, or he's oblivious, having never had a brother before. They chat endlessly about Brendan's childhood and his life growing up as Coltrane McMurray's son. Giles eats it up, and, although he had a happy childhood, he must wonder what his life could have been…if only…

And what about the time machine?

We had it hauled to the rooftop podlot of our seven-story dormitory where we share living quarters on the fifth floor with two other couples and Brendan. Our dorm includes a communal kitchen and bathroom, and each bedroom has an en suite bathroom and a kitchenette. Brendan sleeps on a roll-out bed in the common room. Single-family homes seem to be a thing of the past, long since torn down and replaced with multiperson housing, which block our view of the tree-studded hills across the river.

Giles and I remember the early days of the trend when single-family homes became frowned upon. Decades later, we're told they're a waste of valuable resources. Unsustainable, the fruits of greed. And here we are, at the full tail end of it. Rich people are scorned, and living a simple life is noble.

Nice, however, to have a roof over our heads and some income. But we had to come up with a cover story for our dormmates to explain our oddities. Being from Australia came in handy, and they all seemed to believe that a malfunctioned autopod was a legitimate reason for us to be here. We mention homes and families back in Australia. Thus, if—I mean *when*—we leave, they won't be surprised.

But to Giles I could express my true sentiments. "Stefanie must be frantic that I failed to return. And what do you think Ari and Zach thought?"

"I can guess."

"Kidnapped by aliens," we chortle in unison.

"Zach is probably jealous."

The time we were stranded for a day in 2123? It was nothing compared to seven years. But it's amazing what depths of resilience humans prove to have when they've run out of choices. I've learned to Cloudshop, guide an autopod, and decipher how robots communicate. Since they don't have any body language or varying tones of voice, you have to take everything they say at face value. And their emotions? They state them as fact. "I am getting angry." "That is sad." Giles calls them "Spock machines."

We humans could learn some lessons on honest communication from robots.

The fence behind which Midnight Rider will land seems to sway, but it's wishful thinking. It would take an earthquake to sway this fence. But that telltale hum gives it away. "He's here!" I suck in a rattled breath. "Brendan, hop on board as soon as you can." McMurray will recognize his son, whereas Giles and I will be strangers. So we nominated Brendan for the job, and that's gotta be my fifth reminder.

Our daughter plays with her daddy's hair while Brendan steps forward and peeks through the narrow slits. "Yes!" He turns to us with a fist pump, then gestures us back.

He waves at the fence. The gate slides to the left a few inches, and he slithers inside. "Hey!" calls a female voice. "You can't be here." Where have I heard her voice before? "And how did you get inside?"

"Penny?" Shock tightens Brendan's voice, and my hopes tailspin. We weren't expecting Penny. Is she alone?

"Um, do I know you?" I can visualize her furrowed forehead, her eyes squinting at him.

"Yeah, you know me. Brendan…"

"Never met you in my life. Now back away before I gram the cops and report you for trespassing."

No! She can't do this! I start forward, but Giles holds me back. "No, love, don't risk it."

I want to weep. It never occurred to me McMurray would send Penny in his stead. "But maybe we can talk her into taking us back."

"No, she'll sic the cops on us." Giles slips his shades off and wipes the lenses with his shirt until they are smudge-free. "Do you want to be interrogated again? Remember, we know the exact day and time he'll be here in three years."

"Three years?" Brendan stomps toward us, punching an invisible target. At least he didn't swing at Giles.

He falls into step on Giles's other side as we return the four blocks to our parked autopod. But I halt, the implication sinking in. "We have to wait *three* more years?"

"Thea, our life here isn't so bad, is it?" Giles takes my hand and urges me on. "I mean, if you weren't here, it would suck. But we're together, our baby girl is wonderful, and we can have more kids if you like." Daisy swings her little legs, jostling the pack on Daddy's back. "I kind of enjoy life here, if you want to know the truth."

"Don't you miss our church? The New Seasons deli? Hawthorne?"

"I do, but our church here is fine, even though it's so small."

Brendan points to the BirdNest as its aroma floats our way. "And the food is so much better without all those chemicals they used to add."

So true. "But don't you think it's sad how few people attend worship services anymore?"

Of course, Brendan isn't a churchgoer and couldn't care less. But Giles agrees with a nod. "People seem to have forgotten about the God who created them."

I often wish Brendan would join us for worship, but I don't see that happening. In fact, with the number of women he's dated, it's like he's forgotten he was ever married and had a child. But it's not my place to judge. "What about you, Brendan? I gather you can't wait to go home either." His life as a ladies' man—no commitments, no obligations—does it fulfill him? Does he even miss his family? He never mentions them, at least to me.

"It's okay." Brendan shrugs and thrusts a thumb behind him. "What happened back there convinced me. I've gotta rebuild the time hopper instead of trying to fix it." He rubs his hands together, all grins. "So we may not have to wait three years to get home."

Wait. Is that possible? Having plummeted to the depth of despair, I start to climb back.

Clapping Giles on the back, Brendan quickens his steps. "You'll help me, won't you, bro?"

"Not sure what I can do, but I can give it my best shot."

I smile and break into the "Hallelujah Chorus." Daisy giggles, my high spirits infectious. Thinking back to the life-changing day when we arrived, I visualize the scene outside the vehicle. "If we'd been hanging around on June 8, 2123, waiting to persuade McMurray to take us back, I'd have seen us. But nobody resembling you two stood around in the crowd."

My feet give a happy little skip. "It must mean you're going to be successful."

IN THE YEAR 2120

"Brendan seems serious about his latest conquest," Giles tells me Saturday morning as I sit at the kitchen table doing research on the Cloud. Daisy sits beneath the table absorbed in a child hologram. Despite the blocks and toys and puzzles we've bought her, she prefers the gram. Typical twenty-second-century three-year-old. "Baba win," she babbles.

"Day-zee win," I recite since she still struggles with her name.

"Bab-by days win," she repeats, giggling.

I shift my hologram so Giles can't see I'm researching the subject of our conversation, who fortunately is not here. If Brendan ever made it back to 2023, there should be an obituary for him. I've searched for five minutes, finding nothing. Does that mean he—and we—never made it back? Or he—and we—did, but nothing about his death was ever printed?

I shift to face Giles. "Is she the one who moved into the apartment downstairs with her mother?"

"Yeah, the one named Juni."

"Wonder what makes her different from all the others."

"She's got that wild streak he likes."

Something soft brushes my leg. It's one of our "replacement" cats, one of whom I named Grinchetta, in memory of Mia. The male I named Grimm, in memory of my favorite Portland-based TV show. I reach down to knead Grinchetta's fur. I fear my Grizzy and Rumple got taken to the Multnomah County Animal Shelter when I failed to return in 2023. Poor kitties. So much for my promise to never leave or forsake them. Maybe a good family adopted them. I can't bear to contemplate the alternative. The relationship between these two isn't amicable. Grimm is so territorial. I'm continually reminding him to "Be ye kind one to another, tenderhearted, forgiving one another." But so far, the Word of God has had no effect.

Yellow-furred Grinchetta meows. "My food is stale," her collar translates in a Siri-like voice.

Black-and-white Grimm gives a yowl. "The water is old," he's saying. If I ever get to go home, I'm taking these AI collars with me. And the cats, of course. All cats deserve to communicate accurately. I salute the woman who invented cat-translation collars. I refresh my spoiled kitties' food and water, and they meow their gratitude. "Thank you!"

"You're quite welcome, my lovies."

Our other dormmates are beginning to drift in and out of the kitchen, pouring coffee, rubbing sleepy eyes. The kitchen holds two round tables, so someone is always left without a seat

Which is why we try to be the first ones up. "Mornin," greets Lexel and his spouse, Kate—a nice timeless name that has made a comeback. It adds a sense of normality to our lives. "How you?"

"Fabby," says Giles/Griff, who speaks the vernacular like a native. As do Brendan and I. "Plans for day?"

Speaking the vernacular like a native, we've learned, requires one to keep their mouth half open while speaking and skip filler words and extra syllables.

Kate pulls a coffee cup from the cupboard. "Takin boat to riv for some skiin."Yep, people will still boat and fish and water-ski in a hundred years. Something else that's timeless—outdoor recreation.

Lexel pours coffee into Kate's cup. The aroma wafts my direction, and I sip my dark roast with oat milk. "Want to come with?"

Giles appears unenthused. "No thanks. Got plans."

My outdoorsman husband is not much of a water-sports person. His plans for today are to relax at home, play with Daisy, try to track down Brendan for some money he owes Giles. Maybe go for a hike in Forest Park later. He gets annoyed at having to share living quarters with so many other people. A few years ago, I'd mused, "Wonder why everyone lives in dorms now instead of apartments."

"Remember the high-density housing craze from the 2000s?" Giles replied with a flourish of his hand. "Well, this is HDH taken to the next level."

Only higher-income earners can afford a single-family apartment, with kitchens and bathrooms they don't have to share with strangers. So how can Giles be so shruggy over the loss of our old life? A life of privacy. A life with a yard and trees for Daisy to climb. Here, trees are sacrificed for dorms. On the other hand, our dorm has a tree garden on its roof, as do many dorms, which provides a shady sanctuary from the hot sun. Yet it pales in comparison to the leafy streets of 2020s Portland.

As I tune out the conversation around me, melancholy invades my morning. Of the three of us, Daisy is most content, having never known any other way of life. She plays beneath the table, and when she tires of her gram games, she'll go retrieve her robot dolls and remain serene. Until she gets hungry. Or bored.

Once the dormmates have drifted out and we have privacy, Giles plops beside me and shows me his hologram. "Your wish for a place of our own might be coming true. There's an apartment at Willamette Shores Condominiums coming available in a month." When it's just the two of us, we converse in our normal speech. "I put a deposit down on it, and they'll tell us next week if we're accepted." His voice rises upward, and I'm thankful he wants this as much as I do. I mean, the three of us crammed into one bedroom isn't going to work for the long haul, especially if we have more babies.

I clap my hands, stifling a squeal, as Daisy climbs on my lap and snuggles there. I caress her shiny, soft hair, studying her profile from above. Such fine, delicate features God blessed her with. "You hungry, Baba?" I ask her.

At her nod, I set her down and go into the kitchen to fix her some eggs. As I'm cracking them into the skillet, Brendan bursts in, all animated energy like a sidewalk breakdancer. Behind him trails a girl with hair dyed crimson on one side and blue on the other, like we used to see way back in our old life on college football game days. But football as we knew it was outlawed fifty years ago. Too many injuries, too many concussions.

Then I notice her eyes. One dark, one light. I want to ask if she was born that way, but I bite back the rude question. I remember the commonality of the phenomenon in 2123. Turns out it's not a weird genetic glitch starting to display itself in the human race, but a cosmetic enhancement using colored lenses. Some people go so far as to have laser surgery to change the color of one or both eyes.

Amazing how much medicine has evolved.

"Back at last, bro!" Giles stands, beaming, but the hardness in his eyes betrays his effort at joviality. "Who's this?"

"Juni, meet Marie and Griff. Their pring, Daisy. Juni and her parent moved in last week."

She waves in our general direction but keeps her two-toned gaze on Brendan as if waiting for marching orders. Something about her is familiar, but I can't place it. She's wearing a white mesh sunsuit so popular these days since the mild Portland climate has evaporated along with winter snowfall. Even in

January, the temps rarely dip below fifty. With highs over a hundred most summer days, we dress appropriately.

I need to break through this ice wall she's erected. I scoop the cooked eggs into a bowl for Daisy. "Hi, Juni. Welcome to Oaks Park Dorm." The former Oaks Amusement Park this building was named for is a mere historical memory now. I set the bowl on the table and hoist Daisy into her high chair. "Where did you move from?"

She turns her gaze to me, a smirk flickering on her pink-and-red mouth. "From a distant star, in the far galaxy of Modenza. Just landed here in my spaceship, found this dorble hooman"—she turns a moue on Brendan—"and decided to stay."

I grin. Under different circumstances, perhaps, she and Zach would make a fitting pair. How soon before she finds Brendan's only adorable trait is his looks? Not to mention, he's still married. *Don't let that lack of a wedding ring fool you, girl.*

"Kiddin." Juni tosses the blue half of her hair over her shoulder. "We lived east of here, near Gresham." She presents a jarring image, like a stage actor portraying the two-faced Roman god, Janus.

"We not stayin," Brendan tells us. "Swimmin at the riv."

Giles clears his throat. "Uh, Bren, got a sec?"

"Got two secs," he says, reducing Juni to giggles.

Giles doesn't crack a smile as he gestures Brendan into the bedroom, where I know he's asking about the money.

As I sit next to my daughter and watch her eat, our dormmate Garl emerges from his room, rubbing his eyes. He spots Juni, blinks, and resumes the eye rubs. Taking a second peek presumably to make sure he's not still dreaming, he nods a greeting at her, then beelines to the kitchen. Casting glances over at the visitor, he pours himself a mug of coffee and squirts in the hazelnut syrup he loves.

Yes, Garl, she's really standing there. You can stop staring now. Has he never seen anyone else with the contraface style? True, the trend is in its infancy in the general public, but popular celebrities have been sporting it for months.

Giles emerges from our bedroom, brow lowered, jaw clenched. So he wasn't successful. Maybe now he'll start seeing Brendan's true colors.

Brendan and Flower Child—I mean, Juni—leave, and arms crossed, Giles cocks a hip against the table. "He doesn't have the money right now, but he hopes to next week."

"That's what he said last week."

"I know. And the week before." He sighs, a big heaving breath that warns he's losing patience with his half brother. Giles, the most patient man I know, might reach a breaking point. And then what?

"You ought to refuse any more of your assistance on the time machine until he reimburses you."

"But then he'll stop working on it, the jerk." He keeps his gaze on Daisy, who's finished eating and is banging her plasticized spoon on her unbreakable ceramic bowl, keeping a steady rhythm. "And then we'll never get home."

His eyes have turned dark, flickering with something like desperation. This homesickness must be new.

"Are you in a hurry to get home, love? I thought you liked it fine."

"I do, but…" He scowls at the door his brother just exited. "Brendan and I haven't been getting along. He's difficult to work with. He can get demanding, and when his unrealistic expectations aren't met, I fear he's going to explode."

"If we're able to move to the apartment, that'll give you some space from him."

"We just need to finish the time machine. But he's having some challenges trying to adapt twenty-second-century technology to a machine built last century."

"Hmm." Daisy squirms to get out, and I lift her from her chair. A smear of egg yolk decorates her chin.

I wipe it off with my wet finger. I adore her baby scent. But I also discern another not-so-welcome aroma. "Baby need go potty?"

"Mm-hmm." She wiggles from my arms and runs to the en suite bathroom to do her business. I'm so proud of how well her development is proceeding. Her pediatrician says she's right on schedule for everything. Next year, I'll be enrolling her in hologram preschool. We won't even have to leave home. She'll be interacting with life-size images of other kids and adults as if they're right beside her.

Holographic technology has changed even the simplest of things, like children's social lives. And in the medical field, I'm astounded by what can be done now. For Daisy's checkups, a robot, transmitting to her pediatrician, makes house calls, and the doc can see everything the robot is doing and make diagnoses and prescribe meds, delivered by drone. Best of all, RoboMed is paid for by MedicAll, the federal program replacing Medicare/Medicaid.

"We sure saw that one coming," Giles observed when we first discovered MedicAll. "Didn't we?"

"It was inevitable," I replied, "that the US would someday adopt universal health care."

IN THE YEAR 2120

Word of our approval for the new apartment resolves the Brendan problem. Giles pumps his fist in the air, and we drive the short mile to check it out. The behemoth building overlooks the river and the hills beyond. Sad to see the ubiquitous dorms replace some of the mansions dotting the west side. Our apartment is on the street side, so the rent is lower than the more scenic riverside.

"This is where we spent most of our time in 2123," I remind Giles. "Remember?" I point to the public toilets where I changed clothes. The breezeway near where McMurray landed. The path where Giles was caught on camera. I catch myself thinking of these incidents as already past, even though they're yet to happen.

"When we get to June of 2123 in"—I do the math—"in roughly three years, if the time machine isn't ready yet, should we come back here and spy on our young selves?" I clutch his arm. "Will McMurray still get murdered? Or has time somehow hopped onto a different track, and different events will unfold when we get there again?"

"Love, you're getting into metaphysical territory." He takes my arm and steers us to the building's front door. "Those questions nobody has the answers to, so we won't know until we get there."

I stop, clutching Daisy's hand more as she tugs on me in hopes of escaping. "No, Baba girl, do not let go of my hand." For Giles, I point my free hand toward the river. "Let's say events unfold in the same way. We might be able to see if TigerLily murdered McMurray."

"But if she did, you still won't know her motive."

"You know what?" We approach a plasticized glass door, and our reflections peer back at us. "I'm not sure I care anymore."

It's true. Adjusting to our new way of life, raising a daughter, has taken everything out of me, including the passions and curiosities from my old life. "Sure, we should spy on ourselves. If only there were a way to stop the murder."

"No, don't entertain that dangerous thought." Giles casts a pointed look at our daughter, hopping up and down like the Energizer bunny. "But we might be able to observe without being spotted by robocams if we disable our holograms. Otherwise, we could end up as suspects again."

"How strange if both your current self and your younger self ended up interrogated as a suspect."

In the window reflection, I'm standing stock-still, an open-mouthed madwoman cogitating on concepts too big to wrap her puny brain around. Yet our group of six were the lone suspects interrogated. Either we'll be out of here by then, or we will evade suspicion.

Something else is plying the edges of my awareness. Something about this building. What is it? I observe the clean, stark lines, the faux-brick walls, and a bell clangs deep inside my head.

Shrugging, I pass my hand across the sensor. Whatever it is, it'll come to me.

The proprietor—an actual person!—admits us and leads us to the second-level apartment. One look around proves it's perfect for us. Someone painted a Mount Hood mural on the living room wall in various neutrals, ranging from the stark white of its peak to pale beige shadows and slate gray base. Ashen gray trees on the remaining three walls frames the whole thing in a foresty vibe. Since all these tall buildings block the real view, I'm grateful this anonymous creative brought the view to us.

Daisy loves the walk-in bathtub, and Giles loves the waterless dishwasher. I love it all, especially the six-story set of stairs leading up to the roof. Very cool and retro. Most people use elevators, but I like taking stairs to keep my body in shape. Our dorm, like most, lacks staircases, but here, I can get started on a steady exercise regimen.

The old TriMet bus still sits catty-corner across the street, and we're just blocks from McMurray's landing spot.

Biggest plus: We won't be living under the same roof as the incorrigible Brendan.

With so many pluses, there have to be some downs. But if there are, I'm not seeing them. Yet.

As Brendan and Giles continue to work on the new time machine, I'm optimistic. In those two time-traveling days, we never glimpsed Brendan or a second Giles. This has to work. It just has to. The alternative is unthinkable.

Daily, Giles fills me in on their progress. He's hopeful they'll resolve the glitches, but I don't like what it's doing to his disposition.

He storms into the house and slams the door. "That Brendan is a real pain."

I jump, jostling Daisy who's sleeping with her head in my lap while I watch a holoshow comedy. She lurches, but her eyes stay closed. After my heart rate calms, I whisper, "Then why don't you stay away from him?"

"Can't." He faces me, his nostrils flared, arms anchored across his chest. "Gotta keep an eye on him and that machine. I wouldn't put it past him to take off and leave us behind. I can't let that happen."

But my rebellious, overactive brain is already following a different train of thought. "Love, have you ever wondered about what it'll be like if we do get back home?" I silence the holoshow and shift toward him. "We'll be several years older just moments after we left. Just think how freaked out everyone will be."

"Well, it'll be proof this happened, won't it? Are you saying you don't want to go back?"

What a typical male conclusion. I squeeze my teeth together and let air whistle out. "Of course not. Just letting my imagination run wild."

His face softens, and his smile eradicates those harsh planes. "Of course you are. One of the many things I love about you." He winks, then joins me on the sofa, gazing down at Daisy. "Even after all these years, I still can't predict what'll come out of your mouth."

I snuggle into him, breathing in his rugged scent. Oh, what will become of us? If we never get back, will we grow old together, raise our children, and die in a timeline not our own?

GILES

"TMI, bro. You do remember, don't you, you're still married?" Giles couldn't stop the words he fought to hold back every time Brendan mentioned intimate details of his and Juni's relationship. Details Giles didn't want to hear.

"Not in this life, muff," Brendan snapped. "Yo, bro, hand me that wrench, and cool it with the judginess."

Stuffing his exasperation, Giles reached for the tool and held it out. "I've been wondering, how was your dad able to hang on to that property by the river? How did he know it wouldn't be sold out from under him?"

Brendan grasped the wrench and moved his headlamp closer to the control panel. No natural light reached into the podlot's far corner where McMurray's time hopper sat dormant. Podlots differed little from parking garages, except for the lack of ramps, and most of the time they sat atop buildings instead of underground. "Well, he started leasing the property from the city back in 2020, paying ten years in advance, plus estimated property taxes." The light illuminated the original mechanism McMurray had cobbled together. Brendan wrenched off the metal frame holding the panel in place. "He did so every ten years until the city agreed to sell it to him in 2040. That's when he put up the fence to keep people out. He's set for life."

"It must've cost him a fortune to prepay every ten years."

"It did. He was awarded several grants from scientific organizations. Plus, managed to find some private investors."

"So that property is yours upon his death?"

"Not entirely. It would be split between me and Penny since she's his business partner." A scowl betrayed his true feelings. "The property's registered under his business name."

"Which is...?"

"TimeTrane LLC."

Giles twiddled his thumbs. Brendan still hadn't delegated him any tasks. "Clever."

"Trane as in the second syllable of his first name."

"Got it. Smart man to ensure the property can't get sold without his knowledge. How did the city contact him, say, in 2040?"

"His post office box, which he also paid for in advance."

"Heh, whatcha doin?" a nearby voice intruded.

Two young teenagers, one of uncertain gender, the other a Y, watched from outside the makeshift fence they'd erected from wood scraps to keep trespassers out.

"Workin on my autopod." Giles's empty hands belied his words. "We busy, as you can see." They couldn't afford to attract attention, thus the privacy fence and the evening hours.

The genderless teen, most likely a Y judging by his avid interest in their activities, stepped back, palms up as if in apology. "This look like the time chine that landed here today."

It took a minute for the teen's words to penetrate. Then a chill passed through him. "Um, did you say a time chine was here?" He pointed to the ground. "As in, right here?"

"No, down by the riv. They landed. They stayed while and then, pow, gone." He made an arc with his arm.

Brendan stopped working and came to stand beside him. "What's your name?"

"Eefan."

"So, Eefan. You mentioned they. Who's they?"

"Person workin the vehicle."

"When?"

Eefan shifted from foot to foot, generating brainpower. "Bout lunchtime. Noon, maybe."

"Wut the person look like?"

"Looked like a X. Bout five foot five, plain light hair."

Penny! How had they missed her visit? And why was she making random visits instead of the scheduled ones they knew about?

"Was anything on the news about it?"

Eefan cocked his head and peered at Giles as if a hair had sprouted from his nose. Oh, great. He'd slipped into his natural Aussie accent.

"Anythin on the Cloud?" he corrected himself.

"Oh yeah. But we seen it for ourself."

"Really?"

"Me and Roki, my biff, saw it." He thrust a thumb at his companion, who'd remained silent thus far. "Saw the person get out, go walk round, talkin to peep. Tried to get to em but couldn't get through the crowd."

"You didn't know for sure it was a time chine, then."

How could they have missed it? Again. Almost worse, how could he tell Thea? Not only would this news upset her, but she'd find a way to blame Brendan. Brendan had his faults, but no way was he responsible for this.

Roki stepped forward to offer his take. "The peeps in the crowd talked bout it. Parently operator told em all when they exited they was from year 2023."

"Ah," said Brendan. "And how do you know they wasn't pullin your leg?"

Eefan glanced at Roki for help, but Roki merely raised his brows.

Brendan tried again. "How do you know they was truth tellin?"

"Sumed they was." Eefan shrugged. "Why would they lie?"

Brendan stepped closer. "Maybe they was tryin to impress yull. And yull fell for it." With a chuckle, he punched Eefan's shoulder. "You know time travel's impossible, don't you?"

With reluctant nods, both teens backed away, their sheepish faces disappearing into the dimness. Giles watched them enter the elevator, then landed a shoulder punch on his brother.

"Good work getting rid of them, bro." He checked his hologram for news updates. When he held it up for Brendan to see, a suit-clad newscaster's image filled the space in front of them. "A strange-looking autopod appeared at the riverbank earlier today, but rumors floated that it was a time machine." Newscasters, like robots, spoke more precise English than the typical person on the street. "The person who stepped from the machine told the crowd they was from the year 2023, but this could not be verified."

Giles gasped. McMurray's time hopper materialized, Penny in the doorway, dressed all in black, one foot on the ground.

"The operator would not give their name to the newscloud peep and stayed less than half an hour." The newscaster reappeared with a colleague beside him, giving him a quizzical smile. "But what did they do for half an hour? Bystanders claim the person chatted with them, asked questions about their daily life, and shared anecdotes about life a hundred years ago. Here are some robocam scenes."

Penny made her way through the gawking horde, her cheery, extrovert personality on full display. How she stood out in the crowd, with her twenty-first-century hair and clothing, as out of place as a hoop skirt in the 2000s. Her blonde streaks appeared drab next to the artistically styled dos these women favored.

Brendan clicked his tongue. "We need to persuade her to take us back with her next time she's here."

"Shh. I want to hear this."

"When the pod operator returned to the autopod, they turned to the crowd, waved, and said, 'I'll be back in a month.' When we reviewed the satellite cams, the pod seemed to vanish from sight moments later. Our expert at HondaFord, Dromo Jones, told us the newest autopods have camouflage exteriors, and, with the flip of a switch, can appear to vanish to the casual observer. So was it a time machine? Or some skilled acting? Our conclusion: Inconclusive. What do YOU think? Let us know at our gram."

Giles punched one fist into the other palm. "Okay. She's going to be back in a month. I'm going to park a drone down at the river. Next time, we're going to be ready."

IN THE YEAR 2120

"It's always noon, Thea," Brendan snaps after I have the audacity to question him on Penny's estimated arrival time. "Dad always set the arrival time for noon, for whatever reason. I don't see why Penny would deviate from that."

Forty-five minutes until go time. Brendan has grown more unpleasant, despite his great new relationship with the woman he says is perfect for him. Doesn't seem to have affected his disposition. Was he always like this? Or has our forced ordeal soured him?

We're sitting in the old TriMet bus-slash-deli, immersed in the coffee-and-pastry aroma, almost thick enough to swim in. Juni leans against Brendan, breaking off pieces of scone with a delicate hand and feeding it to him. I'm mesmerized by her long, three-dimensional nails, adorned with flowers both real and fabricated. I've seen nail art even more ornate... tiny 3D swords, cityscapes, jungle animals. Limited only by one's imagination.

"Say ah, sweewee."

I look away, uncomfortable with Juni's baby talk, and place my hand on Daisy's soft head as she drinks from her rainbow sippy cup. A noise outside the window captures my focus. An unkempt Y person is shouting something. He meets my eyes, and his fierce, drugged gaze bores into mine as if I'm to blame for his meltdown.

I turn Daisy away as the scene unfolds.

A couple walks by and makes a wide berth around the "sidewalk shouter," as they're termed now. Both of them jab their holograms. Within seconds, a robot swoops in and grabs the man, who struggles and yells even harder. The robot immobilizes him by wrapping one long arm around the man's upper body and the other around his legs. The man goes limp, and the robot secures him in a police autopod.

More patrons have crowded the window, gawking.

"Bet they goin to the integration pavilion." Juni's odd-colored eyes grow huge.

I shudder. Most of them spend the rest of their lives there.

The drama settles down, noon arrives, and Giles studies the drone footage on his hologram. "Nothin yet."

We're sticking with the vernacular for Juni's benefit. She knows Brendan and Giles are "building" a time chine. She doesn't know about our trip to 2123 or our true history, and we extracted a promise from Brendan not to tell her. Of course, he might break his promise. He's not the most trustworthy guy around. But, if he does spill it, she'll probably find the story preposterous and not believe him.

Brendan frowns. "Keep watchin. It's been zactly a month."

"We don't know if they meant *precisely* one month."

Juni knows we're waiting for Brendan's father to arrive, and she believes Penny is his girlfriend who accompanies him on his "travels." Brendan apparently doesn't mind leaving Juni behind if or when he returns home with his father. Because he's made it clear he's not taking her.

When she gets up to use the bathroom, a child-sized stall at the back, I bring up the subject I've kept my lips zipped about. I remind Giles that we didn't see anyone who looked like us in 2123, closing in on two years from now. Which must mean we'd already left, somehow.

"No," Giles says, "you mean you didn't see anyone who looked like me or Brendan. But you saw two someones who looked like you, a mother and child."

I'd almost forgotten them in the seven years since. "You're right. And I haven't seen them yet. Hopefully in the next three years…"

"Thea, I'm looking at them." His thumb tracks between me to our daughter and back again. "I think those two were you and Daisy."

"What?" I lurch backward as if he'd slapped me. "They couldn't have been. You and Brendan would've been with me."

He tilts his head, considering this. It's true, the little girl would be around the age Daisy will be in two years. I don't even want to contemplate what this could mean. And we can't discuss it further because Juni has returned to the table. The long black feathers hanging from her earlobes brush her shoulders.

"Yull yukkin bout me behind my back?"

Brendan plants a kiss on her bloodmoon-red lips. "Course we were, babe, and it was all good." He grins. "We were talkin bout the time chine."

Juni's delighted grin curves her entire face, big white teeth and all. "Fabby! You mean it's ready to go?"

Shaking his head, Brendan sobers. "No, unforch. Means it only goes one way, not both ways."

"Still can't get it to go back in time? Just forward?"

"Right. We can take it for a spin now. Where you wanna go first?"

"I want to go to 2130."

Giles interjects. "Why that particular year?"

"See if Brend and I still together. If we're still together after ten years, I won't have to break up with em."

"Better make it 2131, babe. That's as far ahead as the chine goes."

Giles laughs, but I'm reeling from his declaration.

Could he be right? And I was looking at myself and Daisy that day? Pursuing myself and Daisy, then losing us? Had I escaped from myself? An earthquake churns my insides, and I shake myself out of my trancelike state.

If he's correct, then he and Brendan were gone in 2123. But Daisy and I were left behind. The woman, that is, I, appeared to be suffering from distress, confusion, loss—something.

And now, instead of anticipating what the future may hold…

I dread it.

The drone footage shows the time hopper's arrival, and we make our way over. Once again, Penny refuses to entertain Brendan's request to "take us for ride." He even offers her a substantial fee, but she shakes her head, although she's friendlier than before. "It's not ready for passengers," she tells him, but this time, her eyes exude concern instead of impatience. "May I ask your names and why this is so important to you?"

Brendan introduces us. "And I'm Brendan. Brendan McMurray."

She fingers the turquoise pendant resting at her throat. "Seriously? Are you related to Colt?"

Brendan nods. "Yeah. I need to speak with em."

"They Brendan's coparent." Juni, no doubt, feels she's helping.

Brendan casts her a dirty look.

And Penny blinks. "How can that be? How are you related to him?"

Brendan's glare, his flared nostrils, punishes his girlfriend. "Long story. But I'd sure like to see em. It's been too long."

"I can pass along the message. Can you tell me what this is about?"

Brendan thrusts his hands in his pockets. "Just a personal matter. Will they be with you next time you visit?"

I step forward, unable to resist some persuasion of my own. "We do need to talk to Mr. McMurray. In confidence." I link my contact info to her hologram. "Can you get back to us as soon as possible?" My voice breaks on the final syllable.

Her brow furrows as she scrutinizes me. "I can't promise anything. And I don't know what our timeframe looks like."

"Just tell them Brendan needs to see them." Brendan pats her shoulder. "Thanks. You're awesome." He sends his contact information to her and beams a shiny smile.

Despite Brendan's faults, he's a good schmoozer. Way to get what you want without revealing sensitive details. Best-case scenario: McMurray will come soon and get us out of here.

Later, Giles and I discuss, rather heatedly, his bombshell revelation. I pace before the front window as Daisy naps. "If you're right, and I was seeing myself, then where were you and Brendan?"

"Well, that I don't know." Giles lounges on the sofa, Daisy's feet in his lap, as if the subject isn't of any concern. "And, of course, I could be wrong."

"You must be!" I cross to the mirror hanging next to our kitchen entrance—a kitchen all our own that we don't have to share with anyone else—and study my reflection. Was this woman I'm looking at the woman I saw that day? No, she was thinner and had a haggard look. I remember blonde hair. I cross to the sofa and scrutinize Daisy's sleeping face. Yes, the girl did bear a remarkable resemblance to my daughter. That day's so clear now, myself looking up at a window, seeing a curtain move. Approaching that big front door. But was it this building? This window? That part's hazy after eight years.

Our new apartment is located in the wing adjacent to the main wing, forming a ninety-degree angle. Down on the sidewalk, someone is passing the building's double glass doors, and I gasp. The memory is clarifying. It was the same door I arrived at that day, the building Giles and I entered. I remember our reflections staring back at us. But was this the apartment whose door we knocked on, where nobody answered? Where I saw a faint outline of someone in the window seconds before?

I step back from the window and grab at the sofa. I want Giles to be wrong. Because my knees won't support the weight of the suspicion pressing into me: somehow, I got trapped in a time warp eight years ago.

And I have no idea how to escape.

GILES

Giles groaned when Juni showed up at the worksite. They'd insisted she and Thea must not bother them. But Juni, unlike Thea, showed little regard for protocol. After a long workday, his patience wore thin as he and Brendan troubleshooted the time machine's control panel—with no success.

"Hey, yull." Juni's wide eyes peeked through the capsule's door.

Brendan, kneeling in front of the control panel, jerked his head. "Juni, didn't I tell you to stay away?"

"Can't I watch? Won't touch anything."

Still on his knees, he frowned at her. "No, you can't watch."

"Does it work yet?"

"Nope."

A pout drooped her mouth as Giles tried to focus on the data of their last three tests on his hologram. "You said it goes forward in time, right? Why can't yull give it a test run?"

Brendan slammed the tool on the ground and stood. "Don't know if we can get back. Don't want us to get stuck in the future, do you?"

She shrugged. Her heavily lined eyes squinted at the interior. "This thing look like somethin outta old holofilm."

Brendan grunted. "Go home, Juni."

"Can't you even tell me how you make it work?"

"Theoretical physics." Big, exaggerated yawn. "Any more questins?"

"Mm-hmm. Want me to ask Penny for help?"

"Penny?" He stepped closer. "How you know Penny?"

"Remember that day Penny wouldn't talk to you? I went back later to talk to em, took Parent with me. Since yull havin so much trouble gettin this thing to work, I thought Penny might be able to help."

"Juni!" A vein beat in Brendan's temple. His Adam's apple worked like it was trying to shift gears. First gear, then second. Back to first. "Nobody is supposed to know about this." He stomped toward her, his hand raised as though he might slap her. "This is a top-secret project. Penny, of all people, can't know about this."

"I didn't tell em bout this. We just picked their brain on how theirs works. Mostly Parent, since Parent teach botting."

Brendan's hand fell to his side. "What did Penny say?"

"Wondered why we wanted to know." She edged nearer the machine. "Theirs looked just like this one. Weird, huh?"

Brendan pressed his lips together, hiding a smile. "Yeah, real weird. Did Penny say anything else? Did they seem, I don't know, sus or anything?"

"Don't think so. We was just a couple curious ones, far as they knew."

Brendan returned to the spot by the control panel. "Please don't talk to Penny anymore."

She clicked her tongue, rolled her eyes, and swiveled, but retreated without further argument.

Brendan watched her leave. "That wench." He returned to his kneeling position.

Wench? Giles hadn't heard that word for ages. "Okay, bro, it's fish-or-cut-bait time. The last three beta tests haven't worked. You really want to keep at this? It's…"

"I know." Brendan's tone lashed him. "Yesterday's test looked like the circuit was starting to engage, then, poof. Nothing."

"And today, when we scheduled the recelerator to drive to yesterday, still nothing."

"The incelerator seems to understand my instructions on advancing to a future date. It's something in the recelerator that's screwing up." Brendan scratched his dyed-red goatee. "But I can't count how many times I've rechecked the circuits. There's no reason it shouldn't be able to drive in reverse, so to speak."

Giles plopped onto the front passenger seat. "That's what I'm saying. It should work, but it doesn't. We're wasting our time." He propped ankle on knee. "I'd like to spend more time with my wife and daughter. Thea doesn't complain, but she can sure drop hints that she'd like me home more often."

Brendan stayed silent so long. Had he come to agreement? Then the guy rubbed his eyes. "Look, how about I do one more tweak on the incelerator tomorrow? I want to explore a hunch. And then I'll do a beta test to the future to see if it will come back. If it does, I'll know my hunch paid off." His gaze pleaded. "If it works, at least we know we can take it on trips to the future without getting stranded. Right?"

"What good will that do us? We want to go home, remember?"

"Well, hey, it could be a moneymaking opportunity." He wagged his finger from his chest to Giles. "We could do what my dad did. He was on his way to being a very rich dude until his death."

"You'd compete with your father?"

Brendan scoffed. "Of course not. It wouldn't be competition. We'd have no competition. He died, remember?"

Giles shook his head in an effort to wrap his brain around such circular reasoning. "But if he'd lived, you'd be competing with him."

"For one, if he'd lived, this baby"—he patted the control panel too hard—"wouldn't be here. It'd be parked in 2023 where it belongs. For two, if he'd lived, we wouldn't be here." His voice rose two notches. "We'd be back home, with no reason to have returned to 'investigate' his death."

Startled by the unexpected emotion dump, Giles nodded like an empathetic brother should. Had Brendan been faking his happy-go-lucky persona all these years? Did it bother him to be here as much as it bothered Giles and Thea? If so, he'd done a good job hiding his feelings.

As had he himself. All these years, Thea believed he was untroubled being stranded in an alien world. If she knew, her distress would only worsen.

"All right." Deep breath. "One more test. If it doesn't work, we're done."

Brendan stuck out his fist for a bump. "Deal."

———❦———

"Did it work?" Evening sun cast a beam through the skylight twenty feet above them, its shaft extending all three stories of the podlot. Giles clenched his fist, steeling himself against unwanted news.

"Good news, bad news." Brendan wiped the back of his hand across his forehead. "Which do you want first?"

"The good news."

"Okay. That tweak was a success. The recelerator is working. Which means, when we go forward in time, we'll be able to get back."

"Great!" Which meant the bad news had to be...

"But the recelerator works in dependency with the incelerator, not vice versa."

Giles's heart sank, and he could almost predict his brother's next words.

"Dad didn't design it to go back, then forward, in time. Only forward and back."

"How did you not know that before now?" He gulped as if he could grab the harsh words back. Too late now.

Brendan spread his arms, his jaw clenched. "Had no reason to know."

Giles dropped into a seat. "We're screwed."

"We are. Unless my dad comes to get us soon."

"We don't know if Penny passed along our message. And even if she did, McMurray may not believe her. Think about it. Someone named Brendan who looks like his son wants to talk to him in the year 2120? How's that gonna sound?" He leaned forward, elbows on knees, head in hands. "Thea's going to be so upset." He lifted his head, meeting Brendan's defensive glare, refusing to shrink back from its potency. "When is your dad's next scheduled trip?"

Brendan gazed out the pod's window in the direction of the waterfront, although the neighboring dorm blocked the view. "Not until June 2123. When he gets murdered."

"Wonderful." Giles shook his head and stood, gripping the seat back. "Well, hey, I have an idea. Take us on a test drive, say, one day into the future. I want to see for myself it's working. If it doesn't and we get stuck, it's for one lousy day."

Brendan nodded, his countenance transformed into that of a young boy showing off his birthday toys. "Yeah, let's go to tomorrow."

"I better gram Thea and let her know." Just in case something went wrong. One more catastrophe on top of the mother of all catastrophes would break her.

As he expected, her joy at their success waged war with her anxiety default. "Please come back, love."

"It's just one day. I'll lose a day out of my life if we don't come back. Think of it like flying to Australia."

"What if something goes wrong?" she fretted, echoing his worries.

How to make her understand?

"If we don't come back, all you'd have to do is wait one day, and I'll be here." Reassuring her eased his fears. He couldn't see a downside to this. Except for explaining his absence to his manager. "Why don't you and Daisy come with, and if we get stranded, we'll skip a day together."

Long pause during which he could hear her brain waves running with the idea. "Only by hologram. I'm never stepping foot in that thing again. Unless it's taking me home."

"I get it. I really do."

"Go ahead and do your run, love, and I'll ride along virtually."

He nodded his readiness to Brendan, who set the incelerator for twenty-four hours from now and the return time for sixty seconds. "If this works, we'll lose one whole minute of our lives," Brendan muttered.

"Horrifying." Giles cuffed his brother's shoulder. "A whole minute lost to eternity, never to return."

Thea, her image perched beside him, giggled. If they ever got back home, he and Thea were going to write all this down for the world to read. In fact, she ought to write a screenplay and pitch it to Hollywood. *Midnight Rider – the Movie.*

The pod jolted, and Brendan belted out the lyrics to "Tomorrow" with Thea and Giles joining in. "We're only a day away." Brendan's high good humor erased his surly mood, and Giles welcomed it, even for a temporary alteration.

When he glanced at the date and time on his hologram, he whooped.

"It worked, good buddy. Now take us back to yesterday, okay?"

Another jolt, surprising Giles since Brendan hadn't touched the panel. The recelerator had kicked in as instructed. They'd returned, making it look easy. Much easier, in fact, than the explaining Giles needed to deliver to his wife on the reason, despite the successful test, they wouldn't be going home, after all.

GILES

"TAKE A RIDE TO THE FUTURE!" The ad broadcast on holograms around town. Brendan McMurray, nicknamed The Two-Timer by local media, but not due to his newly tamed love life, couldn't keep up with the demand.

Giles's day started like any other, with no hint of the cliff awaiting. Breakfast in the sun-splashed nook. Daisy standing on her chair, tugging open the semisheer white curtains. Thea's loveliness enhanced in her yellow floral sundress. Grimm headbutting his leg, and Grinchetta performing a self-massage against Thea's slender calves. "I'm bored. Snuggle me," Grimm meowed.

"You're bored because you're not smart like me, brother," Grinchetta yowled, batting at her toy mouse.

With Thea and Daisy giggling at the cats, the last thing he anticipated was disaster. When your worst fear strikes you unawares, ever notice how hard it works to hide its malicious intent? Ever notice it chooses to smack you down on a morning when you believe all is well in your world? A day of smiling sun, glowing sky, and hilarious talking cats?

"Did Brendan ever pay you back the money he owed you?" Thea picked up a bowl of fresh berries mashed with oat milk, cream, and cane juice from the ancient wood-and-metal sideboard, vintage 2020s, that she'd fallen in love with last month when she and Giles browsed an antique store. He recalled her sense of excitement when it arrived at their home, how she wondered aloud whose home it had occupied, if it had belonged to someone they knew. If the original owner bought it at Kitchen Kaboodle or ordered it from Amazon.

Thea stirred the mixture like mad, then popped it into the microfreeze. Ten seconds later, out came a black mineralized bowl of berry ice cream. The fruity aroma made his mouth water. No twenty-first-century ice cream could beat Thea's homemade concoction. "He had no more excuses since he's raking in the bucks now."

Brendan's backlog stretched to five weeks because passengers were limited to one trip per day to any future date through 2131.

"He couldn't get it to go any further than 2131," Giles told Thea, spooning a delicious bite into his mouth, then swallowing. "He wondered if it's because the world ends that year."

At Thea's horrified gasp, he hastened to backtrack. "He was joking. It's due to his father's programming. He had to set a maximum future limit on the incelerator, and in 2021, he set the upper limit at one hundred ten years, with the hope he could increase it later."

Thea poured Os into Daisy's little ceramic bowl. "That makes sense." She added milk to the bowl and set it in front of their happy daughter. "Ten years from now is way too soon for the world to end."

He didn't bother asking Thea how she made that determination, instead savored the aroma of sweetened cereal wafting toward him. The comforting fragrance of a new day, of family and home. His anchors in an alien world, albeit less alien as time passed.

Thea poured herself a bowl of cereal with almond milk and sat beside him under the broad kitchenette window. "Isn't 2131 where Brendan wanted to take Juni?"

"Yeah, and he did."

Idly stirring, Thea appeared disinterested in her breakfast. "What'd they find?"

"She didn't find what she was looking for, that is, evidence that she and Brendan were still together."

"So did she break up with him?"

"No, but sometimes I wish she would. They feed off each other. And not in a good way."

"Not like Zach and Ari, then. Those two feed off each other in a funny, effective way." She sighed, her gaze out the window as if gazing a hundred years into the past. "Oh, how I miss them."

A knock at the door jerked their attention away from their old friends. Checking her hologram, Thea groaned. "It's Brendan and Juni. What could they want?"

She clicked the door open, and Brendan's voice proceeded him. "Yo, bro. Need a big—and I mean big—favor."

Giles stifled a groan. Whatever the favor, his answer had to be no. Without waiting for Giles's reply, Brendan helped himself to the chair next to Daisy, leaving Juni standing open-mouthed, hand on hip. Today she sported a black-and-white contraface look.

Giles stood and motioned Juni to his seat. "Here, have a seat, Juni." Someone had to be the gentleman here. Anything to delay the inevitable moment when he had to decline.

Brendan wasted no time. "Remember the dudes who converted their income to robocurrency?"

"You mean the ones in prison because it's illegal?"

"They got caught because they didn't have a smart accountant like you."

Easy to see where this was going. Brendan should know better than to try flattery.

"You asking me to partner with you in an illegal activity?"

"But you told me what they did wrong, so you'll know how to do it right." Brendan's gaze flitted to Thea as if he'd suddenly realized she was there. Did he feel no shame in requesting such a sordid favor in her presence? Did he think she'd be indifferent to his business affairs? "So you won't get caught."

"Why would you ask me to do this?"

"With my high income, my tax bill will be way too much."

"My mate so rich, they buyin us a house in the West Hills," Juni crooned.

"Right." Brendan patted her hand. Daisy stared at Juni, as if confused which side of her head was the real one.

Juni grinned back at Daisy, who giggled. "Can't wait to throw a housewarmin party. Will invite yull and everybody we know."

"Bro, I'm on my way to filthy richhood. And I'll compensate you well as my personal tax advisor. As long as you help me convert my taxable income to the untraceable kind, even if not jit."

"No way." Giles firmed his jaw, unable to believe his brother's audacity. He could get into serious trouble with the law. Not only that, what would God think? Thea's eye roll mirrored his disgust, whereas Juni gazed at Brendan as if he were the king of Portlandia. Those two deserved each other as much as Jezebel and King Ahab did.

Brendan's expression darkened alarmingly.

Bracing himself, Giles squared his shoulders. "I won't do it, and don't ever ask me again." He anchored his legs, ready to chase his brother away.

But Brendan shot to his feet and stepped back, his fist cocked. "You self-righteous, despicable muff. I'm so sick of your high-and-mighty attitude."

With no warning, Giles landed on the cold, hard floor, massive pain shooting from his jaw. As his pained shouts joined Daisy's and Thea's cries, Brendan and Juni spun and left, Brendan's curses following him out the door. Thea knelt over him, ignoring Daisy's frightened wails. "Oh, my love,

I can't believe he decked you like that. You want me to call the police?"

He tried to shake his head. But spots floated before his vision, and darkness hovered near. Cradling his jaw, fear gripped him as he moved his mouth but no words formed. He struggled to hoist himself to a sitting position, but it triggered a new pain where his head hit the sideboard. Above him, the ceiling spun as if he'd downed five whiskey shots.

As the light slipped away, Thea's and Daisy's cries faded into an ever-expanding dark void, an abyss that threatened to overwhelm his senses like a destructive tsunami. Where was he? What was happening to him?

Why could he no longer see his beloved wife, his sweet daughter?

Just when he thought he couldn't endure another moment of darker-than-dark nothingness, blazing light unlike any he'd ever seen chased away the void, and a warm river enveloped him, sweeping away every fear.

He knew this place. He'd read about it in the biblical book of Revelation.

Which had to mean...

Standing before him, a white-robed man with a shepherd's staff held out his hand. As Giles raised his hands in wonder and awe, the light tugged at him, pulled him nearer, rendering him speechless at the burning peace invading his spirit.

For the first time in his life, he was complete.

PART III

IN THE YEAR 2123

June 2123

Brendan and his time machine disappeared after he landed the fatal punch on my husband. I suspect where he went but have no way to follow him. "You think he traveled to the year 2131?" The investigating robocop's expression and tone didn't flinch, but for sure, he was judging me as insane. I shrugged and told him, tongue in cheek, to arrest Brendan in ten years.

I thank the good Lord for my new husband, Qory, who has kept me from losing my mind in my grief and anger. Anger at the massive injustice, at Brendan's flight. Did he somehow know he'd killed Giles? He must have, otherwise why run? My tears have dried up like a summer billabong in the Australian outback, and time has softened the blow.

Yet something in me died that day along with Giles.

I met Qory at church—a kind and decent Christian man, also widowed. His two teenagers love Daisy, and she loves them. But Qory doesn't know my history. He thinks I moved here from Australia ten years ago. It's a great excuse for why my speech is inconsistent at times.

But Giles will always have my heart. Poor Qory. I sometimes sense he knows he's not the love of my life. After our coupling ceremony, he and his girls moved out of their crowded dormitory, and now we have a household of five. Daisy shares her bedroom with Qory's two girls, and Qory fills the empty spot in my bed where Giles should be.

If only he could fully inhabit the Giles-shaped hole in my heart.

Introverted Qory can't compete with Giles's winsome friendliness that inspired confidence and put people at ease. Although gifted in his way, Qory's pedantic mind can't measure up to Giles's brilliant curiosity. Qory's physique, tall and lean, suggests basketball player, as opposed to Giles's soccer-player build, well-proportioned and toned, that attracted me from the get-go.

So, why did I marry a man who doesn't measure up to my first husband?

I've been asking myself that ever since. In a moment of loneliness and desperately missing the intimacy of married life, I agreed to couple-unite with him. I didn't consult the Lord because He felt a universe away after I lost Giles. The old saying comes to mind about when God feels far away, it wasn't Him who moved.

I'm not unhappy, however. Despite my failures as a Christ-follower, God's mercies are new every morning. I like Qory well enough. His sense of absurdity takes me—and anyone else who doesn't know him well—by surprise. His steadfast character proved itself when he took Daisy under his wing. And he parents his daughters with firm affection. Unlike Giles, he's right-handed and no longer mirrors me when we eat, another trait I've had to get used to.

I shouldn't compare the two. And I've promised myself I'll stop. Honest. I'm just not there yet. Giles's death is still fresh. Still, I suspect Qory plays the comparison game also, observing the contrasts between me and his late wife.

On our first date, I asked him if he'd ever played basketball. His dark eyes pinned me with a funny look.

"I play dunkball. Is that what you mean?"

"Yeah, dunkball."

Although basketball died down in popularity fifty years ago, athletes now play a similar sport, which consists of four baskets in a square. Since the baskets are about a foot shorter, no need to be the tallest person in the room to achieve success. For our second date, we played a game of dunkball with another couple. Qory and I slaughtered the other team. All in good, competitive fun, of course.

After we officially coupled, I vowed to God and myself that I wouldn't give him any cause to doubt my commitment to him or allow a crack in the contented demeanor I wore so well. He doesn't deserve it, and it isn't his fault Giles is gone.

Soon after Giles's death, the autopsy found the cause. The antique sideboard's sharp metal corner had pierced the soft tissue of my husband's temple when he fell. I had the sideboard I once loved hauled away to a place I'd never have to see it again—the dump. When the police discovered Brendan and the time machine missing, it was time to fulfill the justice for Giles that the police couldn't—or wouldn't—do.

Days after Giles's death, my insides hollowed out and my tears spent, I found myself knocking on an apartment door blocks away. If I couldn't bring Brendan to justice, then I'd track down his girlfriend, who'd proved a destructive influence on Brendan and ultimately on Giles, Daisy, and me.

The woman who opened the door with a hello bore a strong familiarity. I'd seen that thin face framed with graying blonde hair before, but not recently. Racking my brain, I stepped forward and introduced myself. "I understand Juni lives here. Your pring?" Hesitating as if unsure of my information, I tilt my head.

"Hant seen Juni for days. They and that muff mate of theirs gone off somewhere together."

"You mean Brendan?"

She practically spat. "Yep, the one known as Two-Timer." She opened the door wider. "C'mon in. I'm TigerLily."

She would have noticed my lurch if she hadn't turned her back to usher me in. Then I understood Juni's familiarity. She's a spitting image of her mother. I squelched a gasp. The 2123 murder investigation had yet to take place but remained a memory in my mind. TigerLily had been despondent over the rift with her daughter, who dropped off her kids with her mother and aunt.

Which meant Juni had children. But Brendan hadn't ever mentioned any, nor had Juni. Could it be a different daughter? "Do you have another pring?" I couldn't stop the words. Wow, the woman must've thought me so prying.

She peered over her shoulder at me. "Juni's my only."

"Don't she have a couple prings?"

TigerLily stayed rooted to the spot, twisting a silver ring on her thumb. "They stayin with coparent."

You're only going to live a couple more years, my rebellious brain recited that day two years ago standing in the lobby of Juni's mother's apartment. I had to find a way to learn what happened between the two of them to cause the estrangement. I summoned up my inner reporter and plunged right in.

"You must wonder why I'm lookin for Juni." I tried not to glance around for clues to TigerLily's life. "Their mate was Brendan, the one who operated that time chine, who assaulted my spouse, then disappeared. The one on the news lately. They wanted for manslaughter, and I need to find em."

TigerLily gasped. "Oh, you poor poor thing."

Her empathetic manner opened the word gates. "I fear they traveled together to the future, to the year 2131. If they did, it'll be impossible to arrest em."

"Juni didn't say anything to me bout where they went." She seemed to snap to awareness and then gestured for me to follow her to the living room.

When she ushered me to a compofabric sofa, I sat, the cushionette soft against my limbs, my head still reeling at the twist of fate that brought her into my life. What were the odds? "When did you last see em?"

She picked up a half-eaten cacao Bundt cake from a table beside a shiny black armchair. I felt my mouth water. She sat and crossed her legs without offering me any refreshments. "Few weeks ago." She held the plate as if she'd forgotten she had it. "They and Brendan came over tryin to talk me into goin for a ride on that machine. I said no. Then we chatted a bit. But they owes me money, which I reminded em of, but they says they pay me later." Her leg swung, forward and back, stimulating the mental images. "I look at Brendan to see if they take the hint, but they just stood there smilin." Her bangs trembled against her forehead. "I mean, they so rich now, right? I pulled pring aside and reminded em they got a rich mate now, and can't the mate repay me? They got mad, and the two stormed out. Hant seen em since."

What had I expected? For Juni to stay behind while Brendan escaped to the future? In reality, a dim hope for that scenario had pushed me forward. I should've known better.

I drooped, my hopes dashed. But even if Juni's mother knew where she was, how could it help me?

It couldn't. I fidgeted in a sudden mood to get home. But TigerLily stood, eyeing the Bundt cake. "Got another slice of this cake. Want a piece?"

It felt rude to say no and leave. "Sure." The US food industry has improved in the last hundred years. The FDA banned all the additives and processed foods that were poisoning us. Desserts are now sweetened with unprocessed sugar cane and nothing artificial. TigerLily returned from the kitchen and handed me a plate with an identical cake. Taking a bite, I closed my eyes and savored the purity of the sweet dessert. "Mmm, this is good. Did you make it?"

"Ha, wish I could take credit. Bought it at BirdNest."

Another big bite. "Love that place."

"Same here. We should do lunch there."

As it turns out, we never did. I couldn't bring myself to kindle a friendship with someone who churned up shame in me. Knowing her fate but unable to share it with her would've eaten me alive. Better not to go there.

But TigerLily was never far from my thoughts. Oh, if only I could warn her of her soon demise without being hunted down and sent to the integration pavilion.

I squelched my guilt by reminding myself I wouldn't know who to tell her to beware of anyway. The truth of her death remained a mystery on that dreadful day in 2123 when we were shoved ten years into the past. Was she murdered, or did she do herself in? It's difficult to believe the latter. You couldn't ask for a more upbeat personality, the type least likely to commit suicide. So either tragedy struck her in such a way that she could no longer face life—

Or someone else was responsible.

IN THE YEAR 2123

Tuesday, June 8, 2123

On the morning of the day I will see Giles again, I awaken from another dream about him. The umpteenth time so far this year. In the dream, as always, he hadn't died. Sometimes in my dreams, we live in twenty-first-century Australia. But this morning, the fading dreamworld leaves me with pounding heart and dry mouth. Maybe it's a portent to what awaits me this day.

As the images slither away like a clandestine cat, Qory senses something wrong. He bounds awake and grabs my hand. "What, dear? Bad dream?"

I rub my eyes. "I dreamed about the integration pavilion."

He tilts his head. "Really? Why the pavilion? You nev even seen it. Have you?"

My unsteady fingers grip the sheet's edge. "No, just heard terrible things about it."

I'm still trembling, but I don't know why. What horrific thing had I seen? "Nor do I want to see it."

Qory, radiating warmth like a space heater, pulls me snug into his side. "Maybe a visit is what you need to calm your fears."

"No!" My gut reaction takes both of us by surprise.

"Don't ya think it'll help you member your dream?"

I wrap my hand through his resting on my waist. "I don't need to remember my dream."

He squeezes my hand. "But this is bout the tenth time you had this dream. If you see the site in ordinary daylight, it loses its power to scare you."

Maybe, maybe not. My thoughts soon fill with Giles and the time travelers, due to arrive in a few hours. Although I haven't glimpsed Penny this week, I'm aware of her presence, recalling McMurray dropped her off earlier this week. It must've been a clandestine operation because not a peep made it to the news. Whatever project McMurray has her on, she's keeping it on the down-low. Can't blame her, considering all the media attention she attracted last time. If I do encounter her, would it do any good to ask her if she passed along Brendan's message? And if she did, would she know why McMurray never came for us?

I shrug. Too late now.

A noise comes through my hologram speaker programmed to pick up sounds from Daisy's bed in the room she shares with her stepsisters. She's awakening, her sweet chanting warming my heart. "It morning time. It morning time. Oh hello, sun. Oh hello, sun..."

Rustling sounds tell us she's getting up and will soon be poking her head in asking after breakfast. I'm happy to have an excuse to end our conversation about my dream. Normality has returned, and today is the day I've been awaiting for ten years.

Not only the day I get to see Giles again. But also the day I find out how TigerLily dies. And McMurray, while I'm at it.

Lord willing, I'll obtain information to take to the police. And if I can save a couple of lives, well, I'd be altering history, wouldn't I?

Qory doesn't know I plan to wait in the crowd for McMurray's time hopper. A pang squeezes my heart. He'll be working and won't know I'm spying on my late husband. Qory is a botter—a robot programmer—for Finity Drones and, like Giles, doesn't have to leave his living room. Robot programmer—it sounds like a higher-paying job than what it is. His salary covers our living expenses, plus some play money. Giles left no life insurance. Why would that occur to either of us? Qory, with his loving and generous heart, has never protested supporting a spouse and another man's child.

He deserves a woman wholeheartedly devoted to him. Not one still in love with her late husband.

While my spouse showers, I riffle through my wig collection and select a short platinum one. Giles and the others won't recognize me. After I've tucked my long hair beneath it, I insert a dark contact lens in my right eye, then paint my prominent cheekbones with bright blusher and embellish my eyelids—one crimson, one blue. Today, I need to look like everyone else. In this upside-down world, plain faces stand out, overly adorned ones fit right in. I study my thin, milky-white face. Amazing how food science has succeeded in reducing the caloric content in common foods. How modern drugs have turned everyone, not just me, into walking, talking skeletons.

By contrast, my twenty-first-century, one-hundred-twenty-five-pound self was downright plump.

Sometimes I feel like I'm Alice just landed in Wonderland.

My jumpy mood must be rubbing off on Daisy, for she's peevish at the breakfast table, whining about this and that, kicking the table leg, till I want to snap. I toss a help-me look at Qory, but he's oblivious.

A deep breath smooths over my annoyance. "Daisy, darling, don't you want to go play at Lark's after school?"

She nods, her cute little pink mouth turned down in a pout, her fingers tugging the neckline of her favorite fuchsia shortie. It must be getting tight, seeing as it's over a year old. I should encourage her to change into a newer shortie, but I already know how that will go over. I don't want to fight that battle today.

"Then stop kicking, be a good girl, and eat your cereal."

The other two girls, Aeryn and Nebula, have missed breakfast and are still sleeping. Not a whole lot different from when I was their age.

A drone drops a hard-boiled egg on Qory's plate and a cacao muffin on mine.

Daisy's trying, she really is. Her lower lip quivers, but she takes a hesitant bite of oat cereal.

I can't focus, however, my to-do list monopolizing my brain. I'm scheduled to meet TigerLily for that long-overdue lunch. Her joy at hearing from me last week assures me I'm doing the right thing, and I was right to time it for today. I'll ensure she's nowhere near her apartment or the Time Machine this morning.

I take my first bite of muffin, barely noticing the burst of pure cacao on my tongue. Today, perhaps I can keep death at bay.

But if I do, how will it alter the present for my younger self? If I prevent McMurray's death, we six time travelers will go home at the scheduled time. There won't be an investigation into his or TigerLily's death, and I'll have no need to return for answers.

We'd likely never meet Brendan, and Giles would still be alive.

And I wouldn't be here.

Will my memory of these past ten years be erased? Or will Qory remain a pleasant interlude, sweet while it lasted?

"Thea?" Qory's voice jerks my attention back to my off-yellow dinette. Outside the window, the oak's thin branches wave in the morning breeze, greeting us with a leafy good morning. Will I run into Penny today? She'd claimed she'd been here for a week, but I haven't seen her, despite keeping my eyes peeled whenever I'm out and about. Yet she won't know me, so how could she be of any help?

Breakfast ends as the clock ticks over to 9:00 a.m., and I grab Daisy's hand. "See you later, love," I call, hoping Qory won't be too curious about my whereabouts.

But no. "Where you two off to?"

"After I drop Daisy at school"—I keep my tone light, casual—"I'm getting together with my friend TigerLily."

Daisy's "school" is a mural-bedecked room the size of a gymnasium spanning the top floor of our building. All the kids from the complex gather there and learn via hologram. We kiss Qory goodbye, then ascend to the floor below the podlot. A hundred or so chairs are arranged by grade. Students inhabit about three-quarters of them, and the din of childish energy echoes off the high ceiling. The high schoolers sit in a separate corner with their bored, skinny faces. Somehow all of them manage to look alike. Much like high schoolers in my day—proudly conforming to their nonconforming peers.

The changes in education still astound me. Two or three parents, depending on the number of students, stay in the room to supervise, but the teachers work from their homes. The parent supervisors rotate, and I dread my turn every three weeks. The unrulies still dominate the supervisors' attention, picking on the younger kids or having meltdowns. As they have since schools were invented.

Somehow, the twenty-second-century public schoolrooms are all holo-organized by grade, subject, building, and teacher.

But how they do it is beyond me. Private schools work differently. The students attend onsite, but the organization of it all is identical to public schools.

"Good girl for getting your math assignment done last night." Head bent to my daughter's ear, my words of encouragement are meant to fuel Daisy's motivation. Sometimes, they do, but sometimes, they fall flat, depending on her mood. In three hours, her mood will bubble with anticipation when robots deliver sandwiches, snacks, and drinks.

From her smile and hug, my words have their desired effect today. She runs to sit beside her best school friend, Lark, whose mom, one of today's parent supers, approaches me. "Mornin, Starr," I greet her, then turn to leave, my mission foremost in my mind.

On my way to the café to meet TigerLily, birds chirp and sing in the trees lining the street. How strange to know I've lived this day ten years ago, my alternate life running parallel to this one. But I'm unable to remember TigerLily's time of death. All I know for sure is, for my timetable to work, I must be near the time machine at noon if I want to glimpse my late husband. Will he notice me? Recognize me?

When I walk into Riverside Deli, TigerLily's sitting in a blue sheath dress and oversized fabric straw-colored sun hat. Penny, in that familiar red sundress, shares a table with her.

Déjà vu slams into me, and I grab the doorjamb. Steadying myself, I wait for the surreal sensation to pass, then approach the table, breathing deep savory aromas like fresh-brewed coffee and hot pastries.

How do these two know each other?

A vague memory emerges. Penny sharing with us she'd chatted with the dead woman the same morning her body was later found. And didn't Giles mention Juni's parent met her on one of Penny's earlier trips?

As I pass by Togg and give him a nod, TigerLily sees me, and her face lights up. "There they is," she calls.

Penny, heavier than I recall, regards me with a pleasant smile but no recognition. No wonder. My wig and contacts render me a different woman.

"You must be Marie." The twenty-first-century cadence, familiar and comforting, falls like a beautiful song on my ears. A half-eaten muffin rests on her plate. "Hope you don't mind my crashing your party." The tone, the manner, is so vintage Penny I nearly blurt her name.

Pulling myself together, I take the chair across from her. "Yes, I'm Marie. You?"

"Sorry for not introducing myself. I'm Penny."

Words claw at my throat—that I was one of the desperate stranded travelers who begged her for a ride home three years ago, and why didn't McMurray ever show? But something stops me, an intuitive twinge in my gut. I clamp my mouth. Best to see how this plays out.

TigerLily's glossy mouth contrasts her eager gray eyes. "Marie, would you believe, Penny is from the past?"

I force my mouth open. "Really?"

"That time chine everyone talkin bout?" TigerLily picks up the cup a robot places in front of her. "They came from the year twenny twenny-three."

"Wow!" I turn an appreciative gaze to Penny. "Weren't you on the news a few years ago?" Despite my cheery attitude, I'm flailing inside. Penny's presence is throwing a wrench into my plans. How long is she planning to stay?

As if reading my mind, Penny makes a don't-mind-me hand gesture. "I'm leaving soon. My friend and partner, the time machine operator, will be here at noon, and I need to pack up my stuff and go meet him. But this nice lady and I have gotten to know each other better this week, haven't we?"

But didn't she already know her? I bite my lips—hard.

Penny places a hand on her new friend's shoulder. "I'll miss you, my friend."

"Wish you could stay longer. I'm fash with your robot experiments."

"Robot experiments?" I don't recall Penny mentioning that.

Penny beamed. "Yeah, I'm working on a project for my boss involving robot programming. Or botting, as I believe it's called."

"Wow, that's awesome." But the passing time makes me antsy. "I'd ask you to explain, but I'm afraid it would be over my head."

TigerLily stops her with a hand gesture of her own. "But I bet Marie wants to hear all bout life in the past." She turns to me. "Don't yull love how they talk? So elegant."

Groan. I have no choice but to sit and listen to Penny regale us with her rendition of a life I love and miss. And pretend it's all news to me. We sip coffee and nosh on pastries and eggs while I conjure up my inner actress and give suitable replies and reactions, even throwing out an appropriate question or two. An hour passes as I grow frantic. In one more hour, both TigerLily and McMurray will be dead.

And I don't have much time left to prevent two deaths.

IN THE YEAR 2123

"TigerLily." Rude or not, I interrupt Penny's narrative. I'm running out of time. A robot has cleared away our dishes. "What's new with your pring? Juni? Ever heard back?"

"Oh yeah! The best news. They popped in last week to show me my new grandpring."

"Really! Amazing!" She gives me an odd look. Oops. I slipped into my natural speech. "So, uh, where they livin now?"

"They wouldn't say. But they comin by for another visit at noon."

"Brendan too? Is Brendan the coparent?"

"Yeah, to both." Her face droops from an angst too deep for words. She must wish her daughter had chosen a better man to have a child with. "Wasn't Brendan the one hurt your spouse?"

My throat seizes, and I choke the words out. "Yes. My spouse died after Brendan assaulted em."

TigerLily gasps, her hand on her heart. "Ah, forgot that."

Really? How does someone forget such a thing? Yet it happened over two years ago, the news dropped the story after a week, and Juni hadn't been in contact with her mother all this time. Maybe she did forget Giles died.

"Well"—Penny stands and pats her mouth with a napkin—"sounds like you two have some catching up to do. Marie, I hope we meet again, and I'm so sorry to hear about your spouse. What a difficult thing to go through."

I nod. If she knew she was about to meet a very much alive and younger Giles, her head would spin, wiping that cheery expression right off like a cosmic eraser.

Penny leaves as the clock nears eleven. I let out a sigh. "Nice person."

"And brilliant too. I first met em few years ago, asked bout how their time traveler worked. Marvy interestin. I returned the favor this week by teachin em botting."

"I'm surprised Penny'd be forthcoming with the information."

"No, it was fairly general, no specifics. But enough for me to get a good overview. I promised to teach em what I knew bout botting. No prietary secrets there."

"Brendan knew a lot about the time chine also."

"Only because they picked my brain after I picked Penny's, hopin to get theirs workin again."

"You mean the brain? Or the chine?"

"Ha!" We share a giggle. "Both!"

Didn't his father teach him everything he knows? But if TigerLily wants to take the credit, who am I to object? She must not be aware of the connection.

But wait. When the police interrogated Penny and Giles on the day of the murder, didn't Giles tell me Penny was here at this café at 12:17? And the hologram proved it?

It's almost 11:30 now. If I'm recalling his words, then I have to wonder: why is she coming back?

Unless repeating this day has somehow altered the cosmic timeline.

In that case, will the two deaths still happen?

A silence between TigerLily and me pulses. Great. I'm not listening. And then her hologram flashes, and her countenance lights up. "Juni!" she greets her caller.

And now I understand. Brendan aims to kill TigerLily before she can kill his father. His words from our first meeting echo in my memory. "If I could, I'd travel to the future and do her in myself." That day, I glimpsed the depth of his corrupt character. Too bad, I didn't heed my instincts. Because I've become more and more convinced TigerLily is innocent.

Had Brendan not realized before today who Juni's mother was? He'd had ample opportunity to carry out his threat before he disappeared. But now he's reappeared, and the threat awakens.

So I'm not surprised when TigerLily's mouth moves in silent conversation with her daughter. I'm not shocked when she turns to me and says, "Gotta run, friend. Pring will be here soon."

"Wait." I put out a desperate hand to stop her. "Can't sh—*they*—meet you here? We haven't even had a chance to visit yet." I force a smile. "Haven't seen you for two years. Got some catchin up to do."

I'm gabbling, frantic not to let her out of my sight.

"They meetin me at my place, but you can come with." She stands and beckons me to follow her. "Would love to see that muff arrested for what they did to your spouse." She follows this with some spicy swear words, shocking me with their intensity.

I have no choice but to accompany her to her new place, an apartment on the second floor. As we get off the elevator, we pass the office where I will be interviewing Nogard Riden tomorrow. There he is, the six-foot-seven oddity. TigerLily's apartment is at the end. "Juni should be here in a few mints." Her finger swipe slides the door open.

"Heh, Parent." The familiar voice startles me. I didn't expect them to be waiting inside already. Juni's holding a blanketed bundle from which a tiny hand protrudes.

Another familiar voice greets me. "Hello, Thea. Fancy meeting you here." Brendan, whom I haven't seen since he disappeared two years ago, is barely recognizable with blue-and-gray contraface and a long dark beard. Of course, he doesn't want to be recognized as the perp wanted for manslaughter. He narrows his eyes at me. "Wasn't expecting to see you."

I swallow away the rasp waiting in my throat, but can't do anything about the pounding of my heart. "Ditto, Brendan." How did they get here?

Ah. He fixed the time machine to travel back in time.

He turns away as if I'm no longer significant. "Sit down, Lily." My friend's mouth twitches downward as if she's hiding her annoyance, but she obeys, no doubt sensing, like me, something dark and frightening beneath his placid exterior.

He settles in the easy chair across from her as Juni perches on the wide arm, caressing her baby's tiny head. I remain standing and shifting from foot to foot, my hands hanging at my sides. Brendan seems to remember my presence.

"Thea," he says to me.

"Isn't their name Marie?" TigerLily adjusts her hat, fingers trembling, squeaky desperation in her voice. She knows Brendan's up to something. She also doesn't want me to leave.

I have no intention of doing so.

He ignores her. "Thea, why are you here? This family visit doesn't concern you."

"I invited em." TigerLily's recovered her poise. "They is my friend."

"That's right." I cross my arms. "We weren't done visiting. Maybe you two could come back later? Say, in an hour or so?"

TigerLily's eyes flicker with an appeal as her gaze meets mine.

But Brendan scoots down in the chair and places ankle on knee, clasping his hands over his belly, the image of a man of the house relaxing after a long day of work. "I believe you're the one who should come back later, Thea. We won't be here long, right, Juni?"

She nods, her mouth still twisted in a smirk over how Brendan is taking charge. The bundle moves, and she shifts the baby to her shoulder.

I stay rooted.

Brendan's eyes bear an oppressive darkness, stark and threatening. "You can wait for her downstairs in the restaurant. When we're done, she'll come down to meet you. Okay?" His wheedling tone, like that used on a child, doesn't fool me.

My hologram shows the time as 11:36. TigerLily and Juni are watching our little drama, TigerLily with no clue she has minutes left to live.

I imagine blurting out the truth. Would it prolong her life?

No. They'd gram emergency services and accuse me of delusional behavior. A robot would haul me off to the integration pavilion. No questions asked.

Everyone's staring at me. What if I were just to stand here for half an hour? Surely, he wouldn't try anything?

As possibilities dart in and out of my mind, TigerLily intervenes. "Marie, it's fine. Just go downstairs and wait for me, okay? Just plannin to hold my grand for a few mints."

"No, I want to stay." Obstinacy drives me forward. I point to Brendan, finger trembling. "This muff's responsible for my spouse's death. I'm not leaving you alone with him."

Brendan bounds up from the chair, startling me backward. Grabbing my arm, he opens the front door and ushers me into the corridor. My heart pounds so hard he must see the pulsating in my eyes.

"You were told to mind your own business," he hisses.

"Giles's death is my business." My fingers twitch toward my hologram, about to summon help.

But his gaze follows mine. He reaches over and touches it. The screen goes dark.

"What are you planning to do to TigerLily?" I screech. Nobody is about, nobody who can help. It should be obvious to any bystander this qualifies as abuse. His fingers still grip my upper arm so hard, it'll leave a bruise.

"Nothing. Thea, listen to me. I am sorry about Giles. I never meant for that to happen. But I can't go to prison, you see. I have big plans for my life. So you'll turn yourself around right now and go home. You won't tell the police where I am." He clamps my other arm and propels me toward the lift. My feet have no choice but to obey or risk a fall. "I know where you live, so if you don't want trouble, if you don't want anything to happen to you or your daughter, keep your mouth shut."

I lurch. Daisy! I need to get to her, make sure she's safe.

Brendan shoves me into the lift as two stern-faced, plainclothes robots exit and turn in the direction I came from. They saunter down the hall before stopping at TigerLily's door.

Whew! She must have managed to call for help. Thankful she has a chance at rescue, I let out a breath as the door closes, shutting Brendan from my sight. Yet the lift's hum as it descends echoes the vibrating anxiety over this new threat to Daisy. I reactivate my hologram and get Starr on the screen.

"Is Daisy okay?"

Starr's dark brows lift. "Sure, they fine. Why?"

"They—I'll be there soon to take em home early. They can finish their assignments tonight."

"Everythin okay?"

The lift opens, and I scoot around two people waiting, hoping they don't notice my panting or my fear-widened eyes. "I'll explain later."

In the café, I hustle past the table, now empty, that I occupied a mere fifteen minutes ago, clueless as to the danger I was about to face. As I exit into the summer day, I glimpse Penny's red Nordstrom dress. She's sitting at the back of the patio, her gaze fixed on her hologram. A robot sets a plate in front of her, but she doesn't look up, nor does she notice me as I hurry on by. Did she go to her rooms first, then back here? Or did she move to the patio when she left me and TigerLily?

God, please rescue TigerLily. Don't let Brendan and Juni succeed in their scheme.

But if this day is meant to unfold the way it did ten years ago, TigerLily is screwed.

The hot sun and silvery-blue sky beam down on me, betraying no hint of anything but warm good cheer. *Lord, I know You can do anything. You can even change history, if You so choose. I pray it's not too late for TigerLily.*

Sticking to the riverside path, I pass the spot where her body was found. Beyond it, the peaceful river shimmers in the soft breeze. I recall when the cops retrieved the corpse—the strange-looking ambulance, the shouts, our impatient biding of time. The immaculate river is no place to hide a murdered corpse. Didn't the perp realize the Willamette wouldn't keep such a sordid secret to itself? I continue on past the fenced-in cement slab where McMurray, Giles, myself, and friends will be appearing in fifteen minutes. Wishing I could tarry until it arrives, I hurry on to my apartment building and reach the classroom at straight-up noon.

Daisy's cute but confused face is balm to my anguished soul. I sweep her up as she's finishing her turkey sandwich. Grabbing the rest of the food, I carry her out in front of all the other kids.

"Daisy!" Lark calls. "Where you goin?"

"Parent?" Daisy says, her small voice tight. "Why you makin me leave?"

"I have a surprise for you," I tell her. "It's down by the river." Keeping tight hold of her, I make our way back to the time capsule landing site and join the mingling crowd.

And there we are, our younger selves, blinking in the bright sun, our heads moving to and fro, absorbing everything around us. The other Thea can't hide her anxiety, and she takes Giles's hand.

Giles! I drink in every plane of his face, every hair on his head. My heart rate surges so much I nearly drop Daisy's hand and run to him.

But I must resist that temptation.

"This is the time machine we've been hearing about," I whisper to Daisy. We move closer, near enough to touch young Thea.

Which Daisy does. "Wut year yuh from?" she says to the other me. I recall this part, when I glanced down at my little clone, unable to understand her speech. My younger self twists her face, frustrated at the garbled question, and walks on, hand in hand with beautiful Giles. That Thea won't recognize me with my short platinum wig and two-toned eyes. If only I could run after her and warn her to turn around, go home, and never come back.

Exactly as Brendan did to me.

I lurch. Did Brendan kill his father? Despite his warning not to go to the police, I will if he's guilty of murder. Daisy'll be safe with me when I do. Then Qory and I must move.

Preferably to a different city, far away from here. Where Brendan won't ever find us.

IN THE YEAR 2123

Brendan's words from that long-ago tomorrow drift into my head and clarify my next step. *"The only way you're going to learn what happened is to be there to witness it."* Daisy is restless as we approach the arborvitae hedge hemming in the breezeway. My heavy boots handle the slippery river rocks to the rarely seen side of McMurray's fortresslike fence, parallel to the Willamette. Time to implement my plan. Using a thin cloth so as not to leave prints, I release two drones: one programmed to launch to the other side of the fence, the other to confirm Giles told me the truth about his disappearing act that day. Young Thea has no idea how grateful she ought to be that her fingerprints will not be detected when the cops find the drone.

Daisy's soft hand tugs at me. "Why we here?"

"Thought it would be nice to finish your lunch by the river. Then we'll go home."

"Why got a drone?"

Exactly what I feared—Daisy questioning me. "Tell you later." I stroke her velvet-soft hair, hoping my answer appeases her.

She falls quiet as we stomp along the rocks and sand for an eighth of a mile further upriver. A black compometal bench overlooks the water and the wooded hills beyond. I put her on my right where she can't see my screen and then retrieve her half-eaten turkey sandwich from my pack and hand it to her.

Odd that I'm more curious about what Giles is up to right now than who killed McMurray. At this moment, Thea and Giles are in the public restroom. I guide the drone that direction.

There's my Giles! Traipsing toward the capsule, just as he said, strides purposeful, head down, hands in pockets, sunglasses atop his head. He's about five feet from the fence when he slows, looks up. Directly at the drone hovering ninety degrees from his left ear.

My heart clutches as his wide hazel eyes meet mine through the drone cam. *Giles, oh, Giles! How I miss you!* I sniff away the tears, which will only lead to more questions from Daisy. I drink in the close-up of my late husband, nearly bending over in my effort to stanch my weeping.

Giles stops, scratches his head, pulls his shades over his eyes, and pivots, strolling back the way he came. I disable the drone, and it falls to the ground, having confirmed for me Giles's integrity.

Not that I doubted him. But seeing the proof was good. And the drone that seemed so insignificant when he mentioned it on our drive home...not so insignificant after all. His instincts were spot-on. He *was* being watched.

I must not weep, or I won't be able to see the other drone's path. Daisy, tossing rocks in the river, giggling at the ripples, hasn't noticed my quiet crying.

My hologram screen provides a clear view of the time machine's rear as the second drone hovers. Through the back window, I see McMurray moving around. What could he be doing in there? Whoever murdered him will be showing up any minute. Will it be Brendan? Yet I can't quite wrap my mind around the idea of him, with premeditation, murdering his father.

Oh, how I wish I could stop him. But I'm no match for him, and he might come after Daisy if I make the slightest wave. All I can do is watch, my heart in my throat, and, if possible, use my evidence to bring him to justice.

No cameras are set up on the river, so Daisy and I won't raise any suspicions as we enjoy a picnic lunch, even if we're seen from the satellite cameras.

"Parent, this nice."

Daisy's finishing her sandwich, so I take out two bags of potato chips—the twenty-second-century version—sans additives—in a biodegradable wrapping. Even without the flavoring, they still manage to satisfy the palate.

"My mum and dad used to take me picnicking by the river when I was your age."

She chews the last bite of sandwich. "Was it this riv?"

"No, was in Australia. Remember that big brownish circle on the globe I showed you?" I stick a chip on my tongue and relish the satisfying crunch. "That's where I grew up."

"Why so far way?"

"It just is. The world's a big place."

Daisy forms a circle with her arms, her fingers touching at twelve o'clock. "This big?"

"Much, much bigger." I point to the ground. "If you were to dig all the way through the earth, on the other side would be Australia."

Her round eyes and the tiny line between her feathery brows tell me her understanding isn't quite there yet. I've crunched my way through half the chips while I've waited for something to happen. A rustling and movement from the screen wrests my attention. A clang, then a robot, face shaded by a straw hat, lurches toward the back of the capsule. Exactly as Giles described the murderer in the hologram scene, except we never knew it was a robot.

Daisy taps my leg. "Parent?" I shush her with a finger over her mouth, and she scowls. I don't dare even breathe as the humanoid fingers the keypad on the rear door, its clothing, hidden by the hat on the street cam feed I once saw, identical to one of the robots at TigerLily's door.

Not a robocop after all, but a robokiller. The door opens, and it goes inside. My drone hovers.

An electronic voice reverberates. "Where's the book?"

"The book?" I recognize McMurray's stunned cry.

The robot collapses in upon itself like a Transformer toy, leaving it half its former height.

McMurray strangles out, "Nel's book?"

"The book." The robot lunges for McMurray, who collapses against a seat. My mouth gone dry, I guide the drone closer.

And too late, realize my mistake. The robot turns its head, spots the drone, and bats it away.

The screen goes dark.

———◆◇◆———

What book? And who is Nel?

Whatever mysterious book the robot sought, I'll never know. A book so valuable, or so incriminating, someone murdered for it. I rue the timing of the drone destruction, causing me to miss out on seeing the rest of the drama unfold.

Since McMurray is dead, he must've resisted the robot's demand. If he didn't give over Nel's book, did the robot find it somewhere in the capsule?

Or perhaps he didn't have it with him. Which could also have caused his murder.

At least I have an idea of the motive, which seemed so murky before. I need to find out who Nel is.

Now what?

Gram the police? But as I recall that day ten years ago, Giles did so. But what if I were to gram them early?

Yet what could they do? Is murder by robot even prosecutable? As far as I know, this is a first. Besides, it's no longer possible to contact the police anonymously. Everyone is connected to the Cloud. If I gram the cops, they'll beam me up and question me. How would I explain the drone?

Best to let Giles contact them. I have a strong urge to find and follow him. I know where they are, after all. I twine my fingers through Daisy's, who has been tugging at my skirt for at least a minute, and grab the empty picnic basket. "Let's go take a walk, lovey."

We proceed away from the river, jostle through and around other walkers, and there they are, Giles and Thea, walking toward BirdNest while discussing the murdered McMurray they discovered. Should I follow them in so I can feast my eyes on a very much alive and animated Giles? I stay a decent distance behind, yet without letting them out of my sight.

Daisy chatters, but I can't concentrate. I give her the appropriate mm-hmms at regular intervals, but my mind won't stop churning. Did Brendan program those robots? Giles believed Brendan considered his dad competition. Still, would he murder his dad? And what was his motive for sending the robots after TigerLily? Or was that Juni's idea? Still, the murky motive stymies me.

And something else slithers at the edge of my memory, a sneaky wraith who doesn't want to be discovered. Something to do with the robots, perhaps? Nothing unusual stood out about the two robots at TigerLily's. Perhaps a snatch of conversation? TigerLily relating a story to Penny this morning or vice versa?

It will come to me, given time. Such an odd sensation, reliving this day. Like I've landed in that old movie *Groundhog*

Day. But one repetition is plenty for me, thank you. The same autopods crisscross the same periwinkle-blue sky. The whispery warm breeze ruffles my short platinum wig at the same time it lifts Thea's long dark mane.

Everything is the same, yet so different. Young Thea still has Giles by her side, unaware what her future holds. Eager to get back and start on that article, which, as it turns out, never got finished.

As for me, my heart aches at the sight of Giles.

Giles and Thea and their friends halt up ahead, having reached the café, where they enter. I won't be recognized, yet still, I hesitate. Across the street, the answer appears. "Baby, let's rest over there at the taxi depot."

I tug Daisy's arm and lead her toward the spot where the old TriMet-bus-turned-deli used to be—the sole remaining connection to my old life now sacrificed in the name of progress. We dodge idle autopods and waiting taxipods. Crossing streets is no longer dangerous, thanks to faultless radar on all vehicles. Sparsely occupied benches line the opposite walkway.

"I need to get off my feet for a few." And I can watch Giles at his window seat. Not once does he turn his head in my direction, and Thea is just out of sight. I relax and observe unobserved. Soon, the two cops, Ruba and Robocop, rush in, and it all unfolds as I remember. So surreal, like a dream, from this perspective. The blue lettering on the café door starts to blur under my intensified scrutiny.

"Parent, can I go play with the prings?" Daisy is focused on two children about her age, standing in the street playing Dox, a game where two drones chase each other, guided by remote controls. If one drone catches up with the other, the loser aborts, and a fresh drone replaces it. Whoever loses the fewest drones wins.

"No, baby, we're going home now." A drone falls, and the girl reaches into a shiny metal canister, releasing another drone. She squeals as her drone disables the boy's. The drones remind me of the Lunar Module, shrunk to a hundredth of its size. It's so hypnotic to watch them swoop around like buzzing bees I almost forget why I'm here.

But then the six travelers and the two cops exit the café, their hurried movements and worried faces wresting my attention. I half hear Daisy complaining, but I must keep a steady pace behind, my head craning around the crowd. Although I don't need to. I know where they're going.

My brain whirs as my legs eat up the sidewalk. If our being sent back in time had some cosmic purpose, what was that purpose? Seems to me it was to solve the mystery of two murders—or to confirm the murder-suicide.

We veer around a slow older man walking with a cane. He hasn't had bionic leg surgery yet.

I have no way of knowing who programmed that robot. Most people know the basics of robotics, but to have the advanced knowledge it would take to send a robot after a person to kill him/her? Only a handful of trailblazers are that far along.

Like Brendan.

Oh, and Penny too.

The capsule appears in the distance, glowing white under the noonday sun. My steps quicken, and Daisy whines. I pick her up, heedless of her dead weight. What had Penny said in the deli? Something about learning robotics. Snatches of TigerLily's conversation I hadn't heeded come back to me.

I first met em few years ago, asked bout how their time traveler worked. TigerLily's words are fresh in my mind. *I returned the favor this week by teachin em botting.*

Then what? I'd been thinking about the passing time. TigerLily's words filtered in one ear, passing nonstop through my brain, and out.

But wait. Maybe not. Now I remember.

As I'd tapped my toes, she'd added, "Penny's boss wanted em to figure out if a robot could be botted to locate a person. I said you bet, works same as drone locating."

Could a robot be botted to murder a person as well?

Only two people, besides McMurray, would've known about the other gate and the secret rear entrance.

Brendan.

And Penny.

IN THE YEAR 2123

Which of them is the culprit?

The cops escort the time travelers away from the time capsule, which is blocked off with crime tape and guarded by two robocops akin to Star Wars stormtroopers with their helmeted heads and metallic bodies. Had their designer gotten their inspiration from that ancient movie series?

No reason to stick around now. Curious as to whether Brendan is nearby, I stop by our old dorm's podlot. As I suspected, the fenced-off corner is empty. He and Juni must've made their escape right away. And now I know where to find them. My grip on Daisy's hand loosens, knowing she's not in any immediate danger.

Tomorrow, when Thea, Giles, and Brendan return for the interviews, I'll search the time machine for that mysterious book. Assuming the robot didn't get it. And then I will go find Brendan. He needs to be held accountable, plus he may know who Nel is. And my suspicion as to Brendan's whereabouts makes sense.

When the time travelers return from the police interrogation, Daisy and I are in the crowd to see them off.

The cops've just learned of another death, and they are about to discover TigerLily's body in the river. This strong déjà vu sensation is rattling, but the chain of events clarifies as I stand on this side of the timeline. One of the robots must've hauled the poor woman out of her apartment and dumped her while the other one hunted down McMurray. But how did they manage to do so and nobody notice? Did Brendan send them?

If I find him tomorrow, will he kill me too?

Maybe I should rethink my plan.

I watch Thea and the others, remembering that feeling of sweet relief at heading home. Longing to join them pierces me.

Thea's gaze turns my way. She searches my face, then meets my eyes. The eeriness of staring at my other self jolts me, and I gasp and look away. I must get away from her/my searching gaze before my brain implodes. I tug Daisy's hand and lead her home, answering with nonanswers her curious questions about the people who dress and talk funny.

"Parent, why that person look like you? Why do them wear weird clothes?"

"They're from another time," I tell her. "I don't know why the person looks like me. I heard everybody has a twin somewhere."

Now she wants to talk about twins, but I spot a robocop up ahead and flag it down. "Can you tell me more about the dead person found in the river?"

"We are still conducting the investigation."

I take a deep breath to calm my racing heart. The last thing I need is to get hauled in for questioning. "But do you have any suspects?" Keeping my voice level, I ease my grip on the robot's arm.

"We will release more details when we discover them."

He's no help. Daisy pesters me about the dead person all the way back to the apartment where she reacts to my lack of attention by creating as big a racket as possible.

I wish I could promise her that, after tomorrow, life will flip to normal again.

But I'm not sure I know what that means anymore.

I wait until the next afternoon to put my plan into action. School isn't meeting today, so I have to cart Daisy everywhere I go. Otherwise, she'll interrupt Qory too much while he's working. Lark's family went to the beach for the day, but didn't think to invite Daisy. Maybe because their own three kids are handful enough?

I never mind spending the day with her. But this is different. I'm on a mission—and not a child-friendly one. I try to stay out of sight of Giles and young Thea and watch them from a distance. Thea's already curious about me and Daisy. I don't want her to start following me and asking too many questions. How awkward. Like I'm supposed to tell her

I'm her older self abducted by a time warp? Really? And the man who's tagging along with them killed the man she loves?

How preposterous. And I can't think of a reasonable fiction to pass off.

Best to keep my distance.

But she glimpses me and Daisy as they're about to have lunch. They don't know it yet, but they'll be eating at BirdNest soon. I have about forty-five minutes before they return.

Oh no. Now they're tracking us to our apartment. Thea's walking right up to the door. I don't have time for this interruption. And what would I say to her anyway? She plans to show me a photo of herself as a child and pretend the photo is her niece. Over Daisy's protests, I take her into the bedroom, pull off my wig and contacts, and carry her to the back stairs, slinging my compoplastic bag over my shoulder. I know the perfect place to hide her while I do what I need to do. Qory asked no questions, merely waved.

We stomp to the top floor. Once in the podlot, I lock her in from the outside, with strict instructions to stay hidden in case Brendan happens to come looking for us and to gram Qory if I don't return in forty-five minutes. Her toy drones will keep her occupied until then.

I hurry to the site, this time with no crime tape blocking it off, scan my prints, and slip through the gate before it's fully open. Nobody is paying me any obvious attention, yet I'm aware of eyes all around from robocams and overhead satellites. All my movements are being tracked, so I need to act quickly.

As I close the gate, something hums nearby, one of those ever-present drones, so common we no longer notice them, in the same way twenty-first-century citizens don't notice aircraft sailing through the sky. The capsule door slides open, and I step inside.

And so does the drone.

Only one person would send a drone after me. Daisy found my stash of real drones in the autopod. Apparently, she's outgrown her toy ones without my ever noticing. Her curiosity is going to be the death of me. If it isn't the death of her first.

"Baby, if this is you, you better have a good reason to be spying on me." The drone hovers inches from me, but I can't let her see what I'm up to. I grab it and disable it, dropping the useless implement into my bag. Now, the book. *Lord, let it be here.*

There aren't many hiding places. The driver's chair is basic vinyl, no compartments that I can see. So if he had a book on board, where would he have stashed it? Or did he have it on his person?

If so, and he didn't give it to the robot, the cops would've found it. The cops said nothing about a book. *Keep looking.*

I scan the rest of the interior and examine each seat before realizing my vulnerable position. What if Brendan were to show up and see me here? Young Brendan is having lunch with Thea and Giles. Current-day Brendan, however, I suspect fled to 2131 and plans to stay there if he was responsible for yesterday's murders. But what if he returns to check out the aftermath of his dirty deeds?

A renewed urgency drives me on. Hands on hips, I resume my scrutiny of the driver seat. A picture arises in my mind's eye of Penny feeling around under it, and I rush to do the same.

Nothing but cold vinyl and hard metal. But what did I expect? If anything were under there, Penny would've found it. What could she have been looking for? Surely not the book. Why would she?

I turn in a slow circle, trying to see through the eyes of Penny, who knows every nook and cranny and is likely familiar with each hidden panel. Whatever she'd been looking for, had she found it? Could she have known about the book and decided to search for it? Or am I reading more into her actions than is warranted?

After we returned, the police blocked access to the vehicle. Did she even have time to come back and search before we left again?

Hope is a funny thing, keeping one going against impossible odds. I glance at the time. Thirty minutes remain before I need to be out of here.

An odd sight on the ceiling catches my eye. One of the lights is blinking slower than the others. I squint. The first time an acoustic panel is out of alignment with the others. Excitement mounting, I climb on the seat Ari used and wrestle with the square plastic piece. After a few moments of jostling, it falls into my hand.

Along with a black, five-by-eight leather-bound notebook.

I gasp. Assuming this is what Penny sought, how did she miss it?

Or had she decided to return later to resume her search after finishing her police business? But then Brendan confiscated the vehicle before she could.

I open the precious leather cover to pages covered in tall angular printing that reminds me of a cityscape. Letters like high skyscrapers and squat office buildings. Checking the time, I sit down and begin to read.

NEL

After graduating from college with a degree in mathematical physics—I switched from computer science midway through my sophomore year, ensuring another two years of grueling coursework—I lost track of Nel, eschewing any reunions or social events where I might run into her. My desire to get as far from her as possible landed me in Australia, a land I'd always wanted to visit, where I could sew the proverbial wild oats for one carefree year. But once back home, I reunited with my college sweetheart, married, and embarked on my engineering career.

But I never forgot Nel and how persuaded I was she'd gotten away with murder.

Dissatisfied with my level of knowledge, I enrolled in Stanford's master's program in quantum physics. While working on my thesis, I stumbled upon a formula that could make time travel possible. Somehow, word got out. (My professor was so excited about my discovery, he must've spilled the beans to his friend at the Chronicle.) My completed thesis was discovered, and I was the new media darling with local and national podcasts and TV documentaries focused on me.

In a nutshell, time travel breaks through the fixed space-time continuum the same way a rocket ship overcomes the forces of gravity, by generating a power mightier than the forces holding it in place. Eventually, I invented the incelerator, the time-traveling "engine," so to speak, that would generate that necessary power. I won't overload my page with the technicalities, but the public ate it up. I set to work building a machine to house my invention, but after many months of frustrating work, I could do no more. The instruction panel codes couldn't understand how to get the incelerator to launch. I needed a partner, a second brain, to work through the bugs.

The inevitable happened next. Nel reappeared in my world, having heard of my invention and wanting to know more about it. Of all the people I'd worked with, she was the only one with the needed brainpower to help troubleshoot my incelerator and get it working. Yet how could I trust her, knowing what I did?

"Stop calling me Nel, Colt," she insisted after she walked into my laboratory uninvited. "I go by Penny now."

"Fine." Anything to stay on her good side. Penny—Nel—both nicknames for her cumbersome birth name of Penelope. I gave her a general idea of the incelerator's circuitry, but no specifics lest she steal my idea.

She patted my machine's fuselage. "And why haven't you taken this baby for a test spin yet?"

"Because the control panel won't talk to the incelerator."

"Ah, I see." She scrutinized the machine I'd dubbed Midnight Rider, and I caught a flash in her eyes. A brainstorm was brewing

in that brilliant noggin. "The problem is, they aren't speaking the same language."

"I know that. Lost in translation, you might say. But I haven't found a way to bridge the two."

"Hmm." Her thoughtful murmur worried me. Was she about to trample over my carefully laid boundaries? "Remember that old book from the eighties, Men are from Mars, Women are from Venus?"

I nodded. "Remember the name. Never read it."

She grinned. "I read it in college. And even though it was dated, I loved it. Quite true, and so helped me understand 'male speak.' And what's true for the genders is also true for computers. Your two computers don't have to speak the same language. They just have to learn how to decipher the other's 'speech.'"

"Y'know, you might be onto something." Nel's—I mean Penny's—intellect always wowed me. But I was impressed anew by the combination of her female perspective working hand in hand with her brilliant mind. Maybe this problem just needed a woman's touch.

If only the woman didn't have to be her.

"In fact, I can show you how to get the two of them to talk to each other. If you'll let me."

If I let her. Somehow, I had to forestall this chain of events, give myself time to think. "I'll let you know tomorrow."

Appeased, she went away. The next day, I was ready with my answer.

"I drew up a partnership contract to ensure everything's aboveboard," I told her. I'd gotten the form off the internet and added several phrases in my scramble for peace of mind after a sleepless night. After all, I fought to convince myself, I don't know she committed a murder. Mere speculation led to that conclusion. She might have been a difficult person in grade school and high school, but people can change, can grow. And if she signed a contract, she wouldn't be able to color outside the lines without risking a lawsuit.

I made sure to specify I had the final say on all decisions.

Most importantly, if I were to achieve my dream of time travel, only one person on earth could help ensure its success.

Penelope Nichols.

Fiddling with the pen, she scanned the document once, then twice, lines popping out between her light brows. If she saw anything objectionable, she said nothing. After clicking the pen two or three times as if warming it up, she signed.

She was my official partner in TimeTrane LLC.

IN THE YEAR 2123

Stunned, I snap the book closed. No wonder someone wanted this book so badly. Penny is still in 2023, all smug and carefree, having gotten away with murder. She must've been guiding the robot as she sat in the café yesterday and then used us to make her getaway.

A clever scheme, a scheme she'd have pulled off if not for my skepticism, my doubts. My stubborn compulsion to investigate.

I have fifteen minutes to decide my next move.

The compulsion to return to 2023 and show this to the police sends me pacing up and down the narrow aisle. Only one person has the know-how to get me back, but he's in the year 2131.

I tuck the exposé into my bag, replace the ceiling panel, then approach the dashboard. The apparatus makes sense now. I know what each of those commands mean. Go. Lock. Set Date. I must've absorbed more of Giles's and Brendan's exchanges than I realized. Dare I send this thing into the future to find Brendan and plead his assistance? Dare I enlist the cops' help once I get there?

Would Brendan be willing to help me after what he did to Giles? And can I trust him? After all, Penny murdered the father he admired and looked up to. If I strike a deal with him, promise him immunity from the law, will he see that returning me to my home year is in his best interests too?

Well, I can't just stand here. Reviewing Brendan's instructions to Giles, I suck in an anchoring breath and tap the date selector, poised to enter the year 2131. But what day would Brendan have chosen? If I choose a day later in the year, odds are he'll be there. I puzzle over it, press in 11/1, then the year, my fingers trembling like gum tree leaves in a summer breeze.

Wait. 2113?

My heart lurches. Oops, of all times for a dyslexic moment to strike, this is the worst. I press abort.

Nothing. The year 2113 still gleams green on the display. My heart is still playing hopscotch, my breath coming fast and hard.

Abort.

Nothing.

Fist slam.

A malfunction? Or sabotage? But who would sabotage this thing with its tight security?

Déjà vu quivers around my awareness. Why does this feel familiar?

I have to get out of here before this thing launches me into the past.

Back to November 1, 2113.

Oh, horrors.

I hurry out the door, knowing the fate awaiting young Thea and Giles. I could wait for them right here, warn them not to get on, and risk sounding like a maniac.

Or I can let history play itself out as it's meant to, let it lead younger me through ten years of joys and sorrows to this moment. Through the highs of childbirth and the abyss of death. Through endings but also beginnings. And long-sought answers.

No more messing with destiny. Squaring my shoulders, I retrace my steps toward home. My priority is to get back to my Daisy.

Then take this book to Ruba and tell her everything.

———◆◇◆———

"TigerLily Malone did not kill McMurray," I tell Ruba. "And she did not commit suicide."

I launch into my story. At first, Ruba doesn't believe me. I can't blame her. With my rambling, fantastical tale of malfunctioning time machines, circular time glitches, and robocrimes, she's every right to think I'm unhinged. What saves me is the book and the drone footage on my hologram. Ruba can't deny what her eyes are seeing. And when I read the book aloud since nobody in this world reads script handwriting anymore, understanding flashes in her eyes.

"Thanks for sharin that," she answers my questioning gaze. "It *was* you that day." Her chuckle comes out gravelly.

"Thought maybe I goin cray, seein double like. Good to know my eyes can still be trusted."

I grin back, relieved to have that secret out in the open.

"But what I don't get"—she leans forward, the top of the desk pressing against her waistline—"is why Penny would kill TigerLily."

Ah, the million-dollar question. "I've been giving that a lot of thought. Only one scenario makes sense. Knowing Penny, I suspect she planned to get rid of McMurray and take over his business. Then when she comes here on an experimental run, TigerLily comes along asking a lot of questions. It had to have raised her hackles. Why all the questions? Did TigerLily plan to compete? Then she learned about TigerLily's career—botting—and I also believe TigerLily let slip about Brendan's time machine. Penny realized she needed to eliminate him as well as TigerLily and McMurray. What better way to eliminate all her potential competitors without detection than by using robots? The whole crime smacked of insider knowledge. For so long, I suspected Brendan."

"But Penny didn't kill Brendan."

"No, he escaped when he forced me into the hall. Remember Penny was in the café when McMurray's murder took place. She was right downstairs from TigerLily, guiding those robots to her door in order to kill her and Brendan. She used TigerLily's own technology against her." My outraged voice rises. "The robots would've killed me and Juni as well, just because we were there. Imagine, Brendan saved my life and his own by pulling me out of there."

"Hmm. So one of the robots framed TigerLily and got rid of their body, the other headed to McMurray."

"Penny was one smart lady."

Ruba just shakes her head, over and over. "You know I could prosecute you for interferin with a police vestigation?" But a tiny smile belies her threat.

"I know. And I'm…"

"But I'm not goin to. You had insider knowledge we didn't."

Squelching a relieved sigh, I grin. "So is there anything you can do about the murders?"

"Problem is, the murderer's livin in 2023. Doubt they be comin back any time soon. Not possible to extradite them either. If I were them, I'd stay far away from the scene of my crime."

Now, I do sigh. She's right. I'm as certain Penny won't be returning as I am certain the sun will rise tomorrow. Clouds may obscure it, but they can't stop its appearance.

My evidence can't bring Penny to justice in this world.

But it can in hers.

Somehow, I have to return to 2023. But how?

I thank Ruba and extract a promise from her to arrest Penny if she ever shows her overconfident face here again, despite the infinitesimal odds. Ruba keeps a copy of the incriminating pages, and I, clutching the precious book, return home to Qory and Daisy, stay quiet about my mission, and carry on my life as if all is normal.

And life does go on as normal, even as justice isn't yet served. I sleepwalk through each day after my family wakes up, as we eat our meals, go to school and about our daily business, even visit with friends. Because Penny is still free. McMurray and TigerLily and Giles are still gone. Justice can't bring them back. All she can do is ensure the guilty pay the consequences. Someday, all wrongs will be made right when Christ rules in His kingdom, but how many years off will that be? In earthly terms, the wait seems like eons away.

And then, a week later, a knock on the door while I'm readying for bed changes everything. "I'll get it," I tell Qory, who's just about in dreamland already. Not seeing any light from the slit under the girls' bedroom door, I go to the front door.

When I open it, my chin drops. Juni stands on our welcome mat in the hall light's snaky glow, unsmiling, the furrows on her brow having multiplied as though she'd aged five years since last month. "Juni?"

I snap my mouth shut before she can ask if I'm trying to catch flies. The old Juni would have. But this Juni is subdued. She's altered her hair to a softer greenish-blue shade. Luminous under the light, it reminds me of the river on a sunny spring day. Her light gray eyes peer at me through slitted lids. Gone is the contraface and the high-octane snark. Has Juni grown up?

She anchors her green shoulder purse under her arm. "Come in?"

I block her access by thrusting one foot forward. I can't think of a single good reason she'd show up here.

"I know you not happy see me." A rare hesitance quivers in her tone.

No kidding!

She schools her mouth into a rigid grin, steps forward, and grips the doorjamb as if she belongs here. "But I came to talk you bout Brendan."

Still silent, I cross my arms, barricading any further words, while listening for any stirrings from Daisy or Qory. The sleeping silence behind me hangs heavy.

"Don't looka me like that." The old Juni seeps out through the almost harsh words. "This is serious. If you not gon to invite me in, can you step out here for a mo?"

"I'd like to know what you need first." Her flinch tells me she heard my no-nonsense tone. I keep the threshold between us.

"Well, Brendan found out from the Cloud my parent's and their coparent's murder was solved."

"Yes. And?"

"It said a nonymous source had evidence that the assistant killed em. Was it you figured it out?"

I nod, my iciness thawing a little. "Only because I spied on the scene. Did Brendan send you since he can't face me after what he did to my spouse?"

Juni shakes her head. "No. I mean yeah, they sent me to see you, but not for the reason you think. They sent me to ask you cause they stuck in the year 2140."

Seventeen years from now? It would explain her baffling maturity. "Then how did you get here?"

"The time chine. Brendan rebuilt it so it can go forward or backward in time."

"Really?" Curiosity propels me out the door and to her side. "How did he get stuck in 2140, and not you?"

"Long story. But they wants to see you. They wants to see justice done for their father's murder."

"But if he's stuck in the future, how can he help the cause of justice? Especially since he himself got away with manslaughter."

Tight silence, then, "Who said they got away with it?"

When I can't think of a suitable reply, she piles it on. "You don't have a clue what happened to Brendan. They just wants to see you. They has an idea...."

"What idea?"

"An idea on how to travel back to 2023 and get Penny arrested." Her tone hardens. "Penny killed my parent as well as Brendan's."

Travel back in time? After all the fruitless work Giles spent only to learn it wasn't possible? I squelch the temptation to laugh. "Why can't you just take me, since you have a working time machine now?"

The snaky glow covering her head shifts from her left to her right as she crosses one foot over the other like she's in need of the facilities. She better not ask to use mine. "Could do that. But you'll have to trust me."

My sarcasm must've been lost on her. Can I trust her? Then a memory arises, a vision of a robot, bent on harm, pounding on

TigerLily's door. Another one penetrating a solid security gate and slaughtering an innocent man. A desire to see Penny—and Brendan—held accountable for their crimes presses down on me, sagging my shoulders and spurring me on.

Is Juni my only hope for justice? My mind searches for alternatives, anything to get me to my objective, but nothing presents itself. In this world, Penny is long dead. But in her world, she's in the prime of life, ripe for more crimes, ready to endanger more souls.

I can't see any other options.

Juni's watching me, her glowing head tilted, anticipating my reply. I rub circles on my temples. "Give me till tomorrow to decide, okay? This is sudden, and I need time to think about it."

She nods, plants her feet like a robot. "Fine. I'll be back tomorrow morning, then."

"Wait."

She stops midspin.

"What did you mean, Brendan didn't get away with it?"

She flings her purse behind her back. "I meant, they in prison. In the integration pavilion."

I gasp as my hand flies to my heart, my usual gut reaction to those two petrifying words. "What for?"

"False accusation of theft by the company they worked for. Now they in jail."

"Can't he appeal?"

"Yeah, they workin on it. But's draggy process. Brendan's certain who's the perp. But's the boss's pring, and they was Brendan's accuser. Brendan couldn't win."

And now I see how the cosmic hand of justice must have her way, even when dealing an unfair hand. Justice had to make Brendan pay for Giles's death.

And now he is.

"By the way, Juni, I've been curious about something."

She nods.

"What did you do when the robots came to your parent's apartment?"

"I thought they were Pope comin after Brendan. So I ran to the back door and down the stairway to meet up with him. I went back later to see if Parent was okay, but it had turned into a crime scene. They told me Parent was found dead."

"Well, it saved your life. Brendan didn't return to the apartment?"

"They did return, but saw the robots, turned round, and got out of there."

I swallow hard. "And I have a confession to make."

Juni tilts her head, but remains silent, waiting for me to spill my guts.

I rub the nape of my neck and watch my toes squirm in their slippers. Then I look up and meet her suspicious gaze. "It's my fault Brendan had to rebuild the time machine." My voice comes out whispery. "I broke the incelerator."

"How?"

I relate the catastrophe that flung us back in time. "The incelerator can only go forward, right? And the recelerator kicks in on the return trip. So when I keyed in 2113, the incelerator was still engaged. Even though it followed my instructions, the confusion caused it to short-circuit."

"Wow." Her mouth stays open. "I had no idea. And I don't think Brendan ever knew either."

"Can you pass along my apology? If not for me, none of the subsequent events would've happened."

"But I wouldn't have met Brendan. And you wouldn't have solved the murder."

"But Giles would still be alive."

Behind me, a throat clears. I whirl to Qory, rubbing his eyes and yawning. "Dear? Who is it?"

I close the door on Juni and go to my spouse's side, my mind a whirlpool. How much can I tell him? If I tell him an accurate history, at what point will I strain his credibility?

Probably the point at which I entered the time machine.

"Love, you shouldn't be up." I hasten to reassure him. "It was just an old friend."

But wait. Tomorrow morning, I'm traveling back in time, assuming Juni can be trusted. Doesn't Qory deserve to know my intent, especially if I don't return?

And what about Daisy? How can I leave her behind?

It wouldn't be fair to Qory to take Daisy and leave him behind.

I take him into the bedroom, and I tell him everything.

IN THE YEAR 2023

"So glad you insisted on coming with me, love." I squeeze Qory's narrow shoulders, meaning it. But he shrugs, still blindsided by my late-night confession. Not only did I go lone wolf and solve a murder, I kept from him an entire segment of my life. What he doesn't know—I intended to return to 2023 alone until he refused to let me—won't hurt him. Despite his quiet outrage, he's a protective man, worried about me being alone with Juni, but worse, risking another malfunction and getting stranded in the past.

I awoke this morning queasy, but now I'm glad we're going as a family. How fun to show them all the sights from my old life! Will Qory loosen up enough to appreciate my world? Will Ari and Zach recognize me?

The possibilities and what-ifs entertain my mind like an unstoppable dream. Qory's still hurt I waited so long to confess my history. As we stroll with Juni to the time machine parked in my former dorm's lot, he focuses on Daisy, and his pace lags mine. Last night, in the face of his skepticism, I retrieved my wallet from my hidden backpack to prove my 1998 birth date.

Once he held proof, it took all my persuasive powers to convince him I had good reasons to keep it from him. "Would you be okay with all the attention if word ever got out?" I retorted. "You remember how much attention that time machine attracted."

"Still, this is huge."

"I know. What would you have done had I told you earlier?"

He refused to answer. He knows as well as I do it would've been a deal-breaker. In time, he'll adjust to this new reality.

"Parent, what does travelin to the past mean?" Daisy gives a little hop, then another, fueled by whirling thoughts too big for her seven-year-old brain.

I cast a helpless glance at Qory, who, judging from his glazed eyes and stiff steps, still struggles to comprehend it. Nor can he help me explain it to our daughter. "This sounds like a movie screenplay," he said last night when my flow of words ran dry. "Not real life."

"Juni." Near the dorm lift, I halt her with a touch on her elbow. "I assume you or Brendan tested it to make sure it'll return to 2023?"

"Course I did." She resumes her bustling pace. "But not Brendan, like I said. They just showed me how to work it while they in prison."

I can't read her body language to gauge if she's lying. But, as Qory reminded me last night, if she's up to something nefarious, we'll be together.

Funny, Giles said the same thing when the worst happened. And his presence saved my sanity.

But Juni wants justice for her mother's murder, so why would she have some other agenda?

"What did you think of 2023?"

A smirk crosses her face, then vanishes. "Primitive. Smelly. Loud."

I can't help chuckling while elbowing my spouse. "See, love? I can vouch for Juni. It is stinky and loud compared to this." Another spasm of nausea threatens as my arcing arm encompasses quiet, odorless autopods traversing through the sky, drones slipping to their destinations, people conversing in calm voices. Wiping sweat from my brow, I point to the cloudless blue sky. "But it's also much cooler. Which is why I told you to bring extra clothing." My only jacket is tucked in my backpack along with my 2023 belongings. "You'll feel like you're in Alaska."

We arrive at the podlot. Sure enough, there's the McMurray capsule, about twenty-five feet from its original site, still fenced off. Though graffiti mars the old fence, it's still intact. "Oh, it got moved."

Juni winks. "You'll see why."

"Parent, wut this?"

I pull Daisy closer to my side. "This is the time-travel autopod. Come on. Let's get in."

My eyes burn with unshed tears as Qory sits beside me, Daisy on his lap, and Juni launches us back to June 2023, the day after we took off the second time. If Penny is lying in wait at the Oaks Park site for our return, she'll be waiting awhile. We're several blocks away.

The podlot walls blur, then disappear, and I grip Qory's hand as if we're taking off to the moon. My heart pounds as if it thinks so too. "I'm so grateful you're here."

His beaming smile rewards me.

The vehicle thumps its landing as we're dropped five stories.

Juni clears her throat. "We made it."

I hadn't realized how much I missed my old life. Until I'm forced back in time to face it. We've landed in the rear of a dark parking lot next to a convenience store. Its neon lights cast a rainbow glow over the night. Smart move on Juni's part to arrange a middle-of-the-night return, like we're a band of undercover agents. Juni shows me Brendan's upgrades, which include allowing the operator to specify the exact altitude of the landing. "See, when we return, it will take us back to the podlot and not the ground floor. Slick, huh?" Juni's grin rivals the neon lights' brightness. "First time I made this trip, I landed on the roof, like Santa Claus. Brendan thought he better make some adjustments."

Daisy and Qory are speechless. The sudden scene change must feel like being inside a holofilm.

My fingers explore inside my backpack for the tenth time, ensuring McMurray's journal is tucked away, as though it might've sprouted legs and run off in the last twenty minutes.

"How about we go into the store first? I need to charge up my cell phone first thing and make sure it still works."

After ensuring the capsule is locked, we troop across the lot through the sharp nighttime chill to the store's glass door. Its Open sign welcomes us home. I shiver. "Forgot how cold fifty-five degrees feels," I mutter to Qory. The bell tinkles, and the recognizable aroma of brewing coffee stops me in my tracks. "Doesn't coffee sound wonderful right now? Daisy, love, would you like a juice?"

She nods, her voice out of operation as it always is in an unfamiliar situation. She scoots closer to me as we three adults help ourselves to coffee from a machine that looks and feels antiquated after ten years away. When the other two gawk at the machine, I hasten to assist them, and then we approach the counter, the coffees warming our hands.

The fortysomething beer-bellied man lounging behind the counter looks up from his newspaper. "Three coffees and a juice. Will that be all?"

I dig out cash from my wallet, the smooth bills alien under my fingertips, and hand the man a twenty. "Yes, please. I also need to charge my phone. We'll just sit over there at the table, if that's okay."

When he nods, a display of prepaid phones catches my eye. "Oh, wait. My husband will need one of these as well." I hand the man my debit card, crossing my fingers that it still works. It's not degraded after ten years hidden away in the dark for it goes right through. I rack my brain to remember how much remains in my bank balance. Oh well, if my phone still works, I'll check my bank app.

The others haven't spoken more than a few murmured words, letting me take the lead. It must all appear as strange to them as their world looked to me. We settle with our beverages at the table, and I plug in my phone. The warmth of the paper cup permeates my icy hands. While my phone charges, I show Qory how to work his. My explanation last night failed to prepare him for this primitive forerunner of a hologram. Ha. Now he has no choice but to give me his undivided attention. Does he regret agreeing to this?

My cell phone beeps. It's 4:34 a.m., and several messages light up my screen. One from my bank to remind me my credit card payment is due. One from Ari: *Hey gf, hit me up when you're back.*

Won't she be surprised to see me?

A text from Mia: *You back yet?*

How will I explain my altered appearance?

The cold hits me then. Shivering, I put on the well-loved jacket I haven't needed for ten years. Why did I wait so long?

Oh, right. I'm not used to donning a jacket. And neither is Daisy, who gives her jacket a suspicious look when I help her into it.

Juni swivels in her seat, sipping her vanilla-flavored hot brew. How my opinion of her has altered. She's my rock, my anchor, my hope for justice. "What next, peeps?"

I shift on the hard chair, jamming my still-chilly hands into my deep, fleece-lined jacket pockets. "The cops."

"In the middle of the night?" Qory retorts, evidently still perturbed, yet his widened eyes betray his awakened sense of adventure.

"Sure. They're on duty twenty-four seven. Same as criminals."

"And how will we get there?"

"Remember I told you about Uber?" I open the app and show him. "A car can be here soon to pick us up."

Speaking of cars, one roars by, making us all jump. Daisy hides her face in my jacket, and I return to my seat, stroking her soft head, my fingertips circling her temples.

"Wait." Qory's backward glance at our vehicle framed by the window can't conceal his longing for the familiar. One loud car chased off his sense of adventure? "One of us needs to stay with the vehicle, don't you think?"

"Good idea, love. Are you volunteering?"

He shrugs. "Sure. I can stay here, but how do we keep in touch?"

I point to his new phone. "With that. And if you can keep Daisy too, I sure would appreciate it."

IN THE YEAR 2023

At five thirty, sunrise beams are lightening the eastern sky as Juni and I get an Uber to the police station. The queasy feeling returns when the driver swerves around a rumbling TriMet bus, and thinking of my upcoming appointment only intensifies it. What if the police don't believe me? What if I throw up all over this nice driver's new car?

Lord, please make sure I don't!

I'm dying to get to my apartment and see my cats, but they must wait. My script races through my mind as the car travels Division Street. Juni fixes her gaze out the window. Her expression mirrors what mine must've looked like when we arrived in 2123.

The officer in charge of McMurray's case, Detective David Major, waits for us. He's a big guy, a typical Portland cop, but his kind face reassures me. I say a prayer he'll believe my testimony.

We start with introductions. Then he asks to see the evidence I promised him on the phone. Retrieving the book, I explain that we traveled with McMurray into the future and drone technology enabled me to witness the crime. He'll believe me because, according to him, Penny already explained the robotics of the future. "Plus, when you read this, take note of his final sentence."

He opens the book, skips to the end, and reads aloud, "'In case anything ever happens to me, the most likely culprit is Penelope Nichols.'"

Wow. No wonder she was so eager to get her hands on that book. She had to be frantic when she found the capsule gone.

"Penelope Nichols? The primary witness we interviewed? He's saying she's the culprit?"

"Yes, sir. And she was responsible for the murder of my friend's mother, as well." I indicate Juni beside me.

"In that case, I'm surprised he hid this in the vehicle she had access to."

"Maybe he was still writing in it, and he intended to find a better hiding place once he got back home."

"Guess we'll never know." He casts a glance over my shoulder. "Well, speak of the devil. Here she is."

My heart jumps into my throat. I pivot.

Penny marches along the hallway with purpose beside a tall, slender man in uniform. Heading our way. But there's no place to hide. Nausea churns in my gut.

"I asked her to come in first thing this morning for more questions. But I didn't expect her this early."

"Wait." I lurch to my feet. "I can't let her see us. She'll recognize us."

"Come this way." He leads us to a door behind his desk and an interrogation room, just like the one in 2123. In fact, this might even be the same building. "Wait here. I'll ask her to come back later. Then we'll talk some more."

He closes us in, and his deep voice muffles through the crack under the solid metal door. "Hello, Penny. Thanks for coming in."

I can't make out her muted reply.

"Something has come up, and I won't be able to meet with you until later. Would you be able to return around nine thirty, ten?"

Another muted reply. My phone chimes with a text from Qory…his very first.

How goes?

Fine, I type. *We'll be back soon.*

Good. Daisy getting restless. Running out of ways to entertain them.

Download Crazy Gears.

Was he listening when I explained apps? Detective Major opens the door, then beckons with a sweep of his arm. "Coast clear."

An idea brews in my mind. I run it by him.

Crossing his gaze from Juni to me, then back again, he nods. "That might work. Worth a try, anyway. I'll text Penny and ask her to return at noon instead."

Knowing Penny, she won't be suspicious. She'll walk with blind faith into the trap. After I promise to return before noon, Juni and I grab an Uber. "The best secondhand stores in town are within a three-block radius on Hawthorne," I tell her. "We're sure to find the perfect outfit in one of them." The thought of visiting Ari flits through my mind, but I think better of it. I need to warn her first of my altered appearance, even send a photo, so she won't faint.

But first, our mission. "Think back to that last day with your...parent. Try to remember the scene."

Juni scrunches her eyes, snaps her finger. "Okay. I'm seeing it."

The Uber driver returns us to Qory and Daisy, the latter nearly in tears from my long absence. I nestle her against my chest, whispering apologies into her hair. Then we all return to the Uber. "We'll go to my apartment first. You two can stay there while Juni and I go shopping."

"You still have keys to your place, dear?"

I dangle them on my finger. Daisy wipes her eyes, and we proceed to Sellwood. The Davenports better not think I'm a stranger. If they catch a close-up of me, how will I explain?

But we make it inside with no unwelcome encounters. Two loud meows assault my ears. Grizzy and Rumple sit on their haunches near the food bowls, staring at me with reproach. More meows, and I scoop up my poor rumbling fur bundles. Oh, how I missed them! In Thea time, it's ten years later. In cat time, I've only been gone one day. "Do not fear, for I am with you," I murmur into their soft fur. "Be strong and of good courage, my sweets."

"Meow." But no translation follows. In my haste, I didn't bother to bring the translation collars. My best guess? "Mommy, where did you go?"

Once I replenish their food, they're happy to leave my arms. Taking in the tiny flat I haven't seen for an entire decade, I marvel at the familiar turned unfamiliar. I turn on the TV to the kid's programming, which passes muster under Daisy's wondering scrutiny. "Make yourselves at home, loves. We'll be back in a few hours." After rapid-fire instructions on how to operate the TV remote, I kiss my husband and daughter, their heads still swiveling in awestruck wonder. At least, they have a safe place to wait.

Juni and I hop on TriMet and head for Hawthorne Boulevard. After ten years of not navigating the bus system, I'm surprised how easily it all comes back to me. The second shop we visit has what we need, so we return to my apartment with new outfit, wig, and makeup.

We're ready to set my plan into motion.

IN THE YEAR 2023

It's almost noon on a sun-dappled June day, one of those cloudless summer days twenty-first-century Northwesterners wait all year for after enduring months of rain and cold. At the police station, Detective Major awaits Penny's arrival. According to her text, she's five minutes away. Juni and I are seated on the other side of the interrogation room wall where we can hear and see Penny but she won't know we're there. I sip a Sprite, which always helps settle my stomach.

Then, at the appropriate moment...

But I mustn't get ahead of myself. Juni and I chat with the officer seated next to me, Detective Latifah Robinson. The detective clutches a copy of today's *Portlandia*, Part I of my article on the front page. She peppers us with questions about life in 2123, the murders, and drone technology.

Until Penny arrives in a cloud of dynamo energy, all innocent smiles and I-want-to-help handshakes. "Hi, there."

Detective Major ushers her into the interrogation room, and a spasm of surprise crosses her face. Does she recognize it also?

The good detective has his partner bring her coffee. The other man leaves the room. Then Major gets down to business.

"Ms. Nichols." His back is to me, but I have a clear view of Penny. "We have some new information on McMurray's murder, and we think you might be able to help."

Another twinge of surprise. The second of many, if all goes as I hope. Except for a noticeable twitch of her eyelid, Penny's doing a good job playing it cool. "Oh? What information?"

"A witness has come forward claiming McMurray was killed by a robot, not by Ms. Malone."

Now the twitch accelerates. Major's partner returns with coffee, a thin poltergeist of steam slithering from the vent hole, and she grabs onto the Styrofoam cup like a drowning woman. "Really? A robot? Who's the witness?"

"We can't reveal that yet." He leans back, relaxed. His next question is delivered in a warm, almost friendly tone. "I do have some questions related to technology. Yesterday, you told me you spent a week in 2123 learning botting, as you referred to programming robots. What led you to pursue it?"

Penny blinks once, then twice, her gaze fastened on the room's upper right corner. "Colt asked me to." She swallows, and her voice croaks. She takes a sip of coffee. "He wanted to incorporate robots into our business plan."

"For what reason?"

"Reason? Why, I suppose"—another big swallow—"because robots can do so much. By the way, how could *you* know there was a witness in 2123?"

"Like I said, they've come forward."

"Come forward? How is that—" From her sudden intake of breath, she's realized how it's possible.

Major picks up the black book from the chair beside him. "Ms. Nichols, did you know Mr. McMurray kept a journal?"

Penny eyes it. A split second of fear contorts her face. She clears her throat. "He did mention it, but I've never read it."

"Someone found it." Major opens it, thumbing its pages. "Hidden in the time capsule."

"Oh." The strain Penny is under, trying to pretend she isn't nervous, shows as she bites her lower lip hard enough to dent her coral lipstick. "He must've wanted to keep the work on his incelerator invention secret."

"Yes, he did include a brief description."

She nods, her smile breaking free with the release of tension. "I bet most people would find it boring reading."

"Could be. But I found it enlightening."

"How so?"

How gratifying to see Penny lose her confident aplomb. Her innocent act fell away sometime in the last five minutes. She knows something's up and can sense the sword of Damocles above her head about to drop.

Major ruffles the pages again, as if he's in no hurry at all. "He also wrote about a good friend of his named Nel."

Penny's head is cocked, a half smile hovers, like a polite audience member listening to a less-than-interesting story but poised to move on at the earliest opportunity.

"Interesting," is her ironic reply.

"Do you know Nel?"

She shakes her head, of course, her mouth twisted into a fake smile. "I don't."

"Really? You're his business partner, and you don't know his good friends?"

Penny shrugs, her stare fixed on the open journal.

"He also mentions you."

Forced chuckle. "It better be good."

"There are a few complimentary mentions of your brilliant intellect."

C'mon, Major, get on with it. Apparently, the good detective has all day.

"I saved his butt. If not for me, Midnight Rider wouldn't have ever gotten off the ground. No pun intended."

"But he says it was Nel, not Penny, who came to the rescue."

Even from the other side of the glass, I can see Penny's heart rate speeding up, running like a rabbit being chased by hounds.

She's not sure how much McMurray incriminated her in his journal. Thus, her frantic search. She must've been so panicked when the killer robot returned with no book. Then, when Brendan took us back, she saw us leave. I bet she meant to stop us so she could do a more thorough search.

If she's smart, she'll request an attorney right about now.

Instead, she leans back, her expression wiped clean with an invisible hand. "Where are you going with this? Why do you need my help?"

He turns to his partner. "Drake, bring the witness in."

Juni, beside me, straightens her shoulders. It's showtime.

She follows him in, Penny's eyes goggle, and I see what Penny is seeing.

TigerLily in the flesh, returned from the dead.

With a grayish-blonde wig, some makeup tricks, and a cobalt blue sundress, Juni can pass for her mother.

Juni stands with feet planted, hand on hip. "We meet again, Penny. Just got one question. Why send robots after me?"

Once Penny gets her jaw off the ground, she recovers, rolling her eyes. "What *is* this?" Turning a stormy gaze to Major, she springs to her feet. "Is this some kind of trick?"

"So you know this woman?"

Penny's trembling hands clasp together on her abdomen. "It's someone pretending to be the woman who committed suicide. The one who killed McMurray." She gathers up her purse and swivels to the door. "This is ridiculous." Her heels clang as she storms to the door.

Detective Drake intercepts her. "You can't leave."

"Yes, I can. You expect me to fall for your shenanigans? I'm going to report you to the state board."

Drake forces her back to the chair as Major taps the book. "We have evidence pointing to you as the mastermind behind McMurray's homicide."

I didn't think her eyes could bug out any more. Penny gapes at the journal, her mouth opening and closing like a hooked trout.

"Penelope Nichols, I'm placing you under arrest for the murder of Coltrane McMurray. Anything you say can be held against you in a court of law. You have the right to an attorney...."

IN THE YEAR 2023

"Penny refused to confess." I bite into a PB&J prepared by Ari, who's sitting across Hawthorne Food Carts' picnic table from us. "But she's in custody." It feels so good to speak in 2023 language again.

Juni wipes a spot of jelly off her mouth. "But we was told if they goes to trial, we'll be subpoenaed as witnesses. Which means we might hafta stick round while."

I check my phone for texts from Qory. Still nothing. *You two doing all right? Is Daisy being good?*

Found a show called Sesame Street. *They seems to love it. It's funny.*

I grin, imagining Daisy's glee, envisioning her laughing at Oscar and Big Bird and Elmo. Then the smile turns to a frown as my thoughts lead me to the future. And the awkward position my spouse and I are in.

Ari interrupts my musings. "I still can't believe Giles is gone and you have a new hubby."

"You have to come over and meet him."

"And that you're thirty-five, not twenty-five, and it's been ten years since you've seen me." She glances over at her husband, bustling at the order window. "So trippy! Zachy will love this."

She waves at him, then turns a toothy smile on me. "You are staying, right? I mean, your job and everything."

I can't admit I don't know. I told my editor what she wanted to hear. Of course she's excited for another article on my ten-year sojourn into the future.

I also told Mia what she wanted to hear. Even though I shouldn't be making such promises.

On one hand, a lot is riding on my staying.

On the other, Giles is gone. I have a new family whose only life is in 2123.

We return to my apartment at three in the afternoon. All I want to do is nap. In fact, it's bedtime according to my 2123 body clock. But Qory and Daisy need me. So I squelch my yawns and update Qory while Daisy and Juni watch TV. When I notice Daisy yawning, I tuck her into my recliner, and she's soon out.

Juni leans back and closes her eyes. "Can I crash on your sofa?"

"You totally can. Love, come check out my comfortable bed. You'll love it."

Qory gets to his feet, stretching his arms over his head. "We need to talk."

"Yes, we do."

On the bed, he lays face up, his hands cradling his head. "I been thinkin all day."

I wait, already sensing what he's going to say.

"You belong here. This is your home, your life. You have friends here. A little girl you're mentoring. There are photos of you and Giles all over. Don't you agree would be best if you and Daisy stay here and I have Juni take me back tomorrow?" His tone dips, as though he's not as confident as he'd like me to think. "Even though I love you and want to share life with yull, this isn't my home, and I can't see me fitting into your world."

I flinch, but still can't speak. So I take his hand and twine my fingers through his slender ones. His face remains expressionless as he stares at the ceiling. Is he sorrowful? Resigned? Swallowing, I breathe a prayer for guidance while my heart breaks in two.

And it dawns on me, too late, that I love him back.

"I love you too, and I get what you're saying," I half whisper, drawing out the words, reluctant to add drama to an already impossible situation. He doesn't need a guilt trip. "But why don't we get a good night's sleep first and talk about it more in the morning? Maybe we'll both see an option we can't see now."

He pulls my head onto his chest, and we lay there, his heart beating into my ears until I fall asleep.

When I awaken, it's nearly midnight. I've slept for several hours, and Qory snores beside me. The first thing I notice is that my nausea has worsened. I run to the bathroom, reviewing my meals from yesterday. The last thing I ate was Ari's sandwich. No way would Ari have used spoiled ingredients. She's super diligent about the purity of her food inventory. I've eaten nothing since, and the combination of hunger pangs on top of nausea unsettles me.

I run to the toilet, but nothing comes out except bile. Yet my stomach demands food. What a strange sensation. I tiptoe into the kitchen. If I turn on the light, Juni and Daisy will awaken. But maybe that's okay.

Keeping the light off, I grab a Sprite from the fridge, the first of a six-pack I bought two days ago in 2023 time. After a few sips, I feel better. Daisy is stirring, rubbing her eyes. "Parent?" Her little voice comes out as a croak. "Parent!"

I hurry to her side as the unfamiliar surroundings creep into her awareness. She probably thinks she's dreaming. "C'mon, lovey, let's get you some breakfast."

We head to the kitchenette. Soon, the aroma of eggs and toast wafts through my small digs, bringing Juni and Qory out of their slumbers. As Juni sorts through my clothing for something to wear, I realize I need to make a trip to the 7-Eleven down the street, so I let them serve themselves while I drive the few blocks.

The store seems deserted this time of night. A twentysomething couple is buying beer. I'm the only other customer. The fiftyish guy behind the counter looks like a bouncer. I bet the store has very little crime when he's on duty.

I find the product I need, plus some food items, then pay the bouncer, and head home where I beeline to the bathroom. "Be right there!" I tell the others.

And there on the little pink strip is the answer I've been waiting for.

———————⊷⬦⬦⊶———————

Qory stares at the positive pregnancy test in my hand. "Yull right, dear. This put our dilemma in a new light."

I close the bedroom door. "We're going back with you," I declare in my most no-nonsense tone. "We're going to have a child together! A new family. How can I stay behind?"

He plops onto my unmade queen bed. "But what about your job? Mia? The court date?"

I sink down beside him, my arms encircling his waist. "I have a plan, my love. I need to run it by Juni first, but she'll agree."

He nods, his face breaking into a smile. Then he grabs me in a bear hug. I breathe in his fresh-shower scent, marveling at awakened feelings I haven't experienced since the day Giles died. "Wow. A baby. So marvy."

Thank You, Lord. Qory is going to be an awesome coparent. And I marvel at God's amazing grace, blessing me with another precious child.

Juni is delighted by my idea. "Totally will bring you back for your court date or to visit friends or whatever. Long as you pay me my regular fee."

"Hey, maybe you'll meet a nice, old-fashioned, twenty-first-century man while you're here."

Juni's face droops. She must be thinking about Brendan locked away in the integration pavilion for another two years. After his release, who knows what their fate as a couple might be?

I'll keep my apartment so we have a place to stay for my court appearance or for when I visit Mia or submit articles. Oh, how I wish for an easier way to span the centuries.

As we Uber back to Midnight Rider, Qory and I can't stop kissing and embracing. "Yull gon get a room when we get back?" Juni drolls.

Qory laughs, I giggle, and my heart rejoices as my family and I sail away to a bright future. "Daisy, love, how did you like visiting the past?"

Daisy grins that heart-melting smile of hers. "It's fabby," she says.

EPILOGUE

Portlandia, **May 25, 2035**
OBITUARIES
Penelope Rae Nichols—born May 18, 1980, Ellensburg, WA. Died May 1, 2035

Longtime Portland resident Penelope Nichols, known as Nel or Penny by her friends and associates, passed away May 1 of insecticidal poisoning at Coffee Creek Correctional Facility in Wilsonville, OR. Ms. Nichols had served nearly twelve years of a life sentence for homicide at the time of her death. The business partner of the notorious time-traveler, Coltrane McMurray of Portland, she was convicted of first-degree murder after he was found dead in the year 2123. Ms. Nichols is survived by her two daughters, Jessica Nichols Stuart (Mervin) of Santa Fe, NM, and Rachel Nichols Bradford (Ben) of Chico, CA, and four grandchildren. She is interred at Lincoln Memorial Gardens.

THE END

Excerpt from

Time Passengers Book 3 –

NIGHTS IN WHITE SATIN

TODAY

Panting, I look over my shoulder for the fifth time. I could've sworn I heard footsteps behind me, but the dark sidewalk is empty. The stately homes across the street point their blank faces to the night.

The constant barrage of news on our local serial killer has turned my world into a sinister place. A world where I can't feel safe. A world in which I'm ever on guard. I quicken my steps toward the distant yellow glow on the next block. My sanctuary. My escape.

Hurry. At last, I rush up my dark concrete steps, my key already clutched in my shaking hand, and fumble for the lock. My full shopping bag knocks against my off-white front door. Snowflake shapes float in my vision, so I take in the deep calming breaths my yoga instructor taught, then exhale out the anxiety. Another backward glance shows me an empty sidewalk twenty feet in either direction.

You're going to be okay. You're going to be fine. Mom swore by the mantra, but I won't be fine until I'm safely inside.

A shiver jostles me through the door of my three-story charcoal-gray townhome, and I slam the door with a satisfying thud. The deadbolt's click concludes my safety regimen.

Our local serial killer, known as The Ladykiller for obvious reasons, has plagued the city for months. Women who used to frequent Portland's awesome food scene and trendy neighborhoods with carefree abandon now carry pepper spray or even concealed weapons. I feel sorry/not sorry the next time Ladykiller tries to butcher an armed woman.

LK always strangles them and dumps their bodies in remote corners of Forest Park. The authorities believe LK lives near the park off one of the steep roads leading to the Thurman Street trailhead.

A road much like this one. Stewart Street, a mere block from Thurman in Portland's Alphabet District.

A bottle of Chateau St. Michelle Sauvignon Blanc beckons me from my shopping bag. I need my drug of choice in the worst way. No time to chill it. What a day it's been. A day that started out as a normal workday ended with a threatening sight at my neighborhood grocery store.

Cops. At least five of them, racing west up Thurman Street, sirens blaring, toward Forest Park.

It can only mean one thing.

Someone found the latest victim.

ABOUT THE AUTHOR

Welcome to the world of D. K. Till, where The Future and The Present collide.

D.K. Till writes Time Travel Fiction with A Twist, a blend of the dual timeline fiction she enjoys mixed with a big helping of the sci-fi she loved as a child. The indie author from the land of microbrews and coffee snobs fell in love with books in kindergarten when her older sister taught her to read. She used to impress her parents' friends by reading aloud the entire short story The One Hundred Hats of Bartholomew Cubbins. In first grade, she knew she wanted to write stories, too. Throughout her childhood and teens, she either had her nose in a book or was attempting to write one.

But life got in the way, marriage and children set her dreams aside for higher purposes. Today, with children grown and retirement achieved, she's reopened that dream package and is now living the life she had only imagined.

The author is a huge fan of the Back to the Future trilogy, inspiring her to write time travel, too. Thus the Time Passengers series was born. A classic rock lover, she names her titles after classic songs of the 60s and 70s like Starry, Starry Night (Don McLean, 1972), Midnight Rider (The Allman Brothers Band, 1970), and Nights in White Satin (Moody Blues, 1967).

Sign up for her newsletter at dktill.com.